CW01468687

Destiny of a Free Spirit

Stephen Ford

LEAF BY LEAF

Published by Leaf by Leaf
an imprint of Cinnamon Press,
Office 49019, PO Box 15113, Birmingham, B2 2NJ
www.cinnamonpress.com

The right of Stephen Ford to be identified as author of this work has been asserted by him in accordance with the Copyright, Designs and Patent Act, 1988. © 2023, Stephen Ford.
Print Edition ISBN 978-1-78864-956-8

British Library Cataloguing in Publication Data. A CIP record for this book can be obtained from the British Library.

All rights reserved. No part of this publication may be reproduced, stored in a retrieval system, or in any form or by any means, electronic, mechanical, photocopying, recording or otherwise without the prior written permission of the publishers. This book may not be lent, hired out, resold or otherwise disposed of by way of trade in any form of binding or cover other than that in which it is published, without the prior consent of the publishers.

Designed and typeset in Adobe Jenson by Cinnamon Press.
Cover design by Adam Craig © Adam Craig.
Cinnamon Press is represented by Inpress.

Destiny of a Free Spirit

Living in the Wild

The smell woke me.

It isn't that sabre-toothed cats stink, but they do have a distinctive odour. I'd struggle to describe it. In other circumstances I may not have noticed. Living in the wild, one is tuned to the unusual, a sound, movement, change in the light or, in this case, an out of place smell.

I opened my eyes and saw the enormous predator silhouetted in the doorway. I felt a slight movement of the cold night air on my face from the draught let in as the cat pushed aside the heavy blanket curtain that normally hung over the entrance into the communal living space.

The cat crept soundlessly, scanning the room for prey. It focused on what appeared to be the easiest and least risky, the sleeping infants, five year old Bjorn and his sisters, three year old Helga and baby Inga.

I reached silently for my dagger, but realising it would be insufficient, in the split second I had to react I looked for alternatives.

I sprang from under the fur covering of my bed in a fluid movement, reaching the central hearth where embers from the previous evening's fire smouldered. I grabbed a heavy rock from the hearth and launched it. The cat already faced me, so the hunk of limestone struck the side of its face and bounced off its shoulder.

It snarled angrily and rushed me. I grabbed a half burned length of wood protruding from the fire and lunged the glowing embers into the animal's face. It yowled as smoke and red hot fiery fragments went into its eyes. I backed away, narrowly escaping lashing paws.

I swept up my dagger and, seizing my chance while the cat was disoriented, plunged it to the hilt into the beast's chest.

A smaller animal might have been dispatched, but this one would not be killed so easily. I was unable to escape a blow from its mighty paw. Its claws slashed my upper arm, gouging into the flesh. The force sent be reeling across the floor. As I saw the sabre teeth loom above, about to slash down into my torso, I thought my time of Earth had come to an end.

Fortunately the commotion had roused the others. Gudrun, the children's mother, and young Freya, had rushed to safeguard the children. It was Torsten who saved my life, thrusting a spear from behind into its belly.

Still the cat twisted, snapping the shaft off the spear as if it was a matchstick. It advanced on Torsten.

Knut, Gudrun's husband, finally slew the beast, thrusting another spear under its ribcage, twisting as he did so, ripping and tearing through to its pounding heart.

For a while the mortally wounded cat continued thrashing ineffectually on the floor, initially with dangerous strength but ebbing in intensity like a clockwork toy as its spring unwinds.

Old Ranulf was with us too, armed with another spear. Still tough and wiry, but not as muscular and fast as he had been in his youth, he had wisely allowed the younger men to step out in front.

As a group we gathered to observe the dying beast, saying nothing, wary while it still squirmed and thrashed.

Gudrun broke the silence. Content that the children

would be safe, her attention was drawn to the blood running freely from the gashes on my arm. She gestured me to where the pitcher of water stood. "Come. Let's take a look at you."

Gudrun must have been around thirty, yet already the family matriarch, the undisputed mistress of the homestead. She set washing my wounds and applying a dressing of honey and rosemary.

"Praise be to Gaia," said Freya. "Vulcan nearly had us all."

Freya, at around nineteen, was at that stage of physical perfection when a girl has only recently blossomed, her soft hour-glass contours tight and smooth.

"Yes, Gaia was with us today, thanks be to Commissum," said Ranulf.

"We've not had one of these before," observed Knut, indicating the corpse. "We've only ever seen them from a distance until now."

"I've been wondering when one might come sniffing around," Ranulf remarked.

"Fortunately I sniffed it out before it could do anything," I quipped.

As I said it I realised how improbable that seemed. How my nose could have possibly picked out the smell of the big cat over the pong in that room was beyond comprehension. The dense fug of body odour from the occupants who last rinsed themselves in a stream months before, thick damp clothing that had never been laundered but might have been rinsed in the stream while it was worn, body warmed bedding, fire smoke, cooking smells and old food remnants dating back weeks, should all surely have swamped out everything else.

"Just as well," said Knut, looking over gratefully to his children. Knut, about thirty, was still in his physical prime, not bulky but with a solid strength and neat but defined musculature, his short brown hair trimmed in the pudding bowl style of Medieval kings, his beard cropped short to barely more than a heavy stubble.

"Yes, but good that you guys stepped in when you did. I thought I was done for."

It was too late to go back to bed and anyway we wouldn't have slept. The first hint of dawn was showing from outside.

"Let's get something to eat, set us up for the day," said Gudrun.

She, Freya and Ranulf set about preparations. Knut, Torsten and I were excused after our exertions. Breakfast was a porridge of ground roots and seeds with the remains of the previous evening's vegetable and rabbit stew stirred in, served from a large earthenware pot.

"Praise be to Gaia, the bringer of nourishment and bounty," pronounced Ranulf, before Gudrun served the meal.

"Big beast that," Torsten observed, looking over the stretched out carcase. "It'll have some good meat on it."

His observation was right. In length its body was longer than a man is tall and it must have had the weight of three grown men.

"You should have those big teeth," Knut said to me, indicating the large sabre fangs that were close to a foot long.

"No, that's alright. You and Torsten can have them," I

replied. "I wouldn't be able to take them back with me anyway."

"You wouldn't need to take them back, if you stayed here with us," said Freya.

Knut and Gudrun nodded slightly and smiled, Runulf raised his eyebrow in a hint of approval. Torsten's face remained blank except for a slight curling of his lip as if he wasn't entirely happy with the idea of me staying indefinitely but didn't want to say it. I changed the subject.

"I guess that there is no reason for us to go out hunting now."

Knut looked in the direction of the huge dead creature and nodded. "Not for some time."

"I'm going to need some more roots though, turnips and stuff," Gudrun said.

I looked at the rough shelves being used as the family food store. There were still some sealed earthenware pots containing foodstuffs preserved from the previous year's harvest, but, now, in March, these were running down. There was only a small remaining heap of root vegetables. The few residual mangold wurzels, turnips and potatoes were old and shrivelled.

"I'd gladly help out, but I'm not sure that I'd be able to find where they are," I said.

"Come with me. I'll show you," said Torsten.

I selected one of the spades from where they stood against the wall. Torsten had a look of distaste as he took hold of the other spade, as if he was picking up something dirty.

Leaving the others behind to begin work on butchering the deceased sabre cat, Torsten and I set out into the cold of the winter morning. There was a coating of frost on the ground and foliage that was just beginning to melt where the bright rays from the sun had reached.

The family lived more by gathering than farming. The wild landscape was their farm, but it was not one where every patch was tended and cultivated. Nor was it theirs exclusively. They shared it with the wild birds and beasts that lived alongside them.

Although they lived by gathering nature's bounty, they did give Mother Nature a helping hand. In the vicinity of the homestead was a cultivated plot for vegetables, but this was largely dormant during the winter. The family would bring it to life around April and it yielded crops until November.

The homestead was an Iron Age style hut consisting of a framework of roughly hewn logs filled in with wattle and daub panels and topped with a conical roof of thatch with a hole through which smoke from the central hearth could escape.

In the wild country beyond, the family helped nature along with strategic planting, especially of root crops such as turnips and parsnips, spreading them widely to be retrieved later as needed. Torsten knew where these had been seeded in previous months, which is where we headed.

We wandered with our spades, selecting a small number of plants to collect before moving on, never stripping a place clean. That way the gaps we made would be filled naturally with fresh crop in due course.

Our wandering took us over the crest of a ridge, where we spotted the tops of turnips. We had barely put our spades into the soil when we heard the rustling of something brushing up against shrubbery. Ever alert we each swung towards the source of the sound.

Approaching were three people from the neighbouring Henrik family. I had met them before when Ranulf's and Henrik's families had feasted together. There was Otto, a stocky bearded man of around forty, and his son, Manfred, a youth of about sixteen and daughter Ursula, a young woman of about eighteen. They looked at us with a combination of annoyance, wariness and distaste.

"So, young Torsten, what are you doing over here?" Otto wanted to know.

"Gaia's Greetings, Otto," Torsten replied. "We're gathering roots for the pot."

"Not from over here, you shouldn't be, and especially not with those implements of Vulcan," insisted Otto, gesturing with disgust towards the steel-bladed spades.

Unobtrusively, so as not to escalate, I felt for my dagger, hung around my waist. Our three potential adversaries looked tense and determined.

"Oh, why not?" asked Torsten.

"Your ground ends at the top of the ridge, where the water flows in your direction."

Torsten looked around to check his location.

"A thousand apologies, Otto, you are right. We have strayed too far."

"You weren't taking liberties, were you?" said Otto, accusingly.

"No, an honest mistake, Otto, I promise you."

Otto nodded. The Henrik family's faces, strained with anger and fear, relaxed.

"Alright, but don't let it happen again. Anyway, how are all you Ranulfs? Doing okay?"

"We're good," said Torsten. "We had a sabre cat come over this morning. Big beast. Dead now. Plenty of meat on it. Want some?"

"Don't mind if we do. We'll do you a swap. You can have these roots you're after, but drop us round a bit of meat later on."

"Will do," said Torsten.

"So how did you kill the cat then?" Otto enquired. "They're big beasts. Wouldn't go down easily."

"Spears. I put one in its guts," Torsten boasted.

Ursula gazed at him with admiration. Torsten was a rugged young man in his early twenties, nearly six feet, square-jawed with a shaggy unkempt mane of curly blonde hair and trimmed beard, already strongly built and weather beaten despite his youth. Good looking, if you are looking for a bit of rough manliness.

"Wow. So you killed a sabre cat? Amazing!" crooned Ursula.

I didn't say anything. I could have mentioned I was the one who had originally tackled the beast and diverted it from killing the children, suffering wounds in the process, and that it was Knut who had ultimately killed it, but who was I to tarnish Torsten's heroism in the eyes of his admirer?

"So when are you going to bring over the meat?" Otto enquired.

"Later on," said Torsten.

Ursula gazed at him, anticipating his later arrival.

After the Henrik family's departure, it took us a couple

of hours to fill our large leather rucksacks with as much as we could carry. That would be sufficient to keep the family fed a couple of weeks or so.

"Going back then, are you?" said Torsten, as we hauled our harvest for our return trip.

"Yes, tomorrow."

"What will you do after that?"

"I don't really know," I said truthfully.

"You'll be back here again, though."

"Yes, I should think so."

"You can't keep doing that, though, can you? Back and forth, I mean."

I grimaced and clenched, as I struggled to answer. Torsten had confronted an uncomfortable issue. I couldn't just drift indefinitely, indecisive about my future, but I did not want to confront that thought. "I suppose not."

"So you'll need to decide where you belong. Here or over there."

"Yes, I suppose I will."

"Which will it be?"

"I don't know just yet."

I wondered why Torsten was pressing me. I suspected that his feelings for Freya were involved but preferred not to discuss it.

We continued back in sullen silence with our load of victuals.

By the time we returned to the homestead Knut and Freya were already well advanced with butchering the big cat and Gudrun had a large pot of meat and vegetable stew heating on the hearth. The meagre remains of root vegetables had already disappeared into the stew leaving the shelves clear for Torsten and I to pile our replacement supplies. Ranulf had the smoke house going to preserve the strips of meat that were surplus to what we could consume within the following days.

Torsten indicated a heap of worn clothing that had seen better days. "Here, see what you can do with that. I'd better take over the meat that we promised the Henriks."

He gathered some generous hunks of steak and set off.

I selected a torn jacket and a pair of moccasins that had their soles worn through. Finding some spare leather, a knife, a sharp stone hole maker and a bone needle I set to work making repairs. Meanwhile Knut set to work on fitting a new shaft onto the spear that had snapped off in the struggle with the monstrous cat.

As we worked the delicious aroma of the stew permeated the room, whetting our appetites. The children, little Bjorn and Helga, romped around and insisted on helping me, which didn't assist very much but felt sociable, as if I was really part of the family.

Torsten was back shortly before it got dark. I speculated about how it might have played out between him and Ursula, but I kept those thoughts to myself.

We stopped what we had been doing and gathered to eat. Runulf voiced our praises to Gaia for her nourishment and bounty and we set to work on filling our empty stomachs.

Gudrun had made a substantial quantity so as to consume the maximum amount of the copious meat that had descended into our laps that morning. The cat meat tasted something like pork, but leaner, tougher with a stronger iron flavour. It would have been tough to chew on were it not for the long slow cooking in the pot. It was delicious blended with the root vegetables and the sauerkraut accompanying it from one of the storage vessels. The mugs of ale Ranulf poured out for us helped wash it down.

As we settled back replete, Ranulf recited the story of how our world came to be. Five year old Bjorn absorbed his every word, three year old Helga listened intently but only understood in part and baby Inga gazed and took in the atmosphere, but as yet for her the words were only a comforting melodic sound.

In the Old Times our Earth Mother Gaia had domain over the world while Vulcan, the Lord of Destruction, slept in his underground lair, turning in his sleep only now and again to shake the Earth and spew fire.

The people discovered the powers of Vulcan, starting small with fire and metals, but over time digging ever deeper into the depths to reveal Vulcan's secrets, volatile fuels to provide power and movement, explosives to unleash destruction, poisons to desecrate Gaia's creation, spreading Vulcan's devastation ever wider across the surface of the Earth.

Only the True Followers of Gaia resisted Vulcan's pernicious influences, holding true to the True Natural Path.

Then came the Cataclysm, when Vulcan awoke to unleash his fury. Poisonous fire erupted across the land killing people, animals and plants alike in their multitudes.

Out of the swirling clouds of debris that filled the air, the great Commissum arrived. Supported by an army of metal soldiers, Commissum beat back the forces of Vulcan and set to work nursing the grievously wounded Gaia back to health.

Commissum saved the True Followers of Gaia providing for them a home in the natural environment of Ecologia.

Balance was restored by the establishment of the two Realms, Ecologia and Economica, to be forever held separated for the preservation of Gaia, our Mother Earth.

The Mark of Commissum

There had been no more uninvited nocturnal visitors when, settled as a family, Ranulf led us in giving thanks to Gaia for our breakfast of porridge and warmed up stew.

This time we would have had more warning because Ranulf had set up a rickety construction of sticks outside that would have made a clatter, had any unwanted visitor come snooping.

"Do you think that cat we killed yesterday has any friends or relations that may want to pay us a visit?" I remarked, wondering what the others may think.

"Quite possibly," Ranulf replied. "Those big cats are something new, recently brought back in by Commissum. He wouldn't have brought in only one."

"Back from where?" I asked.

"From the Old Times," Ranulf explained, "before they were wiped out by the forces of Vulcan."

"But if they were wiped out, how come there are any left to bring back?"

"Commissum gave flesh to their spirits that lived on, as he did for many of the other beasts we have around us, mammoths, aurochs and so on."

"Those other beasts have been around here for a while now," I observed, "but the sabre cat is something new, isn't it?"

"Yes," Ranulf agreed, "Commissum has been bringing them back one by one over time. They didn't come back all at once."

"Right, so it's like Commissum's restoring the Old

Times a bit at a time."

"We shouldn't really make presumptions about Commissum's intentions," Ranulf cautioned, "but I think that you are probably right about that."

"It is a problem for us when things get changed."

"Yes, it is," Knut agreed. "We now have the wolves, bears and pumas well trained to leave us alone, but the sabre cats are a challenge. We'll have to teach them respect."

"We need to put the fear of Commissum into the bastards," said Torsten. His family looked at him with concern. Even the children sensed the tension and looked around at the adults for reassurance.

Knut broke the tension. "What have we got on for today?"

"We need to go out and check the rabbit snares," said Torsten.

"There's no rush for that," said Gudrun. "We're not short of meat."

"We still need to check them," Torsten insisted. "We can't just leave them if something has been caught."

"I've got repairs to do on the storage shed," said Knut, not confrontationally but assertively enough to suggest his mind was made up.

"I've got to go back today," I said. "Sorry."

"You are risking the wrath of Commissum with this toing and froing of yours," Ranulf warned. "You know that it is forbidden to pass across between the realms of Economica and Ecologia."

"I know. But I've managed it for quite a while and so far it's been okay."

"One day it won't be," Ranulf said gravely. "We have seen

many others tracked down and seized by Commissum's metal angels. One day that will be your fate."

"But the rabbit snares still need to be checked," Torsten intervened irritably. He turned to Freya. "Freya, I need you to come out with me."

"No, find someone else," Freya retorted, her face flushed.

"Stop being difficult." Torsten voice rose. "You're coming."

"You have no right to tell me what to do," shouted Freya.

Torsten stood and reached to grab her. Gudrun moved in between them. "Stop that," she said. "We'll have peace here. None of this shouting."

Freya jumped up and ran towards the door. "I'm out of here for some peace."

The rest of the family watched her depart with concerned looks. Torsten stood to follow her, but Knut stepped in to hold him back.

"Enough mate. Leave her alone."

"What was that all about?" I whispered quietly to Ranulf.

"Last time those two were out together Freya came back in tears and she and Gudrun were huddled talking about it for some time afterwards," Ranulf explained "My guess is Torsten tried something on he shouldn't have."

"I see."

"Someone needs to go out after her to make sure that she's okay," said Runulf. "Obviously it can't be Torsten, but would you mind?"

"Sure," I said. "I'll tag along in the background, in case."

I slipped on my modern hiking boots. All my other

clothing was the same handmade stuff worn by the rest of the family, but my feet had never become accustomed to the much softer and less substantial moccasins that the others had. The boots were my one luxury import from my other existence in Economica.

I stepped out into the cold morning air. I could make out Freya a few hundred yards away walking through the gorse and bracken of the nearby heath land. I followed along keeping as low a profile as possible, hoping to keep her in sight without her seeing me.

That idea was unrealistic. Having spent her life in the wild country full of prey and predators she was fully tuned in to her surroundings. She soon spotted me skulking in the shrubbery. She looked straight at me, waving and nodding. I stood upright and gestured back. She made no movement towards me, and, understanding that she probably wanted time to herself, I too stayed where I was. I kept her in sight, but took care not to stare.

For a few minutes all was peaceful, Freya solitary and quiet with her thoughts, and me just keeping an eye on things. Then a faint whirring intruded, an electric motor. I was on alert. Mechanical sounds, even discreet barely audible ones, had no place in this environment. I sunk silently but stealthily to the ground, nestling amongst the gorse shrubs, taking care not to rustle the foliage.

A drone appeared hovering above me. I feared my luck had run out and the powers of law enforcement were about to place me under arrest for my trespassing in Ecologia. But this flying machine was not looking for me. Its attention was on Freya.

Like me, Freya took evasive action, attempting to hide,

but the machine had her in its sights. As it swooped across overhead I heard the dull thump of a dart gun followed by a brief shriek from Freya. For a few brief seconds she was back on her feet, attempting to make her escape, she wobbled, sank to her knees, her body swayed in her kneeling position and then fell forward.

Hovering above the scene the drone lowered a lightweight robotic machine on a thin cord. The robot released itself and trundled up to Freya's prostrate form on its chunky all terrain wheels. For a minute or so it was doing something to her. I couldn't see what, but it looked suspiciously intimate, rather along the lines of the interference by aliens some folk report as having happened to them.

Having completed its task the wheeled small robot reattached to its tether and was hauled up to rejoin its mother ship, departing.

I quickly made my way to where Freya was still lying on the ground. By then she was conscious, but groggy.

"Freya, are you okay?"

She blinked and screwed up her eyes to get them to focus on me.

"Yes, I think so."

She sat herself up and I knelt beside her.

"Are you hurt?"

"Well, there's this," she said, indicating a bruise and a puncture wound on her thigh. It must have been where the tranquiliser dart hit, although the dart itself was gone.

"And this," she said, hitching up her clothing to reveal a small incision that had been made on her hip and sealed with some sort of glue.

"Oh. I wonder what that could be." I examined the small sealed wound.

"Knut, Gudrun and Ranulf have those too," said Freya. "Ranulf says that it is the mark of Commissum, providing us with his protection."

"Right," I said, taking in the situation.

"Some of the animals we catch, deer, wolves and so on, they have those marks too," Freya continued. "We find a little metal object inside."

I nodded. I didn't say anything, but I was thinking it must be a tracking device. The powers-that-be were keeping tabs on the inhabitants of Ecologia. I guess it would only have been the larger creatures they were interested in. I don't suppose they could be bothered with mice, rabbits or insects.

My eyes strayed, wandering over Freya's enticing figure, her smooth skin and rounded form. I sensed Freya noticing where my attention had drifted, but she didn't seem to mind. She made no attempt to readjust her clothing to block my view.

She had seemed to me to have recovered her senses, but her eyes appeared to lose focus and she let her body flop against me, her head resting on my shoulder. I put my arms around her to support her and she snuggled into me like a bird settling into its nest. She appeared to enjoy being nestled up against me and I enjoyed having her there, so we lingered a while.

After a few minutes I felt our cosy togetherness was demanding to be resolved one way or the other.

"Come on, Freya," I said at last. "Time to get you back home."

I stood and helped her up back on her feet. I suspect she was perfectly capable of walking back under her own steam, but she held herself up against me, inviting me to support her as she walked. I was happy to oblige.

Back at the homestead I helped her into a comfortable seat and explained what had happened.

"She is blessed, claimed by Commissum," said Ranulf, nodding. "She is selected as a True Follower of Gaia."

Torsten looked at me, his face expressing a conflicted mix of jealousy and gratitude. He looked as if he wanted to say something, but couldn't figure out what to say.

It was getting late.

"I must go now," I announced.

There was that embarrassing pause when someone is about to depart, the feeling something should be said, but nobody can quite think what.

Ranulf broke the silence. "Go safely, brother Peter, be back to us soon."

"I will, brother Ranulf. I wish I could stay here with you."

"But you can, Peter, you can," Ranulf insisted.

"It's not so simple," I replied wistfully, "I have ties over there."

"Well, go safely. Take care."

I turned and stepped back out into the crisp chill of the morning. I allowed myself only one brief glance back as I walked away. Freya, Gudrun and the two older children, Bjorn and Helga, stood in the doorway watching as I departed. They didn't follow me because it was a rule I must go alone. The portal was my secret and it was important for it to remain so. The others did not necessarily understand, but Ranulf did and had convinced them that it must be so.

I needed to take precautions against the portal being discovered, so I arranged my route not to take me directly there.

About a mile into my circuitous journey I came across a bear with cubs. They were a few hundred yards away and as yet hadn't seen me. Not being seen is a good thing in some situations, but in the case of bears the opposite is the case. Encroaching on a bear quietly so that they become aware of you when you are already close is hazardous, the bear will see you as a threat, especially if she is a mother protecting cubs. Bears rarely wish to come into proximity with people except when they want to steal your food. When they see you at long range they will take care to maintain a distance.

I picked up a heavy rock, strode into the open and threw it down onto the stony ground where it landed with a crash. As I had intended the mother bear swivelled her head to face in my direction. I jumped up and raised my arms to ensure she saw me. I skirted around the ursine family, then turned sharply towards the perimeter of the territory.

In front of me loomed the fence, the great divide between the realms of Ecologia and Economica. As tall as the treetops and robust enough to withstand the most enraged of charging bull mammoths, its statement of Commissum's Law was clear. Nobody will pass between the two realms.

In my case, however, I did not need to concern myself with the fence, because I had another way through, known only to me.

In front of the fence was a rocky outcrop. Clambering down over the craggy rocks I dropped into a cleft. Almost hidden by dense foliage there was a hole that disappeared into the protrusion of boulders.

I dropped into the hole and took a few steps into a passageway cut into the bedrock by unknown hands eons ago. Just under the roof of the tunnel there was a cleft. I slid my hands in carefully and extracted my accoutrements of so-called civilised life, modern clothing, my mobile phone, wallet and a hard hat with a head torch. I peeled off the effects of my Ecologica persona, my rough handmade clothing, my dagger and necklace of stone charms and teeth and placed them back into the cleft.

I was also wearing a plaited leather bracelet threaded with charms carved from pieces of mammoth ivory, a memento from Freya. I decided to keep it on.

I cast my mind back to when I first discovered my closely guarded secret route between the realms.

The Portal

"I wish we could go over there," I said to my friend Tim.

Tim Membury, one of my few close friends from school, and I, both sixteen, were on holiday at the Mendips Scouts Youth Camp. It was the school summer holidays and we were allowed to spend a week on our own, our respective parents being reassured we would be supervised under the care of the Scouts. The Camp was situated within the Mendips National Park, an area of pseudo-wilderness where civilised folk from cities and suburbs within the Economically Organised Areas could amuse themselves with outdoor pursuits while pretending to be living within nature.

We were gazing out from a mound looking over a high fence that cut like a scar across the landscape. On the other side a herd of mammoths trampled the thick gorse and heather, seeking for more succulent foliage with their trunks. Hunkered down in the distance I could just make out a big cat, some kind of puma, stalking deer that were skirting the mammoths, perhaps for protection.

"Don't be daft. There's all sorts over there, bears, wolves, leopards. We'd get eaten in no time," said Tim.

I hadn't fancied the enthusiastic regimentation of the activities the Scouts had lined up for us on our first day so I'd persuaded Tim to slope off with me to explore by ourselves. To escape the infestation of electrically assisted mountain bikes, overriding Tim's reluctance to venture from well-trodden routes, I deliberately guided us onto rough, unofficial paths. These were unmarked and treacherous underfoot. I had no concerns about the deep ruts, jutting rocks and tree roots, happily leaping over the obstacles, but Tim trailed behind painstakingly negotiating the challenges. Ignoring his increasingly worried look, I had taken us to the furthest extent of the park where we encountered the barrier fence that divided the comparatively tame landscape from the altogether wild Mendip NER, Natural Ecology Reservation.

"I don't care. I'd take my chances," I said.

"You really are nuts. Besides, people aren't allowed over there. It's reserved for wildlife."

I didn't answer straight away. I was focussed on what I could see over the way within the NER. A short distance from the deer I could just make out a couple of human figures lurking behind shrubbery.

"Ah, that's where you're wrong," I said triumphantly. "Look over there. They're people, aren't they?"

Tim gazed over. "What are you talking about? I can't see anybody."

"Look, plain as daylight. Behind some bushes, in front of those trees, next to the big rock."

There were three figures visible now, dressed in makeshift clothing and armed with primitive weapons. Like the puma, they stalked the deer. There was a flurry of movement as they dashed forward. They weren't quick enough. The deer sprang out of reach. The puma wasn't best pleased. It stood from where it had been crouching, lashing its tail in annoyance.

"Oh, alright, I see them now," Tim acknowledged.

"So, there are people over there, aren't there?"

"But they aren't people, not really."

"They looked like people to me."

"Well, I mean, not civilised people. They are like cavemen, sort of thing. From before real people came about. Prehistoric."

"Of course they are people. Just because they don't have modern stuff doesn't make them not real people."

"But they're primitive. Not evolved. Still like animals."

"By that argument Australian Aboriginals wouldn't be people either," I countered. "They were Stone Age before Europeans arrived. I think I should report you to the Racial Equality lot."

"Well, I suppose you've a point. But they're not being treated as equals, locked up like that behind that fence."

"We're kept behind the fence too. I'd say we were just as much the captives as they."

Tim looked at me as if I was deranged. "How do you mean? We're civilised and we've got our freedom, haven't we?"

"From here I'd say that they had more freedom. They might not have all the technology we have, but how much of that do we need?"

"You're nuts. We can't go back to being like that."

"I wouldn't mind," I said wistfully, feeling a connection and kinship with those folk not shared by Tim.

"Doesn't make any difference," said Tim. "There's that ruddy great fence in the way."

I looked at the fence. It did look secure. It reminded me of the fences around prison camps as depicted in old films about the Second World War. At intervals it was adorned with signs saying "DANGER, KEEP OUT, Natural Ecology Reservation".

"Oh, I don't know. I could find a way."

"Now you really are getting ridiculous. The whole place is covered with electronic sensors, it's electrified and there's law enforcement robots all over. You wouldn't stand a chance."

"I bet I bloody well could," I said, but without having the remotest idea how I'd manage it.

Unable to press on in the direction of the dangerously enticing wild territory we skirted along in parallel with the fence. We encountered a rocky cliff that forced us away from the fence, rejoining one of the park's paved paths.

A succession of three mountain bikes, propelled at speed with the assistance of their electric motors, brushed past us from behind almost pushing us off the path. A short time later two more came at us from in front. This was exactly why I wanted to avoid these main paths. I felt crowded and irritated, but Tim wasn't bothered.

We came across a notice board with a picture of a tiny nondescript plant with unremarkable little white flowers. The placard informed us we had entered a site of special scientific interest that was one of the few remaining habitats of the illustrated plant, the Plumbium cragwort.

Along the side of the path a little further along were heaps of old gravel, now covered in sparse alpine foliage. Normally I wouldn't have given it much thought, but the alpine flora looked familiar.

"Hey, look Tim," I exclaimed, "it's that cragwort thing, growing over there."

Tim was unimpressed. "What cragwort thing?"

"The one in the picture on the notice back there."

"Oh, really. So what?"

"I'm going to take a look." I sprang up onto the gravel heap and looked around. On the other side of the mound was a gap between rocks, a cavity that seemed to extend into the ground, but it was hard to tell because it was disguised by shrubbery that had grown up around it.

"Hey, Tim, come up here," I called. "Where do you reckon that goes?" I said, after he had clambered beside me.

"I wouldn't know," he answered, looking bored by the whole thing.

"I'm going to take a look."

I scampered down over the rocky ground and peered into the pothole. There was a passageway sloping into the ground. I was no archaeologist, but it did not look natural. It was crudely formed and must have been hewn by ancient miners.

"It's a secret passage," I reported. "We should see where it goes."

Tim had joined me, approaching in careful steps where I had hopped and skipped over the rocks.

"Are you sure? It doesn't look safe."

Ignoring him, I stepped into the hole and made my way along into the passage. Tim paused anxiously a few seconds, grimaced and followed behind.

I had expected to reach a dead end quickly. If there had been a chamber where it ended, that would have been interesting. But there wasn't any end. The passageway kept on sloping down into the bedrock. The deeper we penetrated the further we were from the entrance hole, our only source of light. Ten metres in the passage bent around slightly. Now cut off from the direct light there was only a black void in front.

"That's enough. We've got to get out now," Tim exclaimed, panic in his voice. Without waiting for me to reply he backed out as fast as he could manage.

I squinted into the blackness, my eyes adapting to the low light, but however hard I stared it remained a dark nothingness. I shrugged and followed Tim back into daylight.

For some reason the next morning Tim was unwilling to join me again for more exploration. He might have been deterred by the rough uncharted terrain, not to mention claustrophobia in dangerous holes in the ground. Another factor was that, in persuading him to accompany me on this jaunt to the Mendips, I'd promised him girls, and there were none to be found in the wilderness.

I might have predicted Tim, a social animal, would have been less than enthusiastic about solitary derring-do in the outdoors. However, he was more persuadable than my other close friend, Simon, who was neither social nor outdoorsy, but thoroughly cerebral.

I didn't mind being alone. Tim would have cramped my style in the exploration. For my part I felt a need to go back, a magnetic attraction I couldn't explain.

I slunk out of sight while other teenagers, including Tim, divided into groups to pursue various jolly outdoor pursuits the Scout leaders had arranged for them.

While the central hut was temporarily unsupervised I crept into the storeroom and helped myself to a head torch and one of the hard hats issued for participants in such delights as canyoning, tree top rope walking and rock climbing.

I made my way back to the hole. Some might wonder how I did that, since I had no map, compass or other navigation aid, but I have always been able to find my way. I can't explain how I manage it because it is instinctive and does not involve any method or conscious thought.

Now, with the aid of my head torch and hard hat to prevent me banging my head on the rock of the low passage, there was no need for me to stop when I was out of sight of the light from the tunnel entrance.

There came a point where the passage split. I chose one of the passages, which eventually came to a vertical shaft I needed to be careful not to fall into.

I realised that what I was doing broke every health and safety rule in existence. I couldn't call for help because I had left behind my mobile phone. I often did that. When I was out on my own I wanted to be on my own, not constantly pestered by people calling, not even people I was close to, like Tim. I wouldn't have had a signal under all that rock in any case. I didn't care. Stuff health and safety.

I backed out and took the other passage, which split again. As I went deeper it split yet again. I had somehow got myself into a labyrinth. I had the presence of mind to scratch fresh marks in the rock at each junction, signposts for my way out.

Methodically I explored each passage, tracking back on reaching dead ends or shafts that even I acknowledged would have been too dangerous to pursue. Eventually I sensed a faint light in front of me. The passage sloped up and the light became clearer.

As I reached it was clear that this was not where I had come in, but an entirely different entrance into my newly discovered underworld, being a markedly different shape and emerging into another landscape.

There were no paths I could see. I tucked my hard hat and torch into the small rucksack I had brought with me and set off across the bumpy terrain, picking across tussocks of bracken and gorse, my feet alternately sinking into crevices and tripping over rocks.

After a couple of hundred metres I saw the massive fence separating the civilised world from the wildness of the Ecology Reservation, rather as the Berlin Wall had once formed part of an Iron Curtain across Europe. I moved towards it, hoping it would allow me to get my bearings.

As I approached the fence I noticed something odd about it. The signs that hung from it were mounted on the opposite side facing the other way, so that I couldn't read them. In a moment the significance struck home. I was within the Ecology Reservation, looking out towards the realm of civilised humanity, the EOA, the Economically Organised Area.

I didn't have long to contemplate my situation. There was a hair raising howl a short way behind me, followed by two more from either side a little further in the distance.

I turned to investigate to be confronted by a large timber wolf. A short while later it was joined by several more wolves. They formed a posse blocking my route back to the underground passageway, my portal back into civilisation.

I should have been terrified, but strangely wasn't. I was elated by the danger and excitement.

I had read somewhere that to gain control over a group

of dogs you first had to identify which is the dominant one and then dominate that individual. If you succeeded, the other dogs would follow, taking their lead from their pack leader. I figured that the same principle should apply to wolves.

I stood tall and walked slowly and purposefully towards the first wolf growling in the manner of a savage dog. For a while the wolf stood its ground, its hackles raised. I kept on coming. The wolf backed away slowly, growling as it did so, but clearly in retreat. The other wolves slowly backed away too. I edged towards one side of the group so as to get past.

As soon as I was beside them and was no longer moving towards them, the wolf pack leader felt emboldened and began to advance on me again, cautiously initially, but picking up speed when I didn't react immediately.

I repeated the stand-off, advancing and growling as I approached the wolf, which again backed away.

I again moved along back towards my escape portal. The stand-off repeated at intervals. Seeing me in retreat the wolves advanced, so I had to stand up to them, allowing me to back up a short distance towards my escape route before having to stand up again to the wolves.

It was with relief I reached the entrance to the passage system and dropped into it. With the wolves out there it wouldn't be safe for me to explore further, so I called it a day, retracing my steps back to the Scout camp.

Tim asked me about my day. I thought for a moment and decided I wouldn't be sharing my experiences, even with him.

"Oh, this and that," I answered noncommittally. "I saw

some wolves. They were on the prowl hunting something or other."

"You're obsessed by that Ecology Reservation and its wildlife," Tim observed. "Can't say I'm that bothered myself. Nice to have seen it the once, but not sure that I need to go back. I expect that you're glad the wolves weren't hunting you."

I bit my lip and changed the subject. "What did you get up to?"

"Up in the trees on rope walkways. There was this girl, Laura. Gorgeous. She was scared of heights so I held her hand. Looking forward to seeing her tomorrow."

I pondered. I'd probably had enough wild excitement for the time being. Time to be more sociable.

"I expect I'll join you tomorrow too," I said. "Promise I won't cramp your style with Laura."

Back in the present, the entrance into the portal on the Economica side of the fence remained the same as it had back when I'd discovered it as a teenager. The Plumbium cragwort still thrived on the otherwise barren mounds of gravel. Most important, the portal remained known only to me.

The Old Days

It wasn't until I had had a good soak and scrub in the bath tub at my overnight bed and breakfast place, the Old Vicarage in West Dulcote within the Mendip National Park, a good night's sleep in a normal modern bed and a full English breakfast that I felt fully transitioned from my wild existence back to modern living.

Had such places still been operated by human hosts they might have taken exception to my pungent odour after a week of living unwashed in a smoky hut, but the robotic staff didn't care. The front of house robot took the form of a West Country farmer's wife with rosy cheeks and ample bosom. Her cheery persona and jokey banter made it easy to forget she was a machine.

I took an autotaxi to the hyper-tube station in Glastonbury. Instead of taking the tube back home to Woking I took one to Swindon, where I was to visit my elderly paternal grandmother, which was ostensibly my reason for being away.

It might have been nice to have seen the countryside between Glastonbury and Swindon as one would in the days of surface trains, but hyper-tubes are strictly enclosed and subterranean.

In days gone by I could have made the trip by road and way back, as far as the first half of the twenty first century, I may even have owned and driven the vehicle, but that is no longer possible, even using a self-driving autotaxi. The EOAs, Economically Organised Areas, known collectively as Economica within the realm of Ecologia, now form enclaves, separated off within the NERs, the Natural Ecology Reservations that surround them, known by their inhabitants as the realm of Ecologia. The inhabitants of the EOAs are not permitted to enter or cross the NERs on the surface, nor, in normal circumstances, to overfly them, leaving the hyper-tubes as the only means to pass from one EOA to another.

The hyper-tubes are fast, smooth and well equipped for personal entertainment, music and visual displays of one's choice. I used the 40 minutes of waiting and travel to catch up on news and personal messages.

Celia, my fiancée, seemed anxious to hear from me. I had explained before I left a week previously that I liked time on my own out of contact with the outside world to relax and recharge, but she hadn't really understood. It is inexplicable to many people, my Celia included, how someone could want to get away from day to day contact. I referred her to a learned article about how the frantic pace of everyday life can overstress people, recommending periods of separation for their mental health. She had been somewhat mollified but I don't really think she found it convincing. I let her know I was back in contact, I had been thinking about her and loved her. From her reaction it appeared to me that while I had been destressing she had been stressing about my absence.

From the Swindon hyper-tube station it was a short ride by autotaxi to my grandmother's home, an old terrace house built in the early twentieth century.

From appearances it was my grandfather who answered the door, but of course it wasn't him. He'd died ten years before. It was the robot carer and companion my grandmother had subsequently acquired.

Instead of aging with time, this facsimile of my grandfather had been rejuvenated, seeming now younger, more energetic and a good couple of inches taller than I remembered him from my childhood. Presumably my grandmother had had his robotic representation embellished slightly.

I went along with the pretence, greeting him as Grandad and asking how he was. I have to admit the technology is impressive. He talked to me exactly as Grandad always had, the same accent, the same turns of phrase, the same facial expressions. It was easy to get drawn into the illusion that Grandad remained with us, hale and hearty. Besides, I needed to pretend for Grandma's sake, because, to her, her beloved Tommy was still there, keeping her company and looking after her.

It began not long after Grandad died. To start with Grandma became forgetful and sometimes found things hard to understand. Certain things confused her. She would make mistakes identifying people, calling them by a different name. Initially she knew that her new version of her beloved husband Tommy was a robotic imitation, but there came a point when he was real for her, the Tommy that she had known and loved all those years. The technical excellence of the robotic substitute made it easy to believe. We can thank our modern surveillance society for that. For decades we have enjoyed the convenience of electronic devices within the home that obey our every command, switching on the lights, playing our favourite music, putting the dinner on to cook. For all that time the devices have been watching and listening to us, serving as material to be drawn on when we want to reproduce a loved one in electro-mechanical form.

As I came in I was greeted by the robotic dog. It did dog like things, trotted wagging its tail like a dog, sniffed me like a dog. I could see the advantages. It was more convenient than a real dog. It did not need to be fed or taken for walks. It was fully obedient. It did not leave hairs on the furniture, wee on the carpet nor attempt to have sex with your leg. It did not need veterinary care. Heartache could be avoided because if it became damaged or defective it could be repaired or replaced, which robotic Grandad could take care of without Grandma even needing to know.

I took a seat in the living room with Grandma while robot Grandad brought us tea and cake.

"I don't like those hyper things," said Grandma after I had explained how I had come. "They give the creeps, going underground all closed in like that."

"They're not so bad. They're quick and comfortable."

"I don't know why we can't just drive over or go on the train like in the old days."

"There's the Ecology Reservations in the way now."

"We used to have fields with cows and corn and things out there in the old days. What happened to them?"

"We don't need those fields now. Our meat, milk and so on gets specially cultured."

"I've never liked that. Eating all those chemicals. It's not natural."

"But Grandma, it means we aren't exploiting animals and it doesn't impact the environment as much."

"But we'd still have to have the fields, even without meat. There's the vegetables to be grown."

"Hydroponics, Grandma. The vegetables don't need fields. They are grown indoors under artificial light."

"It's just not natural. I don't like it."

"So, Grandma, what was it really like in the good old days?"

"Well, for one, we could go on holiday. We went to Spain, Greece, Italy and places like that in those days. It was lovely and hot."

"That must have been nice. How did you get there?"

"By plane, of course."

"I've never been in a plane," I mused.

"Why, don't you like flying?"

"It's not normally allowed."

"Oh, why not? We used to fly out somewhere every year."

"It upsets the environment."

"You could go across to France on the train, or a ferry though, couldn't you?"

"No, I'm afraid not. You'd need a special migration permit."

"Couldn't you get one, a permit, I mean."

"Well, some people do, but not many. They normally have to have some affinity or ancestry in the country to qualify."

"Couldn't you just say you did."

"Well, the Commission would check. They'd know if it wasn't true. Even then there'd be a three year course in French language and culture; I'd need to pass a tough exam at the end of it. Then if I did go I'd have to become French, Italian or whatever and I wouldn't be allowed back again."

"I don't like that," lamented Grandma. "Not being able to travel."

"There's always places to go in England," I observed.

"I used to like going up to London," Grandma recalled. "There were theatres, museums. Clubs too. We had some fun there."

"London doesn't exist anymore," I said.

"What do you mean?"

"It got destroyed in the Nuclear War, Grandma. You must remember."

"What became of it?"

"What of it that wasn't blown to bits was too radioactive for people to be there anymore."

"Something must have happened to it?"

"It's an NER now."

"What's that?"

"One of those Ecological Reservations. Apparently the wild animals don't mind the radiation as much as people do."

I pressed on with our conversation for a while, but Grandma would forget what we were talking and return to topics that we had already covered. I take my hat off to the designers of artificial intelligence because, somehow sensing my discomfort, robotic Grandad stepped into the conversation, which allowed me to take a break.

I stood and looked around the room. On one side was a bookcase containing Grandad's extensive collections of real books, with paper pages and cardboard covers. This was unusual because these days few people have any physical books. Anything that you might want to read is available online via a simple search.

I had always found Grandad's books interesting to browse. Before the Nuclear War he had been a professor of theoretical physics at Cambridge. The War had brought that to an end. For one thing Cambridge had been wiped off the map by a thermonuclear bomb. That would have been a setback, but what ended his career in science was that after the Nuclear War the Commission outlawed the study of anything that could be used for the development of weapons, such as explosives, nuclear devices, toxic chemicals or germ warfare, which precluded almost all science disciplines.

At first Grandad hoped to re-establish his academic career in one of the few science-related fields still permitted, pure mathematics. The problem was nearly every other former scientist had the same idea.

In desperation he had explored an opportunity in the gambling industry, figuring out betting odds and ways to fleece the punters without them noticing too much, but this had come to nothing. It wouldn't have suited him as he was nowhere near mercenary and unscrupulous enough.

Finally he set himself up as a tax advisor, helping to arrange the financial affairs of a few private clients. His heart wasn't in it. He practised only just enough to get his essential bills paid, devoting most of his efforts into mathematical research for his own amusement and to get him invited to prestige international symposia. Before the War the international events would have had him travelling far and wide, but in the post-War era these were always held online, so his participation was from the tiny spare room in his Swindon residence.

I scanned Grandad's old books. There were learned

explanations of theories complete with the complex mathematics involved. Isaac Newton's *Principia Mathematica*, Einstein's *Theories of Relativity*, Schrödinger, Stephen Hawking on black holes, Max Planck, Heisenberg's uncertainty principle and other science classics. I had no concept of the science, but I did recognise the names and knew their historical importance. I also knew such texts had long since become unavailable.

Besides the physical science books, there was a Social Science paper entitled the "The Psychology of Opting Out". I leafed through the contents. It was an anthropological study from before the Nuclear War of what appeared to be a hippy cult based near Glastonbury calling themselves "Followers of the True Natural Path". They rejected anything unnatural, such as machinery, electronics and other modern contrivances. They had adopted pagan beliefs involving nature spirits and an Earth goddess called Gaia.

Grandad himself was long gone and they were clearly no longer of any use to Grandma. When she passed on the books would probably just be thrown away.

I turned back to Grandma, who was still being kept amused by robotic Grandad. I intruded into their chat, which in any case was probably just repeating an exchange that they had already had a thousand times.

"Grandma, these books, would it be alright if I borrowed some? They look jolly interesting."

"I don't know, dear," she answered. "They're your Grandad's. Why don't you ask him?"

Humouring her I turned to her robotic carer. "Grandad, would that be okay?"

"If it's alright with your Grandma, it's alright with me," the robot replied obligingly.

We both, the robot and I, turned our gaze to her. "Well, I'm not bothered. Take a look at the books. Nobody else does."

I selected some of the most historic tomes, as many as I could fit into my case and still lift it. I slid along the remaining volumes up to fill the gaps, leaving a space at one end of one of the shelves.

"You might want to put some ornaments, a picture or something there to fill the gap," I suggested to robotic Grandad.

"Don't worry, I'll take care of it," the robot replied.

Books

I didn't take Grandad's books to read myself. They were for my old friend, Simon Spiegelhalter, who I knew would appreciate them. They were heavy so I decided to drop them around to him right away.

Simon lived in a down-at-heel block of modular housing units in a rough neighbourhood on the outskirts of Woking.

The modular housing units were prefabricated, each approximately the same size as a shipping container, and, like shipping containers, designed to be assembled into stacks like Lego blocks. The services, utilities, waste and so on were fed in at one end of each block in a standard plug and play layout allowing them to be connected quickly to assembled services towers. The front door was at the other end of the unit and opened onto modular access cloisters that served a row of modules. These external corridors were also stacked, connected with an elevator tower at one or both ends of the block. Internally each module was laid out with all the necessary living facilities, a living space with comfortable seating and a fold out table, a kitchenette, a sleeping space and a compact bathroom. It was reasonably comfortable for a single person and adequate, if a little cramped, for a couple. The modular design allowed for more spacious accommodation of multiple conjoined modules to be provided for families.

While modular housing provides for the basic needs of their residents, they carry a strong social stigma such that almost anybody who could afford chooses to live somewhere else. These are, in general, the homes of those who depended entirely for their existence on UBI, Universal Basic Income. That amounts to more than half of the population because, since almost all essential services and most clerical work are automated, opportunities for gainful employment are limited.

When he let me in Simon didn't show any noticeable emotion. It wasn't a surprise to him because I had called ahead. There wasn't anything in his manner to suggest he didn't want me there, but neither did he demonstrate enthusiasm for my presence. Someone who didn't know Simon might have inferred from his manner that they were not welcome. I knew Simon well so I was aware he had few friends, indeed it was possible I was his only friend. Thus my occasional contacts and visits were practically the full extent of his social interaction and I knew he valued them. Being as he was, it would never have occurred to Simon he should express this outwardly let alone feign enthusiasm when a friend called.

Neither did he feel it necessary to introduce or acknowledge his companion, Lulu.

I had met Lulu before. She was a companion robot. Unlike Grandma's robot companion, Lulu did not represent any particular person. She was an entry level model of a more basic standardised construction. My substitute Grandad had a build quality that meant most people would take him as being a real person at first glance, but Lulu lacked the cosmetic detail to pass convincingly as human. She was what many would disparage as being a sexbot, exaggeratedly curvaceous and endowed with pneumatically inflated bosoms and simpering pouted lips.

Companion robots do not come cheap, even entry level models like Lulu, so Simon would have struggled to afford her on his basic UBI. He had probably had assistance from his parents for the initial purchase and he lived frugally so he would have been able to cover the regular maintenance costs.

While I couldn't fully see Simon from a woman's perspective, I could see enough to realise that he was unlikely to appeal to many as a romantic partner. He had a thin face and nerdy expression, a slight frame clothed in random garments that did nothing for him, non-existent social skills and zero wealth or career prospects. What those women may not have perceived is that Simon was one of the most intelligent and original thinkers one would ever be likely to encounter, a one in a million intellect. Still, Lulu was a good solution to fulfil Simon's romantic and sexual needs.

Simon held the door open, caught my eye only briefly and looked away, then gestured to the seating area.

"Ah, Peter, come on in. Take a seat," said Simon, his voice emotionless.

"Thanks Simon," I said. "Hello Lulu, good to see you." It seemed polite to acknowledge her.

"Hello Peter, nice to see you again," said Lulu, setting her face in a stereotypical sexy plastic smile.

I dragged my heavy case over the width of the room and flopped down onto the sofa.

"I expect you both would like some tea," said Lulu.

"Oh, yes please."

Lulu bustled out into the kitchenette area.

Simon sat beside me, glanced at me briefly and glanced

away. It was clearly going to be left to me to initiate the conversation. I was used to that with Simon. "I saw the law enforcement robots arresting someone just now as I came up to the block."

"There were 226 arrests in the neighbourhood over the last year."

"Oh, what were they arrested for, all those people?"

"About 158 were drug related, 38 burglaries, 27 assaults and 3 murders."

"You've got a good memory for figures."

"The arrest rate went up after the mobile tracking devices were introduced. People came to know where the fixed ones were located and they used to get vandalised."

"Oh, right."

"In Surrey each law enforcement robot made an average of 102 arrests last year," Simon continued, "but that's below the English average of 131."

"Simon, let's take a look at those books I mentioned that I was bringing over for you."

"Oh, yes. Let's," said Simon. There was just the slightest hint of animation in his voice. Knowing him well I could tell that he was itching to see them.

I opened my case and laid out the books on the table. Simon picked up each one as I did so, examining it carefully. He didn't say anything and there was little expression on his face but I could see he was enraptured.

"What do you think, Simon?"

"There're very interesting. These are frequently referred to in historical writings but the texts are not available to be seen anywhere online. I did once glean a little information from a photograph that had one of the books laid open, but that was too fuzzy to make much out."

"Was it interesting, what you did manage to read?"

"Well, it was a formula relating to Heisenberg's uncertainty principle. I was uncertain what to make of it."

I sniggered at his witticism. Simon stared back vacantly. "That was funny, Simon. What you said."

"Was it?"

I'd noticed this about Simon. There was a part of his brain that did humour and poetry, but it was disconnected from the remainder of his thought processes.

"Never mind. So, you're going to enjoy looking through the books?"

"Yes, I will."

At this point Lulu came in with the tea and biscuits. She laid her tray beside the books, shuffling them up a bit to make room. As she did so she looked over at me with a simpering look, stroking her nylon hair back over her ear and wobbled her excessively rounded bottom in my direction.

"Has Peter come over to have some fun?" Lulu asked Simon.

"Yes," said Simon.

It was clear he hadn't appreciated what the question was implying. Lulu came over and held her voluptuous robotic silicone body up against me. She eased her hand down against my thigh. For a few seconds I hesitated, not knowing how to react.

"I don't think that Simon meant that kind of fun," I said eventually, as her polypropylene fingers felt down between my legs.

"Oh, was it more this sort of fun?" Lulu asked, as she

wrapped her arms around my upper body and thrust her pouting synthetic lips onto mine. Her rubbery robotic tongue felt its way into my mouth, bringing with it a plastic taste as if I was sucking on a polythene bag.

I pushed her aside.

"Simon, please, explain to her. We're just talking, not doing stuff."

"Oh, yes, er, Lulu, we're just talking, not doing things," Simon explained, belatedly.

Lulu languidly detached from me. "Oh, what a pity. Perhaps we can have some fun together later."

"Yes, perhaps later," I said, although what I meant was, perhaps not. As I recovered my composure I grappled to remember where the conversation had left off. "Simon, you said that none of these books are available to read online. Why do you think that is? Surely they should be."

"There is nothing said about the reason officially, but I believe it must be a measure to prevent another catastrophic war. If people don't know the science that lies behind nuclear weapons and other dangerous stuff, they can't make the armaments."

"But the same science underlies most of the technology around us that we depend upon, doesn't it?" I reasoned. "I mean robots, artificial intelligence, green energy, synthetic food production, high speed transportation."

"Yes, it does," Simon acknowledged, "but that technology is provided by the Commission. If you're not the Commission I guess you don't need to know."

Lulu moved across to snuggle up against Simon. "Simon, love, have we done talking?" she cooed into his ear. "Is it time for the fun now?"

Simon didn't say anything, allowing Lulu to stroke him with her plastic fingers.

I intervened. "Lulu, please, not just now. We're still talking."

"What a shame," she said. "I was just getting into it."

"Simon," I said, pointedly making the point that it was him I was talking to, "if nobody gets taught this science stuff, where does the Commission get its expertise from?"

"Perhaps the Commission doesn't need people for its expertise."

I was taken aback. "But they must need people, surely."

"Not necessarily."

Lulu was still cuddled against him, nuzzling him with her lips. I could see his point. Lulu seemed to be doing rather well and she wasn't a person, at least, not a human person. Where does one draw the line?

"Anyway, it looks as if you're going to enjoy the books."

"Very much so."

"What do you like about them particularly?"

"They are a point of view frozen in time, unchanging and preserved," Simon explained.

"But surely it is more convenient just to access the information online than try to find an actual book in an old fashioned library."

"The problem with material that is online is that it gets constantly re-drafted to reflect contemporary mores. It's a kind of re-writing of history," Simon explained.

"But that has always happened, hasn't it?" I objected. "I mean, the Nazis burned books, didn't they?"

"Burning books is for all to see and some books will escape. You don't see it happen when online content gets altered or removed and it is thorough, leaving nothing, except perhaps in people's memories."

Lulu wobbled her huge pneumatic breasts against Simon's face.

"I'm burning with desire," she crooned in a voice that resonated like a seductive French singer in a 1950s nightclub.

Simon was preoccupied. I kept quiet for fear that her attentions might switch back in my direction.

"We should make music," Lulu purred into Simon's ear, "you, me and Peter, all of us together."

"Not just now, Lulu, thanks all the same," I said hurriedly. I wished that Simon would take control over that wretched robot.

I sought to regain the initiative by bringing us back to our conversation.

"Talking of censorship, I remember there was a craze for cancelling and de-platforming things that didn't conform with the moral values of the time. Did we lose some stuff from that?"

Remarkably Simon maintained focus on the discussion despite the constant distraction from Lulu. I couldn't imagine how he could manage that.

"Actually no. It didn't work because you can't turn major historical figures such as George Washington and Winston Churchill into non-people. There was a backlash and these figures only became more prominent and widely known."

"Yet, the Commission has successfully managed to erase swathes of scientific literature without trace."

"They don't make a fuss about it. They just do it.

Besides, it isn't actually without trace. Many historical accounts refer to the works. It is just the works themselves that have gone. We do know they existed though, and here they are, some of them at least."

Lulu was reaching down towards Simon's crutch. "Well, I'll be going now," I announced. "I'll leave you with the books. I hope you enjoy them, if Lulu will let you."

Childhood Reminiscences

Leaving Simon to study the books my mind wandered back to my childhood days when I had first come to know him at school.

Despite the radical changes to teaching and learning that arose in the years after the world moved online at the beginning of the twenty first century, schools as institutions have retained their central role in bringing up children to play their parts in society.

Prior to the cyber age it was teachers who carried out the instruction of pupils by presenting materials in classrooms. From the earliest days of schooling this was augmented by books pupils could read for themselves, which by the middle years of the twentieth century was enhanced using other media such as cinema, radio and television. Nevertheless presentation by teachers in classrooms remained the principal means of instruction well into the twenty first century.

Cyber technology, despite the dogged resistance of traditionalists, turned this on its head. Automated interactive online presentation combined with individual participation by pupils proved more effective. The presentation of the material was of a slick professional broadcast standard, standardised and presented at exactly the pace and depth appropriate for the abilities of each pupil. The pupil's understanding of the material was checked constantly throughout the lessons, with topics revised and augmented with additional explanation until grasped by the pupil. Lessons could be taken at any time and could be extended or shortened to suit the needs of the individual pupil.

This revolution in teaching methods prompted soul-searching and anxiety about what schools and teachers were for. Since it was now possible for almost all academic subjects to be learnt from home, perhaps home schooling should have become the norm?

It became recognised that, far from simply being somewhere children were crammed with academic knowledge, schools played a vital role in socialising children during their formative years, enabling them to both to form friendships, many of which would last a lifetime, and to acquire the skills necessary for forming friendships later in life. It was not only friendships. Schools were required to provide children with the skills to work collaboratively. Far from advancing the cause of home schooling, this realisation killed the concept.

Teachers moved on from being presenters in classrooms to coaches, motivating and disciplining as needed to get the individual online study done and developing the teamwork to undertake the joint projects that were the culminating stages of each academic study area after the individual online tuition was completed.

I didn't have many friends at school. I never fit in social groups. I held out for my right to do things the way I wanted. I refused to adopt the conventions of the well-connected nor to slavishly toe the imposed line. Thus I was not particularly liked either by my peers or those in authority.

A contributing factor was my mother, who was incapable of demonstrating her love for me. I always felt that I was a disappointment to her, unworthy of her love.

I recall on one occasion, when I must have been little more than a toddler, my mother left me in the care of another woman while she had to go on some errand. The woman cuddled me, had me do little things to keep me amused, praised me for what I had done, telling me how clever I was. I think it was drawing a picture of a house and some trees and there may have been some people and a dog there too. It was the usual childish daub, but she told me it was great. I wasn't used to being treated this way. My mother never behaved like that. I rationalised that my mother knew me better, knew how useless I was, but this woman didn't know me yet so she hadn't found out what I was really like.

My mother was damaged. She had come through the Nuclear War, had her home and family vaporised and was brought up an orphan in the chaotic post-war period. To those around her she appeared to function competently, but it was functioning almost devoid of emotion, with an intolerance of anything less than perfect.

Thanks to my mother, by the time I arrived at school I had no expectation anyone would like or approve of me, so I made no attempt to seek popularity or approval, which became a self-fulfilling prophecy.

I found fellow feeling with another loner in our class, the unconventional and eccentric Simon Spiegelhalter. He was an odd fellow, to be sure. He never seemed to pick up on social cues, or participate socially at all. I overheard one of the teachers refer to him as being on the spectrum, whatever that meant.

Nevertheless, I found it perfectly possible to talk to him. It didn't bother me that he avoided eye contact, nor that he didn't express much emotion. I would make a remark or ask him a question about a topical subject, perhaps related to schoolwork or something different. He would respond to it, usually in depth, oblivious to social acceptability, covering aspects and points of view that would never normally have occurred to me. Once he started there was almost no stopping him. I was always stimulated by his unique take.

I recall an occasion when we were twelve. We had just been imbued with the current English national ethos under the title "The Nation, United and Pure". I explored its meaning and significance.

"What do you think about the bit about us all having to stand together to uphold English values?" I asked Simon.

"I don't know what English values are, so I don't know what I am supposed to be upholding."

"Well, you know, playing cricket by the rules, fair play, that sort of thing."

"But we're supposed to be proud of our history. Yet we were among those countries that set off the nuclear weapons that almost destroyed the planet."

"Yes, but our bombs landed on Russia and the Middle East. We had to bomb them because they were threatening us."

"Just because the damage was done to Moscow and Tehran doesn't excuse it."

"We have to stand up for ourselves as a nation, otherwise we'd be finished."

"We very nearly were. London, Cambridge and many

other places were wiped off the map and we still can't go back there."

"But we couldn't just give in, could we?"

"How would giving in have been a problem?"

"We'd have been under the jackboot of a foreign power."

"But we have given in."

"How do you mean?"

"We are controlled by the Commission, aren't we?"

"No we're not. The Commission is there to serve our needs," I retorted.

"It seems like control to me. We can't travel. We obey rules about pollution, preserving the environment and so on. We can't have modern weapons nor develop the means to produce them."

"Well, yes, but those things are for our own good. We agreed to those things after the War. Besides it's not like being controlled by foreigners. We have kept the foreigners out, which has kept the nation pure."

"What do you mean keeping foreigners out?" said Simon. "We are foreigners already. Look at our history. There were Celts pushing out other Celts. Romans. Vikings doing raping and pillaging. Normans. Scots. Irish. French Huguenots. Then a load of people came over from the British Empire and they didn't go away. We couldn't be more mongrelised."

There was a positive to my emotionally starved formative years. From my earliest childhood I have been self-reliant. I found that I could cope on my own, so I stood up for myself, even if that sometimes meant I was in a minority of one.

My contemporaries were wary of me, even in awe, because if they attempted to bully me I would respond robustly.

One day our school yard bully, Duncan McThomas, a nasty vindictive boy who gratuitously picked on those he perceived as weaker and less popular than most, had been needling me for some time. For some reason he had got it into his head that because I was friends with Simon we must be in a gay relationship. He went on about how gays disgusted him, how he hated gays and the unpleasant things he would like to do to gays.

For a period I didn't react, not intimidated, but impassive. This only emboldened him to goad me more, determined to continue until I gave him the reaction he wanted. He got a reaction, but not the one he had expected. It wasn't really a fight. It was too quick. I exploded and in seconds, almost before he knew what hit him, I had reduced him to a bloodied quivering wreck on the floor.

Tim Membury, who was to become one of my closest friends, was mightily impressed as well as gratified because Duncan had been picking on him too. Tim was sociable, witty and popular, which made Duncan jealous. Tim was stunned by how I felled him so quickly, too fast for Duncan's tough cronies to intervene.

"You put him in his place, good and proper," Tim observed.

"He was well out of order."

"Wish I could have done that."

I don't think he could have, I mused. When it came to witty patter and repartee Tim was brilliant, but physically he was timid. It wasn't that he was small or weak, it was more that he lacked physical confidence. If one was being unkind, one might call him a coward, although I would never have said such a thing directly or behind his back.

"It shouldn't ever have to come to that," I said. "It wouldn't, if people didn't go too far."

Tim drew me into his entourage, who, having previously ignored me, found me an interesting and welcome member of their circle.

Tim and I developed a symbiotic relationship. Having me as a close friend and companion boosted his image by association with my physical presence. For my part, Tim was my passport into the social scene.

I maintained my friendship with Simon and Tim throughout my school days and since, but they never really came together. To be fair to Tim, he acknowledged and respected my friendship with Simon, and he did try, for my sake, to reach out to Simon. But to Tim, Simon was an enigma. The style and thought patterns of my two best friends were so far apart there could be no bridging them.

When we were about fourteen Tim came around collecting for the English Wildlife Restoration Fund, a well-respected charity devoted to the welfare of traditional English wildlife such as red squirrels, starlings and chaffinches. At the time he was courting one of our classmates, Fiona Deveryll, whose father was a patron of this cause.

I was about to dip into my pocket money with a few pennies, but Simon replied with a flat, "no".

Tim was taken aback. "But why not?"

"You are asking us to pay for the extermination of

wildlife," replied Simon. "I don't want to do that."

"No I'm not," said Tim indignantly. "This is to preserve wildlife, not hurt it."

"What wildlife are you preserving?"

"Well, there's red squirrels, they need saving, and birds, the songbirds in our hedgerows, noctules."

"What's a noctule?" I enquired.

"It's a type of bat that lives in trees," said Tim. I suspect he had only heard it from Fiona in the past few days.

"Sounds like a good thing to me," I said. "What's wrong with it, Simon?"

"Preserving red squirrels means killing grey squirrels. Preserving noctules means killing parakeets."

"But grey squirrels and parakeets are invasive species. They don't belong here."

"Why not?"

"Because we need to preserve native species," replied Tim.

"There are no native species. They're all invaders."

"What do you mean? Red squirrels, songbirds, bats and so on, they've always been here."

"No, they haven't."

"I don't understand," said Tim, genuinely puzzled.

"Twelve thousand years ago this whole area was under an ice sheet," Simon explained. "There was almost nothing living here then."

"But that was eons ago," said Tim.

"No, it wasn't. The Earth has been here four and a half billion years. Twelve thousand is almost no time at all."

"But we want to re-establish England back to its historical roots," Simon insisted. "That's only a thousand years or so, not twelve thousand."

"Not if it means slaughtering grey squirrels and parakeets."

"But they're foreign. We don't want them."

I intervened at this point. "I like your take on it, Simon," I said. "It's like in that book we've being doing in English Lit, you know, 1984, where things are called the opposite to what they are. So, we've got this English Wildlife Restoration Fund, which really should be called the Foreign Wildlife Extermination Fund."

"Don't you start," said Tim, in vain because I was just getting into my stride.

"Fiona lives in that nice house in Acacia Avenue, doesn't she?" I said.

"What's that got to do with it?" asked Tim.

"She put you up to this, didn't she?"

"No," said Tim, his blushing giving his lie away. "I believe in preserving our wildlife, even if it seems you don't."

"She's got alpacas living on their back paddock, hasn't she?" I observed.

"Yes," Tim acknowledged. "So what?"

"And her Dad has a great display of rhododendrons in their back garden, all nice big coloured flowers in the spring time."

"What of it?"

"Well, are you going to kill off her alpacas and root out her Dad's shrubbery?"

"Why would I do something like that?"

"They're foreign species, aren't they?" I said, going in for the kill. "You know, alpacas, South America, rhododendrons, the Himalayas. Not from round here."

Both our school and the English national establishment in general were enthusiastic about traditional sports such as football, rugby, cricket, tennis and so on. Supposedly it developed team spirit and maintained longstanding English tradition.

It was my mother who had first alienated me from ball games. When I was an infant she would throw me a ball, which I was supposed to catch. Naturally, as catching things is not a skill we are born with, I fumbled and dropped it. She berated my clumsiness. I felt as if I was a hopeless disappointment. She persisted, but by then I was unnerved and lacked confidence, so I dropped it again. Even when I did eventually catch a ball she didn't seem satisfied. I was instilled with a belief that I was fundamentally hopeless at pursuits involving balls.

The games were organised, they had rules, they involved wearing special clothing and were confined to marked-out pitches. I hated the conformity, a feeling shared by Simon, who, unlike me, was afflicted with a dyspraxia that was more disabling than the mere psychological impediment my mother had inflicted on me.

In contrast, my other friend Tim thrived on the playing fields. It wasn't that he was the best sportsman. There were others who were physically tougher and more adept. But he practiced hard and achieved a good level of competence in several sports. For him the attraction was the social camaraderie and competitive banter.

I yearned in vain for the freedom of being in the outdoors without the constraints of rules, enforced esprit de corps, laid out playing fields and health and safety precautions.

Call of the Wild

It had only been a brief escapade that first time I had ventured out into the Mendip Natural Ecology Reservation. For many the face to face encounter with the wild wolves would have been traumatic, frightening them back into the safety of their constrained, ordered lives within so-called civilisation, but that is not how it affected me. It was a watershed after which my life would never be the same. I was exhilarated by the wildness and the dangers only excited me. I relished living off my own wits, unencumbered by the rules and structures of the economically organised world. From the moment I had come back, I yearned to return.

For the remainder of my week at the Mendips Scouts Youth Camp I was unable to get away again from the activities the Scout leaders had organised for us. Both my absence and the temporary disappearance of the hard hat and head torch had been noticed. I was subjected to tough questioning about where I had been and stern lectures about the dangers of carrying out activities alone and without proper safety precautions. I sullenly went through the motions of delights such as hurtling down a zip wire, of course firmly strapped to a fully inspected and safety checked harness.

I observed Tim in his element seducing the delectable Laura. At the time no doubt Laura envisioned Tim knelt on one knee offering her a diamond ring, wedding bells followed by a lifetime of married bliss. That did not happen. After that week I don't suppose they ever saw each other again, Tim having moved on to new amorous conquests.

The yearning to return to the wild territory, already strong even while I was still in the Scout camp, grew by the day after I had returned to my daily existence in the Woking suburbs. I soon became fixated on the Mendips. I grappled for a pretext to return.

My chance came when I had to propose a school project. I declared an interest in the rare plant, the Plumbium cragwort, and a desire to make a study of it. Convinced by my sudden interest in botany the school sought my parent's permission for me to pursue my new interest in its natural habitat in the Mendips.

At long last, after months of longing, I was back among patchy alpine flora that fought for its existence on random heaps of contaminated gravel in a remote corner of the Mendips National Park. By this time it was a wet windswept day towards the end of October.

I quickly re-located my secret subterranean route through to the enticing freedom of the wild country. I brought my own personal hard hat and head torch. My supervising teacher and parents had welcomed my new awareness of health and safety.

As I stepped into the mouth of the narrow pothole that would take me through to the wild country beyond I hesitated, held by a sense that this was a significant step that could change me forever. I did not wait long. It was a fateful moment, one I embraced.

I had the presence of mind to leave my mobile phone and electronic watch in a cleft in the tunnel wall. I was aware it was forbidden for people to stray into the Ecology

Reservation and I did not want to be tracked. With only slight hesitation I recalled the intricacies of the route through the underground labyrinth of passageways and emerged back into the daylight within the wild country, normally forbidden to the inhabitants of the civilised world.

I hadn't the faintest notion of what I would do when I arrived. I just yearned to be there. That was enough.

I cautiously stuck my head out of the hole where the tunnel emerged into the Ecological Reservation. My earlier encounter with the wolves had been exciting, but I was going to at least try to keep out of their way. I scanned as far as I could see. I was situated in a deep hollow, so that wasn't far. I was reassured that, at least in the immediate vicinity there appeared to be no obvious signs of lurking wild beasts.

Having hauled myself out, I took a few steps into the open air. I could now see over a somewhat greater distance. All remained clear so I ventured further, wandering cautiously through the landscape, keeping low, placing my steps with careful precision to avoid making noise.

There was a low hill in front of me. It did not amount to much, little more than an undulation in the landscape, but sufficient to obstruct the view beyond. As I approached it, drifting over on the air from the other side, I could hear animals. There was a background collection of small sounds suggesting a crowd of big beasts treading heavily, scuffling their feet against the ground, rustling of vegetation and the squelching of chewing teeth. Above the scrunching and shuffling was the occasional call, akin to the trumpeting of elephants and lowing of cattle. I raised my head slowly to peer over the top of the ridge.

A couple of hundred yards away on the other side were mixed herds of mammoths and aurochs tucking into the lush grass and shrubs that bordered a small stream.

Not wishing to disturb them I laid myself down gently, slotted in amongst the rocks, tussock grass and gorse bushes. Gazing out at the spectacle, I settled down to observe from my discreet observation point.

The herds consisted of a mix of sizes and ages, from small calves, through half-grown youngsters, young mothers overseen by grizzled old bulls.

As I watched there were occasional interactions. The mammoths wanted their space and the aurochs, being smaller, respected that. In the case of the aurochs smaller is only relative. In comparison to domestic cattle they were huge, something like as large as the mythical yeti is reputed to be compared to a man.

Individual animals would occasionally jostle for possession of a prize piece of grazing. The older youngsters squared up excitedly in exuberant play fights. The very young gambolled for short distances before scampering back to their mothers.

I don't know how long I remained. It may have been an hour or it may have been two. I wasn't in any hurry. It was peaceful, just observing, my mind free-wheeling, experiencing the surrounding sensations. It was a time out of time. I had no commitments, nothing I had to do, no need to conform with convention, the rare chance just to be myself in nature.

After a while I rose from my vantage point, ambling on a little further, venturing to a patch of woodland. I threaded between the gnarled, twisted, unruly trees. The wood was in its natural state, untended. There were no paths. Each fallen branch and toppled tree trunk remained where it lay. Brambles threaded across the ground and over obstacles in a tough wiry entangled network, randomly and unpredictably arranged to snag and trip.

The going was arduous, so I was never going to cover any great distance. I persevered until I had penetrated deep enough to at least feel I had reached the depths of the forest, away from the open vistas and sky, sufficiently far in that the woodland looked the same in every direction. Having first kicked aside poisonous bright red toadstools, I settled into a hollow between two fallen tree trunks. As I did so I slipped, steadying myself by grabbing a bracket fungus growing on one of the dead trees. The fungus broke apart leaving my hand covered in a mass of wet fungal mush.

I rested my head against the comforting softness of some damp green moss. Small beetles scurried across my legs. I didn't mind. A moist atmosphere redolent of damp leaves and decaying wood enveloped me. I lay still and absorbed in the feeling of being at one with my surroundings in the dank gloom under the woodland canopy.

After some time I heard snapping twigs and shuffling leaves. I swivelled my eyes toward the sound. It was a little deer, a doe, timid and vigilant. I kept perfectly still. It couldn't have been more than ten yards away, yet it didn't notice me. Soon more deer arrived. They stayed around for some time, alert, yet oblivious of my presence. I did nothing, remaining motionless, keeping my breathing slow and silent. I stayed, enjoying their presence until something prompted them to move on.

I was wet from the damp ground and the cold was seeping into my bones. It would be getting dark soon. Reluctantly I stirred and unhurriedly re-traced my route back to my secret portal, out and back into the artificiality of the civilised world.

Despite nothing much having happened in the wild country, I was elated. What mattered was the freedom.

From the moment I was back in my daily existence in Woking I was already plotting another pretext for a return, my yearning stronger than ever.

A pattern was set. Over the coming years, at the least every few months I would contrive a brief illicit escape. It was like a drug. Most visits were uneventful, but there were the occasional exciting moments.

Not long after I had my second encounter with the wolves. There was another standoff, but this time the wolves were bolder. The lead wolf must have remembered my scent. We stood facing each other for some time, neither of us giving way, but neither of us going in to attack. Warning growls signalled that this encounter could end in aggression. Being alone and unarmed, any such combat would have been one-sided. Yet I was calm, cautious of the danger, yet detached from it. By some miraculous process, while I was in the wild country, I felt empowered and self-reliant, courageous.

It was fortunate I was not afraid because the wolves would have sensed that, their noses quickly picking up the stench of cortisol in my sweat. They would have moved in for the kill.

Eventually, after a battle of wills that had seemed like an eternity but probably lasted only minutes, the lead wolf advanced cautiously towards me. He wasn't growling and his posture was wary, but slightly submissive, so I let him come. He darted forward and sniffed at me, before quickly retreating. His tail wagged a couple of times. I reciprocated by advancing towards him nonchalantly. I held out my hand for him sniff. He wagged his tail again. We had reached an understanding.

Another time I had an encounter with a herd of mammoths. For some reason the herd's matriarch had seen me as being a threat to her offspring and was intent on trampling me into the mud before she impaled me on one of her tusks. Fortunately the wolves saved me, presenting themselves to the enraged pachyderm as the greater threat.

There was another occasion that found me trapped between a bear that saw me as a threat to her cubs and a herd of aurochs that would have delighted in goring and trampling the life out of me. I was saved by the mutual wariness between bear and aurochs. With them focussed on each other I was able to quietly slip away.

Eventful or not, however dangerous it could sometimes be, my visits to the Mendips NER became my safety valve, keeping me sane.

What do women want?

Leaving Simon's, I smiled about Lulu's antics. At least she was easy to understand. Her purpose was programmed. Real women are not so easy. Well, perhaps other women can figure them out, some of the time. But for us men, most of us, women are an enigma.

One example was Annie Entwhistel, soon to be Annie Membury, my friend Tim's fiancée. Annie happened also to have been my own first serious girlfriend. Perhaps if I had understood her better our lives might have taken a different course.

Whatever it was women wanted, in the years of our youth, it was something Tim certainly had. I doubt Tim himself knew what this attractant was, he just had it and did not hesitate to exploit it, leaving behind a trail of broken hearts.

In our last years at school I used to tag along with Tim. Together the two of us had all the components of a James Bond. Tim had the secret agent's suave well-groomed exterior while I had the rough tough steely core that you wouldn't want to tangle with. The problem was that Tim's urbane charm ran to his core being, whereas, while I might be able to floor a villain with a single punch, I was light on the charming bonhomie.

It was possible my presence lent Tim some macho credibility, but unfortunately for me, the process did not work in reverse. Tim regularly picked up the girls and I just as regularly faded discreetly into the background as he made his conquests.

I had plenty of opportunity to observe Tim in action. Occasionally I would try half-heartedly to emulate his corny chat up lines, but what came across from him as witty charm, fell flat for me. I cringe recalling one devastating encounter when I made a move on Fiona Deveryll, a Tim cast-off.

Fiona had the stereotypical beauty of the models used to promote luxury goods, stylishly dressed and impeccably groomed but clearly unwilling to engage in any activity that might scratch the finish of her immaculate paintwork. Quick witted, knowledgeable and well spoken, her mind was as sharp and ordered as her groomed exterior. Her superior attitude conveyed that she was a cut above the likes of me.

I had attended a social event with Tim, but as usual he had abandoned me in pursuit of a bit of skirt leaving me standing alone. Seeing that Fiona was also sitting alone I seized the opportunity to try my luck with one of Tim's corny chat up lines.

Fiona spotted me approaching. As she glanced in my direction her eyes narrowed and her face creased.

Undeterred I delivered my line with as much conviction as I could muster. "You know, you must be a magnet, because you just attracted me over here."

Her lip curled. She looked me up and down. "That is about the most pathetic thing that I have ever heard." She tilted her head to look down her nose at me.

"Well, I'm here now," I said lamely. "You may as well talk to me."

"Why would I want to talk to you? Who do you think you are?"

"I'm the man of your dreams."

"Ha," she snorted. "The man of my nightmares, more like."

"I could be the one who rescues you from your nightmares," I continued desperately.

She gave me a pitying and contemptuous look. "Just give it up. I wouldn't want you if you were the last man on Earth."

"Why, what's wrong with me?"

"Let's just say, that if I had been your mother I would have smothered you at birth."

With that I was holed below the waterline. Her reference to my mother struck deep, homing in on my deepest insecurity. I retreated and pondered why this kind of thing worked for Tim, but was disastrous when I attempted it. What it did for me at that moment was to confirm the feeling that I had had from my mother as an infant, I was inherently unlovable. With the benefit of hindsight a more objective analysis would have been that while in my heart I didn't really believe in my own desirability, that feeling was sure to come across. It was my body language and tone girls were assessing, not what was said.

There was another girl, Suzy Jenberg, who took tormenting me to another level. At least Fiona and the few others I had taken the courage to approach had the decency to largely ignore me, only humiliating me when I had the effrontery to attempt conversation. Suzy sought me out.

Suzy was a lively attractive young woman, bright and chatty but with a voice that carried over a considerable distance. She liked to be the centre of attention, reflected in the provocative and revealing outfits she wore, her garish makeup and hairstyles and her choice of cheap flashy jewellery. When others were in the limelight she was apt to put them down with provocative jibes and to pulling stunts to get herself noticed.

One evening Tim had disappeared in pursuit of some floosy; I was licking the wounds in my soul, having just been crushed by some other girl who I had had the temerity to try to chat to, when Suzy remarked loudly in my direction: "Bit of a loser, aren't you, Peter. Haven't got what it takes to get a real girl, have you?"

At that point I didn't want to have someone rub it in. I was feeling bad enough. I just wanted to sink into the floor, out of sight. Shortly afterwards I did exactly that. After stepping out, ostensibly for the toilet, I slunk out of the back door.

On another occasion, when I was there, she ostentatiously flirted with another boy, then contrived to walk past me, saying: "I go with real men."

For weeks she relentlessly needled me at every opportunity, taunting me about my lack of a girlfriend.

It was during this time my old adversary, Duncan McThomas, became unexpectedly friendly towards me. I was a little wary after the previous difficulties, but, seeing only benefit from being on good terms with him I went along with his cordial overtures.

One day he suggested we adjourn to a quiet spot behind the school sports pavilion to share an illicit beer. He sat beside me rather closer than I felt was necessary. He rested his hand on my thigh.

"You're a good looking bloke, Peter," said Duncan.

I looked at him askance.

"Ever fancied a bit of you know what?" Duncan continued. His hand reached up towards my crotch.

I took hold of his wrist and shoved his hand aside.

"Thanks, but no, Duncan. I don't fancy it."

Duncan's face blushed.

"Well, fuck you then," said Duncan. He stood and stomped off, leaving his beer behind undrunk.

I was perplexed. What could have led Duncan to believe I would be amenable to his suggestion? Besides, how was it that a guy who purported to hate gays, wanted to have sex with me?

Soon after these incidents there was a final social event to mark the end of our final school year. We weren't supposed to be drinking alcohol, but we did. I probably drank rather too much. I didn't have a girlfriend to mark the occasion and there seemed no prospect of there being any change in that situation, so the alcohol dulled the pain and disappointment.

On this occasion Tim was also unaccompanied. After the party had broken up we settled to reminisce while we consumed what remained of our stash of booze.

"How do you do it, Tim?" I asked. "With the girls, I mean. You seem to score nearly every time and I get nowhere."

"I don't understand it either. They fancy you a lot more

than they do me," he confided.

I looked at him incredulously.

"Don't be ridiculous. They hate me."

Tim shook his head and for once looked sincere. "No, straight up. They fancy you like crazy. I've heard them talking."

I looked at him hard to figure out whether this was some kind of sick joke. "You're winding me up."

"Well, I don't know about all of them," he conceded. "But there is one in particular who has the hots for you. Really bad."

"Who is that?"

"Suzy Jenberg."

"Now you're being ridiculous. She despises me."

Tim vehemently shook his head. "You couldn't be more wrong. She worships the ground you walk on."

"But she keeps insulting and belittling me, like she detests me. Anyway, there always seems to be some other boy around who she's flirting with. She obviously prefers them to me."

"No, you pillock. She's goading you. She's trying to get your attention."

"Funny way to seduce someone, insulting them like that."

Tim took a swig of his drink. We sat silently for a minute or so, ruminating on the oddities of our existence.

"You know what else they say?" said Tim eventually. "The girls, I mean?"

"No, what?"

"They reckon you must be gay. That you and Simon are an item."

I raised my eyebrows, tipped my head back and opened my mouth slightly as I was struck by a realisation. "I reckon Duncan McThomas must have got to hear about that too," I remarked.

"Really," said Tim, with a look of interested enquiry. "What makes you say that?"

I mused for a moment about whether I should put Tim in the picture about my encounter with Duncan. I decided against it. "Just something he said, that's all."

"It's not too late to get Suzy, you know," said Tim. "But you'd need to move fast."

"No, I don't think I'll bother," I replied, after reflection. "I wouldn't really want to be with a girl who treats me like that."

It was during weeks between leaving school and moving on to something else, which in the case of both myself and my friends Tim and Simon, was university, that Tim and I were invited to attend a Youth Parliament debating event. This took place in Birmingham and was attended by young delegates from the length and breadth of England.

A pompous young man from a posh school, by the pretentious name of Theophysus Pottinger, rose grandly to propose the motion "This House believes that England must uphold her proud traditions."

Theophysus stood at the podium and surveyed the room. By his commanding presence the audience was supposed to be silent in anticipation of his wise words. The hubbub died slightly but for a background buzz of isolated chatter, chairs scraped and creaked as people shifted their position and footsteps could be heard as some folk wandered around at the back.

Theophysus coughed and tapped his knuckles against the lectern. The background noise ebbed. He tucked his thumbs under his lapels and made his opening pronouncement.

"Let's ask ourselves, what has made England the greatest nation there has ever been?"

He waited with a smug look, allowing his audience to reflect. Already I didn't like the guy.

"It is our traditions. Fair play and sportsmanship, fashioned by the many sports that were invented here in England. Cricket, rugby, football, tennis." He paused grandly after pronouncing each phrase. "Our proud military history. Ruling the waves. Standing alone against oppression. The miracle of Dunkirk. The Battle of Britain. Our finest hour. Agincourt. Routing the Spanish Armada. Alfred the Great. Boudicca."

There was some muttering of disagreement among the audience. I was thinking that this was the most pompous and ridiculous tosh I had ever heard.

At the first opportunity for someone to respond I caught the eye of the chair and stood to intervene.

"Mr Pottinger might like to reflect that England is a mongrel nation blended out of many ethnic groups, that ethnically Boudicca was Welsh, the so-called English kings of the Middle Ages were French, our current royal dynasty is German, our philosophy originates in classical Greece. Many of the deeds he celebrates were moves to dominate and oppress other peoples. Some, like Dunkirk, were defeats."

I systematically shredded his pronouncements, but

what seemed to impress the audience was not so much my words but the power with which I delivered them and way in which I dominated the unfortunate Theophysus Pottinger.

Theophysus made a feeble attempt regain the initiative but it quickly degenerated into incoherent bluster until he retreated from the stage, his credibility shredded.

It wasn't as if I had set out to crush my debating rival. It felt to me that I was merely entering into a discussion where I expressed myself with clarity and directness. But there are times when I can get carried away so as to appear more forceful than I intended.

When I sat, some folk came up to congratulate me on my contribution. I hadn't expected that.

I had expected what happened a little later even less. There was a break in the formal proceedings during which we could get a drink, circulate and socialise. A good looking girl came towards me. She had a mesmerised look fixated on me. She came up close and gazed adoringly into my eyes.

"I thought you were wonderful out there."

I was taken aback. Nothing like this had happened to me before. Indeed it hasn't happened since either. I hesitated a second or two, but felt compelled to say something in acknowledgement.

"Well, thank you. I'm glad you liked what I said."

I had been chatting with Tim, but at this point he suddenly seemed to discover that there was someone else a little distance away who he should be talking to, leaving me alone in the company of my new admirer.

She reached down and gripped my hand. She used her

fingers to squeeze and stroke my hand as she held it. I just stood there looking back at her, uncertain what I should do.

She leaned forward, pushing her lips towards mine. I froze as fear and panic enveloped me. *She is trying to kiss me. What should I do?* As I stood frozen, her lips touched mine.

My panic took control. I turned around to look for Tim for support, but he was nowhere. I quickly backed away, feigning urgent business on the other side of the room.

Later, on the hyper-tube as we made our way back to Woking, Tim couldn't wait to find out what had occurred between me and my mystery admirer.

"Nothing," I said.

"What do you mean nothing?" Tim insisted. "It didn't look like nothing to me."

"Honestly, it was nothing."

"Come on, don't be coy with me. That was pretty full on."

"She held my hand and tried to kiss me. That was it."

"What did you do?"

"Nothing."

"You can't be serious. You must have done something."

"No, I didn't do anything."

"Well, it was in public. When are you going to see her again?"

"I shouldn't think I will."

"Why not?"

"I have no way of reaching her."

"You didn't get her number, email, or anything?" asked Tim incredulously.

"No."

"But you know her name. You could look her up on social media."

"Actually I don't know her name either."

Tim shook his head sadly, a look of incredulity on his face.

"You have women throwing themselves at you, and you don't even find out their name!"

"It wasn't women, just the one woman."

Tim banged the palm of his hand against his forehead.

In due course, by chance both my friends Tim and Simon and I all moved on to the University of York. It wasn't entirely chance. After the Nuclear War, during which London, Oxford and Cambridge had all been devastated by nuclear bombs, York became England's new capital city, and was home to England's premier university. For all three of us being academic high flyers, York was the obvious location for our continued education.

Simon would probably have chosen a science discipline, had that still been possible, but for him mathematics was the next best thing. The purity of the logic and minimal need for involvement with people other than similar nerdy types suited him perfectly.

Tim chose English Literature. There were a plethora of young women in this field and plenty of romantic prose and poetry with which to seduce them.

I settled on Military History. Like Simon, I was attracted to logic and order, yet, while disturbed by it, I was driven by the need to understand the disorder and irrationality of the society in which we lived. I was driven to understand better how we came to be as we are.

The belated revelation about Suzy Jenberg's desire for me and the brief encounter with the mystery admirer in Birmingham had buoyed up my previous despondency about my romantic prospects. At least I now realised that the chances were I wasn't destined to live unattached for all my days. Yet I remained nervous about the whole business on account of not having the faintest idea how I might progress matters romantically.

Buoyed by the thought that my romantic prospects weren't a complete lost cause, I made further half-hearted attempts at reusing Tim's terrible chat up lines. Unfortunately they all fell just as flat as before. I would either by swotted aside like an irritating insect or looked at in disgust. Seeing the object of my attentions reel in horror made me feel like Quasimodo. It was not only personal distaste I had to contend with, politics came into play too. On one occasion after what felt to me to be a friendly and innocuous attempt at conversation I was shrilly berated for sexual harassment and toxic masculinity. Later in my dreams my mother would tell me that I was useless and nobody could love me.

We were in our second term in York. Every time I met Tim he had a different girlfriend in tow. I once asked about a previous girl and he just said they were no longer an item. I commiserated.

He shrugged. "Not to worry. Plenty more fish in the sea."

"But it must hurt. Splitting up, that is, even if there are more girls out there."

"Well, it smarts for a day or two, that's all."

"How do the girls feel? They tend to feel it more, I'm told. Breaking up, I mean."

"I don't really know. They get over it. Anyway, how about you? Met anybody yet?"

I shook my head.

"I don't get it," said Tim. "From what I've heard, they fancy you like you wouldn't believe."

"You're right. I don't believe it."

"We're both fancy free and I'm invited to a party tonight. Why don't you come along?"

I didn't know anybody at this party and had no expectations, but I wasn't doing anything else.

It was in a terrace house being let out as student accommodation. One or two people came over to me for a chat and I introduced myself to a few more. It was the usual small talk, what was I studying, where was I living, was it okay over there in my digs, did I know anyone at the party.

There was a friendly looking girl on the other side of the room. Many women apply their beauty as a protective layer between themselves and the outside world, a suit of armour consisting of fashionable clothing to flatter their figure, decorative accessories, a carefully arranged hairstyle and meticulous makeup. This girl had no such armour, plainly dressed, simply trimmed hair, no makeup. It was her natural inner beauty that shone through.

She wasn't chatting to anyone at the time. She returned my glance in her direction and smiled. I smiled back. A little while later we were a little closer.

"Hello, I'm Peter."

"I'm Annie."

We did the usual small talk. She was doing English Literature, like Tim, as indeed were the majority of the people who were there. What had made me choose Military History, she asked.

"Humanity nearly destroyed the planet recently," I explained. "I want to understand what brought this about."

"Is it something that could happen again, do you think?"

"I don't know. I'd like to understand that better."

"How could we stop it?"

"Take away the weapons, for one thing."

"That's happened, hasn't it? The Commission took away the weapons after the Nuclear War."

"Yes, but what has the Commission done with them? That's what I'd like to know."

We got deeply into a discussion about the Commission, the nature of it, whether it was a tyrannical power. The party was winding down.

"I've enjoyed our discussion," I remarked. "Would you like to continue with it another time?"

"Yes, I'd like that," she said.

When we met again for a drink it was just the two of us and it seemed more appropriate to discuss the poets Annie was studying. We were getting on fine so we continued over a meal. At the end of the evening each of us felt a tension, as if something should happen. I leaned towards her a little so as to retain deniability, slightly puckering my lips. Simultaneously she did the same. We each leaned over more and our lips touched.

We kissed for a short while, tentatively, nothing too passionate.

All things being equal we would have gone our separate ways, but neither of us wanted to be the one to pull away. I felt that it would definitely frighten her off if I invited her back to my place, so I didn't, but I couldn't think of anything else to suggest.

"We could go back to mine for a coffee, if you like?" she said eventually. "Nothing else, mind. Don't get ideas."

"Yes, that would be nice. As you say, a coffee. I'll behave, I promise."

Back at her place we sat side by side on a small sofa, sipping our coffee. Ostensibly we were there to talk, but we didn't say much. It was as if we both expected something else to be happening, but dare not say it.

She brushed the back of my hand with her fingers, nonchalantly, as if by accident. I placed my hand over hers by way of acknowledgement. We leaned towards each other and our lips met again. Before we could kiss properly she pulled away.

"I'm not going to bed with you, or anything like that," she insisted.

"That's okay, Annie, we can just talk, no problem."

We contrived to continue our earlier discussion about poets but the conversation didn't flow. We both had other things on our minds. After a couple of minutes of stilted talk Annie leaned over and placed her lips on mine for a proper kiss. We had been into it for a couple of minutes when Annie suddenly pulled away again.

"We're not going to have sex or anything," she said. "I'm not ready for that."

"I'm not expecting anything, Annie, honestly. Just what you're comfortable with," I assured.

We tried to talk some more, but the pretence became too much. Annie leaned up against me and within moments we were wrapped in each other's arms in a cuddle. After a couple more minutes for what felt to me like a mutually passionate embrace, in a sudden panic, Annie pulled herself away, flinging my arms apart violently. She shifted across to the end of the sofa, perched on the edge with her arms crossed tightly across in front of her.

I was flabbergasted. I must have done something terrible, but I couldn't think what. She seemed to have wanted us to cuddle up close. Yet I appeared to have committed some horrendous faux pas.

I remained sitting nervously, not sure what I should do. Should I apologise? But what would I be apologising for?

"Look, Annie, I guess I'll be off now," I said after a minute or so.

"No, don't go." A moment later her arms were wrapped around me again and she was holding and kissing me more passionately than ever.

This pattern continued for another hour or so, an on then off again session of heavy petting, until what, in hindsight, must have been inevitable, she took my hand and led me into her bedroom.

I had been led to believe that a lengthy session of foreplay was necessary for the process to be satisfactory to a woman, but this must have broken the world record for fast sex. I tried to do the gentle touching bit, but she was having none of it. She wanted, desperately needed, to get to business. As soon as I entered her she practically exploded in moans and her loins gripped onto me like a vice pulsating in contractions, the force of which was a shock for me. Under the influence of her wetness and passion it was impossible for me to hold myself back and I quickly climaxed.

I was mortified. It had been my first time and I had messed it up completely. I must have hurt her terribly for her to be moaning like that. And here I was now, limp and useless, even if she did still want to make love with me, which seemed doubtful after what had just happened.

"I'm sorry, Annie," I said at last, after I had regained my composure, "I didn't mean it to happen like that. I'm sorry. I'd better go now."

As I left her digs that night I assumed we must have been finished, but to my surprise she called me the following afternoon.

"What's the matter? You went and didn't call," she asked, hurt.

"No, nothing's the matter," I assured her. "Are you okay?"

She hesitated. "Well, yes, I suppose so."

"Oh, good. I was concerned."

"If you were concerned, why didn't you call?"

"I thought that you might not want me to."

"Why did you think that?"

"I don't know," I said; realising that sounded lame, I added "Because I messed up, I suppose."

"How did you mess up?" she asked, perplexed.

"Well, you know, when we went to bed."

"You only messed up by suddenly leaving me like you did."

"But, I thought you'd want me to leave."

"Why would I want that?"

"Oh, I don't know. I just thought you would."

"I didn't. I can't understand why you would have left me like that."

"Oh, I'm sorry. I would have stayed if I'd realised."

"But why didn't you?" she asked plaintively.

I couldn't think of anything to say to this. The conversation was going in a circle.

"Look, can we get together? This evening perhaps?"

"Alright."

It was a little awkward when we first met again. Things got easier when we resumed our earlier discussion about the meaning of life, poetry and the human condition. Eventually we resumed our amorous relationship, but it would never have the same intensity as on our first evening together. It felt as if she didn't trust me. I imagined she had discovered what my mother had instilled in me, that I wasn't loveable.

Nevertheless, it was now established that we were a couple, a relationship that was to persist for some weeks. She would either stay at my digs or I at hers. We were together most days.

My new attached status coincided with a change in my apparent desirability among women. Now I was with Annie I went from someone nobody fancied to having admirers pop up everywhere.

I saw a young woman in the street in central York struggling with heavy cases. I asked her if she needed a hand. She told me she was on the way to the hyper-tube. It was only a short distance so I offered to go with her carrying her stuff. We got chatting. In no time she was sharing all sorts of personal information, such as telling me that she had broken up with her boyfriend and was on her way back to stay temporarily with her parents.

As we walked along we were passed by another young woman I had seen at the party when Annie and I first met. At the time I thought nothing of it, but this chance encounter would haunt me later.

At the hyper-tube station I helped the young woman load up her cases, then told her it had been nice meeting her and I hoped she had a good journey home. As I walked away her jaw dropped. I can't remember seeing anyone more crestfallen. It was only then I realised that in her eyes I had picked her up and was destined to be her replacement boyfriend.

Days later Tim and I had been taking a break from our studies to stroll along the river Ouse. Afterwards we dropped into a bar for a swift drink before heading off home. Taking our seats I noticed a young woman sat at the next table. She had a bag printed with what I recognised as a picture of Guildford. I leaned across and asked her if she came from Surrey.

"Well, no," she said, but she had been there a few weeks earlier for a holiday break.

"So, that's where you got the picture. I recognised it because I came from near there."

We chatted a bit more. Then Tim touched my arm and winked meaningfully, before quietly slipping away. After he had tactfully departed my new acquaintance wondered aloud where we might go on to after we'd finished our drinks. Once more I had picked someone up without effort, but equally without prior intention. Again I saw the crestfallen look on her face when I hurriedly made my excuses and quickly departed.

Annie must have had her spies everywhere because, unbeknownst to me, I had been spotted in the bar by one of her friends.

I arrived at her place the next evening to find her tear-stained face glaring at me. How could I have done it, she demanded. Done what? Chatted up those other women. I had never cared about her. It was obvious from the way I was with her. She could tell I been hiding something, and now she knew what.

From then on I was persona non grata in her social circle. A libertine. A Don Juan.

Perplexed I talked to Tim. After listening to my story he remarked: "Peter, until today I couldn't make you out. The girls fancy you like crazy, yet you seem always to struggle with them. Now I can see what the matter is. You think too much. Your anxiety shows through. When I saw you in that bar the other day, you were brilliant. You weren't even trying, which is why it worked so well."

I made a mental note to look up on the web for tips on how to avoid showing anxiety. I would have to work on that.

Tim and Annie

Years later, I still cringe at memories of my brief relationship with Annie Entwhistel. Having left Simon's I had to face up to meeting up with her and Tim. With them going to be married, Tim and I could find it difficult to have the open and relaxed man-to-man conversations we once enjoyed.

Tim and Annie both worked for me in my role as the Solent and Dorset Regional Manager within Davenhirst Properties, owned by my fiancée Celia's father. I would need to catch up with them at some stage. It was a good idea to get this done before meeting back up with Celia, because once she had me in her presence I would be occupied with wedding plans with no escape.

The arrangement was for me to call in at their home where we would quickly cover the business matters before relaxing over a meal.

I knew Annie was very much in favour of what she referred to as Real Food, by which she meant traditional crops ordinary people had cultivated in the open air by the sweat of their brow.

These days most people subsisted on the processed food provided by the Commission. Nobody knew exactly what that was made from. They mostly didn't want to think about it too much. It was reputed to involve assorted chemicals, genetically modified organisms, microbes, vegetables forcibly ripened in automated underground caverns under LED lighting, cooked up in vats with artificial flavourings and colourings. Despite its unsavoury origins, most would have to concede that the end results were remarkably good, synthetic meat products indistinguishable from the flesh of animals, synthetic wines no wine taster would be able to separate from that produced from real grapes, ready meals any cordon bleu cook would have been proud of.

The changeover from agriculture to industrially produced food had been accelerated by the Nuclear War, which had left huge tranches of land contaminated. In the aftermath the only alternative to continuing to feed people from conventional agriculture would have been mass starvation, so people took their chances. At the time there was widespread radiation sickness and a greatly increased incidence of cancer. To address the issue the Commission ramped up the production of radiation free industrial food and discontinued the use of large tracts of farmland, on which the new NERs, Natural Ecology Reservations, were established.

It wasn't long before the Real Food movement built up their opposition to industrialised food, campaigning for a return to traditional growing methods. Many were prepared to take their chances growing and consuming vegetables in their gardens and allotments, despite the resistance of the authorities who opposed this on health and safety grounds due to the continued presence of radioactive isotopes in the soil. Personally, although I didn't want to live exclusively on traditionally grown food, I was prepared to take my chances with it occasionally. Forty years had elapsed since the Nuclear War and the radiation levels had dissipated.

On the way to see Tim and Annie I called in at an

informal Farmers Market where people gathered to buy and sell vegetables and an assortment of homemade food products on stalls. Being winter the range of fresh produce was limited, but I was able to buy leeks. I also bought a bottle of elderberry wine and a jar of blackberry and apple jam.

Tim's and Annie's home was a suburban semi-detached property situated at the end of a cul-de-sac in West Byfleet. Tim met me at the door and showed me into the large open reception room. The living space had been knocked through so that the kitchen, dining area and living space flowed together, extending on further into a conservatory. Annie was in the kitchen putting the final touches to the meal we would be sharing later on. I put down the items I had brought for them onto the worktop. Annie thanked me for my thoughtful gesture and Tim said we should try out the elderberry wine later on.

We adjourned into the conservatory, which backed out into the rear garden, most of which Annie had laid out as vegetable beds with a small paved area retained for recreational purposes decorated with a few pot plants. The garden sloped onto the river Wey. Rising from the far bank towered the monstrous high fence that marked the boundary with the London Contaminated Zone.

Tim poured us out homemade sloe gin before we reviewed progress on the prestigious premises on the fashionable stretch of the English south coast that formed our patch of the Davenhirst Properties portfolio. Tim had already closed three deals since we had last met and he had about a dozen more in the pipeline. Annie had prepared some nice marketing material ready to go out to a list of potential prospects she had collated. The business side of things having been dealt with, we relaxed into more genial conversation.

"So, Peter, you've been off recharging your batteries in the Mendips," said Tim.

"Yes, that's right. I like to get away now and again."

"But you keep going back to the same place every time. Don't you get bored of it?"

"Funnily enough, no."

"I remember all those years ago when we were still at school and we went together to that Scout camp. That was enough for me. I haven't felt the need to return."

"What is it that you like about it?" asked Annie.

I paused. I didn't want to say too much and hint of my visits to Ecologia.

"It's being close to the wild country."

"But you cut yourself off, no phone or Internet," observed Tim. "I can't understand that. I couldn't do it."

"Actually, that is the whole point," I explained. "Not being contactable."

"I understand," said Annie. "Being at one with nature. Natural things. Phones and Internet would spoil that."

"But there's nothing much going on in the Mendips," said Tim. "I remember from our Scout trip it's got a zip wire and some messing about on ropes in the tree tops, but that's it."

"So where would you go?"

"The World Experience would be hard to beat, I'd say."

"You mean that place in the West Country that you used sell trips to? You surely don't still get commission from them, do you, now that you're working for

Davenhirst Properties? You had better not be moonlighting on me." I looked at him with mock sternness.

"No, of course not," assured Tim. "I still think that it's great though, even though I don't earn anything by saying so."

"What's so great about it?"

"Well, you get to see other places, other cultures. Venice, Florence, Paris, Rome, Istanbul, Marrakesh and so on. It broadens the mind."

"But you don't really go to any of those places, do you? They are pastiche reproductions situated in Devon, aren't they?"

"You mean on the English Riviera," replied Tim. "They are perfectly accurate reproductions. Just like the real thing. Absolutely fantastic."

"But they're all fake," I insisted. "Nothing there that is natural or real."

"But there's so much to do," said Tim. "A rollercoaster that swoops down over the Colosseum, climbing up the outside of London's Shard building, bungee jumping off Tower Bridge, scuba diving across Alexandria harbour."

"But all contrived," I said, shaking my head. "All that health and safety nonsense, crowds queuing to get in, safety briefings, wearing harnesses, rescue robots, all to mess about on something that isn't even real to begin with."

We adjourned to the dining table. Annie served up her meal, consisting of what she termed Real Food, made from actual identifiable animals and plants sourced from her own garden and those of other Real Food enthusiasts. We washed it down with the bottle of elderberry wine I had brought along and then another bottle of home produced plonk Tim already had in store.

"That was great, Annie," I said. "It's nice to know what you're eating and where it came from for a change."

"By the way you tucked in, I can see that you enjoyed it."

"I've got nothing against processed food, mind you. I can see the need for it and I'm sure that it is nutritious. Problem is, it may feed the body, but it doesn't feed the soul."

I sensed longing in how Annie gazed at me. "Yes, the soul," she said wistfully. "The whole person needs to be fed, body and spirit."

"All seems a bit mystical to me," said Tim. "It tastes good. That's good enough for me."

The wine was going to my head. "You know, if I could, I would take it stage further."

Annie looked at me with interest. "How do you mean?"

"I'd go fully wild. Right out into nature."

"You mean camping?" said Tim. "Wouldn't fancy that myself."

I hesitated. Perhaps I should keep quiet. I took another swig of wine. No, to hell with it. "More than camping. I mean really living out there in the wild."

"But you do that already, don't you?" said Tim. "When you go on your jaunts to the Mendips."

I couldn't suppress a slight smile. "Kind of," I said cryptically. "No, what I mean is living like those wild folk do, out in the NERs."

"But they're back in the Stone Age," said Tim. "They barely qualify as human."

"They're as human as you and I. It isn't modern flim-flam that makes us human."

"Quite right," agreed Annie. "They are truly part of nature. In some respects they're even more human than we are. Closer to what matters."

"But they've got no civilisation," Tim insisted. "No education. Nothing written down. No knowledge. No organisation. None of the things that separates us from the beasts."

"I'm with Annie on this one, Tim. Modern civilisation makes us dependent on the supporting technology and social structures. It takes things away from us as much as it gives us things. Out in the wild you really are dependent on your wits. You have only what you can do for yourself."

"But all you'd have there would be brutish existence. You'd lose all our higher thoughts. The things that lift us beyond instinct."

"There is a lot more that goes into basic existence than you can imagine. It can stretch all your human faculties to the limit. It would be a lot more challenging than living in the modern world, mentally and physically."

"You're romanticising it. I expect that the faculties of deer, wolves and squirrels are stretched too, but I wouldn't ascribe any higher mental processes to them."

"Animals can be a lot more mentally adept than you give them credit for."

"Oh, come on now," pleaded Tim. "You'll have antelope spouting poetry next."

Annie's eyes glowed with passion. "No, Tim, Peter's got a point. Animals have a spirit, I am sure of that. We're a lot closer to them than you can imagine."

Tim looked as if he was going to say something and then thought better of it.

"They may not have words," I said. "Animals, I mean, but they do have mental processes and pretty sharp mental processes too."

"You'll have mammoths doing higher mathematics now," Tim scoffed. "Anyway, even if you did get out into the wild, how could you manage to live there?"

"Well, there are loads of plant foods out there to be gathered. You might not have farms as such, but things can be planted out to be harvested later."

"Would that be enough?" asked Annie.

"Perhaps not," I acknowledged. "You would probably need meat. You can get quite a bit, rabbits and so on, with snares. Now and again big game can be hunted."

"The way you describe it, it almost sounds as if you have been there," said Annie.

I just smiled.

"No, but he certainly has a vivid imagination," said Tim.

We finished off the meal. As Annie had prepared our feast of naturally grown goodies it was Tim's task to clear away, which allowed Annie and I to adjourn to the conservatory.

"I never knew you had that in you, that feeling for nature."

"It is so deep that it is part of my soul," I said.

Annie gazed at me. Even now, years after we had first met, she had the same simplicity about her I remembered, the rejection of external adornment, a wish to be at one with nature. The beauty of her inner being still shone through, but it had a more care-worn patina.

"Back when we knew each other before," she confided, "I wish I'd known that about you then."

I looked out into the middle distance. "There is a lot that we didn't know about each other at that time. There's a lot that we didn't know about ourselves, come to that."

"Tim doesn't really get it about natural things." She looked at me intensely, silently.

Tim joined us and the spell broke.

In Search of a Cause

Sitting in the autotaxi as it set off from Tim's and Annie's place my mind drifted to the forks in the road of my past life. When Annie and I had briefly been together as students I had yet to be consumed by cynicism. I still naively believed that all the iniquities of society, the inequality and injustices, could be rectified quickly and easily. All it required was a revolution. Just light a spark and the downtrodden masses would rise up.

It was before I met Annie, during Freshers Week, that, as I wandered through the stalls representing the various clubs and societies, I came across the stand for the WRLP, the Workers Revolutionary Liberation Party. There were posters and leaflets with slogans such as "Equality and Justice", "End the Oppression" and "Jobs for All".

There were two people looking after the stand. One was a scrawny, shabbily dressed young man with a threadbare beard, haranguing any who might listen with his faux London proletarian accent uttered in a squawky voice. The other was a gawky young woman with a thin face, scruffily dressed in torn jeans and a T shirt emblazoned with "Smash the Patriarchy". Despite her best efforts her attire failed to disguise her alluring figure. I couldn't tell if her face was always set in an expression of entrenched suspicion or whether that was just in response to my being there.

The aims of the group reflected my own dislike for the pomposity, self-importance and greed of the current Establishment so I enquired about how I might get more involved. The woman scowled. The man was more forthcoming, suggesting I attend a mass rally on the subject "The Commission, a Capitalist Clique".

The mass rally was on a rather smaller scale than I imagined. A lecture room had been hired for the event. Comfortably full, the room could have held about a hundred, stretching to perhaps two hundred if crammed in complete disregard for regulations. In the event the total attendance was about a dozen. At the front of the room were the two individuals I had already met flanking the guest speaker, a passionate middle-aged man, introduced to us as Dr Theodor Empworthy, who held an academic position within the university in the field of Economic Socialism. In his talk he explained how the Globalist Ruling Class had exploited the aftermath of the Nuclear War, establishing the Commission as an agency to cement and consolidate their power. He went on to highlight how much of our lives were managed and controlled by the Commission and how the working classes were excluded from the process.

I reflected that considering the huge role the Commission played in all our lives, how little ordinary people came into contact with anyone from the Commission itself. There were spokespeople from the Commission who appeared occasionally to make statements to the media and answer questions, but how they had come to hold those roles I had no idea. I had never encountered anybody who had worked for the Commission.

"How does the Commission recruit its people?" I asked from the floor.

"Why, thinking of applying?" responded Dr Empworthy. There was a brief ripple of laughter.

"No, I just wondered who the Commission people were? How they came to be there."

"The Ruling Class clearly makes sure that only their own make it into the Commission," replied Dr Empworthy. "Pure nepotism and old boy network. That's why there are no opportunities there for ordinary people. Positions in the Commission have never been advertised to my knowledge."

After the formal proceedings came to an end I stood around on my own for a bit wondering when someone might introduce themselves, but the convention of welcoming newcomers was evidently not an established practice in the WRLP. It was Dr Empworthy who eventually reached out to me.

"Good question of yours earlier," he said. "The Commission are an opaque organisation, yet they ultimately control everything. Very sinister."

After exchanging a few pleasantries with Dr Empworthy I caught the eye of the skinny man with a sparse tufty beard who I had met at the freshers exhibition.

"Hello, I'm Peter Accrington," I announced, reaching to shake his hand. He looked at my hand a moment before tentatively taking it in his, gripping mine limply and momentarily with bony fingers.

"Er, yes, I'm Archie Stenning," he said, without elaborating.

I looked over in the direction of his fellow organiser, the young woman who had accompanied him at the freshers exhibition and beside him at the front of the room. The slogan on the T shirt she was wearing with her torn jeans now reading "The Revolution is Female". Her well-formed lithe form remained fully apparent. I caught her eye and smiled. The look of permanent scepticism on her face darkened into one of deeper distrust.

Not wishing to be deterred I looked back at Archie expectantly and cast my eyes back in the direction of the hostile young woman. Archie looked uncertain before picking up the cue.

"Oh, this is Tess Frammling."

"Hello, Tess," I said, trying to remain open and friendly in the face of her uncongenial body language.

Her eyes narrowed. After a second or two of deliberation, her mental processes having uncovered nothing untoward, she relented. Her face lapsed back into its usual setting of cynical scepticism. "Hello Peter." Having spoken to me, her brain fired up again. Her acknowledgement of my existence had moved me into a different category. "Are you here to help us fight for the revolution?"

"Well, yes, I'd like to help."

A hint of a smile appeared on her face as if she was a gatekeeper letting me in under the portcullis into the inner sanctum. "We need some people to join us picketing the Militarists. Will you join us for that?"

"Militarists? Who are they?" I asked. As someone who was studying for a degree in Military History I was nervous that it might include me.

"The University OTC, Officers' Training Corps," Tess explained.

"Privileged posh gits who want to join the Army,"

Archie elaborated.

I remembered having seen their stand at the freshers exhibition.

"What are we picketing them about?" I asked.

"Perpetuating militarism, the patriarchy, celebrating empire and slavery," said Tess.

I had recognised the OTC crowd as being very much Establishment types, the very people who had been the bullies in the playground and excelled in all those ball games at school. "Okay, count me in."

Over the coming months, between my studies, I would hang out with my new political friends. There were party meetings, for members only, typically including about a dozen people, which generally involved drinking pints of beer while we discussed our strategy for fomenting a final triumphant revolutionary uprising among the workers of the North Yorkshire region, coordinating with our comrades in other regions to achieve a decisive victory for the working classes across England.

There were mass rallies, which were open to all and typically attended by the same dozen or so people who frequented the internal party meetings.

There was also direct action where we would stage protests about a variety of injustices, such as the rights of minorities, the patriarchy and oppressive authorities.

Particularly hated was the Protective Custody Treaty, which authorised the Commission, entirely on their own initiative, to take anybody into what the treaty referred to as Commission protection for any of a number of supposed justifications, such as maintenance of international order, prevention of environmental damage and supposedly the welfare of the individuals themselves.

In participating in these campaigns, something that struck me related to the theme of that first mass rally I had attended, when Dr Empworthy addressed us. If one followed the threads of any of the issues involved, the Commission was at the root of it.

The Commission had been established to regulate the relationships between countries to prevent the insanity of war. But it was not only hostile relations that had been suppressed, international relations of all kinds had ceased. It was akin to the strong drugs given to the insane to control psychotic symptoms, which suppress not only the disordered thinking but thinking in general.

It was not only in the field of international affairs that national governments had to defer to the authority of the Commission. For many other matters governments depended on the policies and largesse of the Commission.

At the outset of the new post Nuclear War order, one of the Commission's key remits had been the remediation of the environmental havoc that not only the war itself, but the negligence of preceding decades had inflicted on the planet. The Commission was the monopoly supplier of major commodities, electrical power, communications technologies, waste disposal and recycling. The Commission had assumed the power to designate tranches of land as Contaminated Zones or Ecological Reservations, separated off from the modern economy.

Under their remit to prevent conflict, the Commission had assumed responsibility for security, law and order. Law enforcement was carried out by the robots of the Commission administered Public Safety Service. Health services were also provided by the Commission by means of online consultations over the Internet and robotic hospitals.

Those defending the status quo asserted that the Commission was just a civil service that carried out the policies of the elected national government. There was some truth in this. The Commission's law and order services enforced the laws made by the national parliament. The Commission allocated the national income and resources as decreed by the elected national government.

Despite its central role in our affairs the Commission was almost invisible. Only very occasionally would a face representing the Commission appear in the news media. These individuals were polished presenters who had a slick answer for everything, but they were individuals who seemed to have no other existence than their roles within the Commission.

In contrast, national politicians were people with human foibles who had connections within the communities they represented. They were accountable and could, and often were, voted out of office.

I asked myself, who were these Commission officials? In an organisation that did so much that was critical for day-to-day living, it was curious that there was no obvious path for an ordinary person to join its ranks. It was clearly some kind of very exclusive club that granted membership only to the most well-connected. There must have been the most blatant nepotism and elitism involved.

With my new friends in the WRLP we would dig out, share and exaggerate details of the Commission's terrible deeds, building a large dossier of its evils. Among ourselves we could get hours of amusement this way, winding ourselves into a frenzy of righteous indignation. Unfortunately in my fervour I was moved to share my new found understanding of the sinister machinations of the Commission with other people who had yet to be recruited into the cause.

On one occasion when I was with Tim and had been going on rather too long about the evil doings of the Commission, he felt the need to put me straight.

"You really are getting very boring about this Commission nonsense of yours, Peter."

I didn't take the hint. "But it's too important just to dismiss what's happening as boring. We need to get people involved to take back control from this undemocratic monolith."

"The Commission is nothing more than a useful bogeyman to blame for everything you don't like."

"But you can see what the Commission does," I insisted. "You can't just dismiss and ignore it."

"Oh, yes, I can," said Tim. "Quite frankly since you have been involved with those Workers Revolutionary crazies you have been off your head."

To be truthful it was not only my deep convictions about the evils of the Commission that had kept me involved with the WRLP. Every time I looked at Tess Frammling I was horny. There was a sexiness about her, an underlying femininity that defeated her every effort to suppress it. Most women worked to look attractive, but in Tess's case it shone through every means she deployed to crush it.

It was clear from her hostile demeanour that I could only look and not touch. Even looking was problematic. I tried to keep my ogling discreet, but I think that she caught me looking a couple of times, although I tried to maintain deniability and look innocent.

After I had formed a liaison with Annie Entwhistel I scaled back my involvement with the WRLP. In part this was in order that I might spend more time with Annie, but it was also to prevent my feelings from being diverted from her by the sexy but unattainable Tess.

But my relationship with Annie did not last long and after it had evaporated the WRLP once again served as a welcome support network. Seeing Tess again after a break of a few weeks reinforced how sexy I found her, despite her front of hostility.

Within the WRLP we each had our own priority areas for liberating the workers from capitalist oppression. While mine was the diabolical machinations of the Commission, for Tess it was the injustices of Patriarchy.

In the hope of getting Tess to more than just grudgingly tolerate my presence, at her suggestion I attended a mass rally that she had arranged on the subject of Toxic Masculinity.

On this occasion the only men present were myself and the ever-willing Archie Stenning. We were heavily outnumbered by twenty women, the most militant of the radical feminists on campus.

The guest thought leader at the rally was Harriet Henpuddle, a woman in her mid-forties. She was bulky, one could say. It quickly became clear that Ms Henpuddle had a marked dislike, an obsession that almost amounted to a phobia, to anybody or anything that had the remotest connection with anything masculine, an attitude shared by most of her audience. As she told it, masculinity was at the heart of everything wrong with society and in general. Inequality, violence, war, environmental catastrophe and a catalogue of other evils all stemmed from the tyranny of male dominance.

To fervent nods of agreement and encouraging noises from those present Ms Henpuddle catalogued aspects of Toxic Masculinity that needed to be rooted out.

There was Predatory Behaviour, leering at women, invading their space, catcalls.

Sexual objectification, such as ogling and making remarks about women's bodies, was demeaning and to be strongly called out. I looked across at Tess, looking as sexy as ever, guilty that I was only too likely to do those toxic things with her if given a chance. Even worse, Tess caught my eye.

Rape culture, which normalised preying on women who were drunk, was an ugly and ever-present threat and led to many abusive behaviours, such as sexual touching or worse.

Men's entitlement. You could even see it in how men sat, she remarked, looking directly at me, man spreading to take up space. I drew my knees together, but I was unable to do much about the breadth of my shoulders.

The competitive and aggressive ethos promoted by the Patriarchy encouraged men to exploit women solely for sex, without offering a committed loving relationship. There were nods and murmurs from the audience.

Coercive pressure that men applied, for example telling

women that they knew they wanted to have sex with them. Women were perfectly capable of knowing their own minds without men telling them. I tentatively observed that, unless the world was going to be celibate, someone would have to make a suggestion about intimacy at some point. I was quickly shut down by a chorus of jeering and an accusation from Ms Henpuddle of mansplaining.

It was a couple of days after I had endured my ritual humiliation at the hands of Ms Henpuddle and her acolytes that the WRLP held a social event. It wasn't elaborate. There was an assortment of cheap buffet food, beer and wine from the local convenience store. There being nothing much else to do, we got stuck into the booze and chatted to comrades, for the most part about our own political obsessions, the dialogue becoming louder, more vehement and containing more swear words as the alcohol consumption increased.

It was part way through the evening when we had already knocked back four or five drinks. I was standing slightly apart from the main group helping myself to another drink, when, to my surprise, Tess came up to me in a determined fashion. At first I wondered what terrible act of political incorrectness I was going to be accused of, but to my relief I didn't see any anger in her demeanour. Her face did have an expression on it, which I struggled to interpret. If I hadn't known better I could have sworn that she was leering at me, looking at me up and down suggestively.

She reached across and gripped my buttock.

"You know something," she said quietly into my ear.

"You're the most attractive man here."

I looked around the room. I reflected that this was faint praise. The other men were some weedy looking specimens. Her change in attitude towards me and the brazen way that she expressed it had taken me unawares. Being so apparently out of character, I wondered whether it was some sort of trap.

"Nice of you to say so," I replied.

She took my hand and drew me over to a couple of chairs that were out of sight of the other partygoers. Once we were sat, she draped her arm over my shoulders and pushed her breasts up under my chin. Uncertain about how to react I just peered down into her cleavage.

"Come on, now, don't be shy," she said.

"Sorry, but this is all a bit sudden," I replied.

"Don't come all innocent with me. I've seen the way you look at me. I know what's on your mind."

"Sorry about that," I said. "I didn't mean to objectify you. I'll try to be more careful about how I look at you."

"Never mind about that. I could tell that you liked what you saw."

"Well, yes, I did."

"And I like what I'm looking at too," she said, her eyes running over me.

"That's nice," I said.

"Well, what are we going to do about it?" she asked.

"I don't know," I replied.

"Don't be coy. I know that you fancy me."

"Well, yes, I do actually."

"Well, what are you waiting for? You know you want to."

She reached down and squeezed my thigh.

For a while I couldn't get my head around my relationship with Tess. The initial sexual union between us had been an explosion of lust. She had been a huge turn on for me since we had met and, unbeknown to me, the feeling was mutual. After our moment of passion we lingered in each other's arms for maybe half an hour at which point her mood flipped. She was as cold and distant as she had ever been. I tried to stroke her arm and make little endearments, but she brushed me off.

After we parted I assumed that our sexual relations must have been a complete failure for her. I couldn't understand what I had done wrong, but whatever it was, it must have been terrible. Yet, at the time she had seemed to enjoy it and just afterwards we were tender with each other. How was it that her dissatisfaction only manifested some time afterwards?

For the whole of the following day she remained aloof and treated me with the same habitual scepticism she had for men in general.

Then, she flipped back into the sex siren that she had been at the party. In next to no time we were back in bed slaking our lust. The pattern was the same. For a short time we were peaceful lovers resting in each other's arms, before transforming in an instant, as if bewitched by an evil magician to turn back into pumpkins at a given hour, into members of mutually hostile tribes.

After this pattern had persisted a week or so I couldn't stand it any longer. Before we parted company a short time after we had had sex I felt compelled to raise my concerns.

"Tess, can I ask you something?"

She looked at me impatiently. "Yes, what is it?"

"We don't seem to be, you know, that close, you and me. I don't really understand why."

"I don't know what you mean."

I couldn't think how to explain it. Tess made to depart.

"Well, I mean, you know, loving and that," I blurted out finally.

"You like fucking me, don't you?"

"Well, yes, I like that."

"What more do you want?"

"Well, couldn't we be more, you know, affectionate, that sort of thing."

"What do you want that for?"

"Well, to feel comfortable together, like we love each other," I tried to explain.

She looked at me with disdain. "What has love got to do with it? We're fuck buddies, that's all."

Her answer explained a lot. I hadn't expected that from a woman. It's the sort of thing a man might aspire to, but even when it was true most men would have the decency to at least pretend to have some loving feelings. Even the most unfeeling psychopath would probably pretend, if only for his own ends. Hearing it from her said blatantly like that was shocking.

"Really, is that it? You just want the sex and nothing else?" I asked, anxious to clarify that I had understood the situation.

"Yes, what else did you expect?"

"Well, I hoped that we would mean more to each other than that."

"You should be pleased. It's what men want, isn't it? Uncomplicated sex."

"Not all men."

"Not that cliché!" she spat. "You call men out on their bad behaviour and there is always someone who will bleat, 'Not all men.'"

"Funny as it may seem, in a relationship I do actually want more than uncomplicated sex."

"Stuff your Patriarchal possessiveness," she said. "You don't own me."

I felt deflated. For months I had fantasised about what it might be like if we had ever got it together, not that I had expected it to happen. Now it had, unexpectedly, and it was a meaningless nothingness.

"Do you care for me at all?" I asked, already knowing the answer.

"Why should I care for you?"

"I don't know. I just thought you might."

She looked at me with cold contempt. "Sorry, but men disgust me."

"Why do you fuck with me then?"

She twisted her face as if I had confronted her with something she didn't like about herself. "I like to fuck sometimes, that's all. Doesn't mean I like you. You've got a body that turns me on. That's all there is to it."

"And that's it," I said flatly.

"Look," she explained. "I'm not proud of myself for this. I wish I didn't have to fuck men. You bastards turn me on, that's all. I wish you didn't."

I reflected that I had never expected to encounter such feelings in a woman, but perhaps that was just my inexperience and naïvety. It was akin to what I had seen in Duncan McThomas, a supposed contempt for gays, while being gay himself.

"I can't go on like this," I said, my voice flat and expressionless. "I'm not doing it anymore."

"That's a pity. You were good."

I looked at her in disbelief. "I just can't believe a woman could be like you."

"Why not?"

"It doesn't seem natural."

"So, it's natural for a man, but not for a woman. Is that what you are saying?"

"Yes, I guess I am."

She looked at me with hatred. I had contradicted one of the fundamental tenets of her radical feminist philosophy that men and women were fundamentally the same in all respects, any differences in behaviour arising solely from the social conditioning imposed by the evil Patriarchy.

"You misogynist swine."

How me having attributed finer feelings to women made me a misogynist defied logic, but then I was coming to realise that there was very little logic contained within Tess's particular brand of radical feminism. I couldn't be bothered to argue the point. At that moment I just felt sullied by the sordidness of the whole business between us.

"I need to get away," I said. "I'll be away for a few days. See you when I get back."

"Don't count on it," she snarled.

Later as I wandered and observed the wild surroundings of my bolt hole in the Mendips Natural Ecology Reservation,

I felt cleansed.

There was always the potential threat from the animals, but I didn't mind that. Keeping alert and living on my wits made me feel alive in a way that nothing in the so-called civilised world could.

At one stage a herd of aurochs took exception to my presence on their chosen grazing area. It was the bulls that trotted towards me snorting and threatening to gore and trample me, while the cows stood by placidly.

On my last evening in the Mendips I attended an evening of entertainment in a local pub that featured a local band, the Gummidgers. They were handing out promotional T shirts emblazoned with the legend "I'm a Zider Drinker – Oo arr Oo arr".

Back in York when I next attended a gathering of the WRLP I happened to be wearing my new T shirt. On catching sight of me Tess's face assumed a mixed expression of outrage and triumph. She loudly called me out, to coin the phrase used to describe a ritual condemnation, for cultural appropriation and mocking ethnic West Country people.

I replied that I meant no offence, but to no avail. The party activists had already coalesced into a mob united against a renegade member. I lingered a few minutes attempting to join in the activities but the cold shoulders I was given were more frigid than an Antarctic iceberg.

I was informed the following day that after my departure a special meeting of the local WRLP executive committee had resolved to cancel me from further WRLP activities due to my unacceptable conduct.

Tim had already ridiculed me for my revolutionary activities, so I suspected that were I to confide in him he would only gloat, so I turned to my other close friend, Simon.

"It's not so much you Tess doesn't like, it's herself," Simon observed.

"How do you mean?"

"She hates the very idea of men, yet she fancies them, they turn her on. In moments of weakness she gives in to her desires. She hates herself for that."

"Irrespective of whether she hates herself, she certainly seems to hate me."

"True, she hates men in general," Simon acknowledged, "but you in particular also represent what she hates about herself. If she can eliminate you, she somehow cleanses herself."

"But that's pathetic," I lamented. "We are supposed to be campaigning together for the workers revolution. We shouldn't be letting personal matters get in the way of that."

"You are studying history," said Simon. "You must have figured out by now that personal vendettas feature hugely in human affairs, far more so than mere ideology."

"How come misogyny is seen as the worst of crimes, even when there isn't any actual dislike or denigration of women, whereas it is perfectly okay to hate men?"

"Have you only just figured out that there isn't any logic in any of this? That's why I keep away from people as much as possible, especially when they're in groups. At least mathematics is logical."

"But I still want to campaign for the workers' revolution. Should I start my own group?"

"How much has the WRLP achieved?" asked Simon.

"Well, not much yet. But it's early days."

"Really? After you joined them I looked them up. They have been in existence in one shape of form for well in excess of a century, since well before the Nuclear War. They haven't really achieved anything much in all that time."

"Perhaps if I set up a new group it might fare better."

"You would have even fewer members than the WRLP and you would waste your efforts fighting them instead of combatting the Establishment."

"Well, I can't just give up the struggle."

"What are you struggling for?"

"Against inequality and injustice. For the liberation of the workers."

"What workers?" Simon challenged.

"Well, those who produce things and keep things running."

"But almost everything is automated these days. The mass working class Karl Marx sought to empower doesn't exist anymore."

"I mean all those downtrodden people just barely existing in their modular housing units."

"But almost none of those people actually work."

"Well we need to give them jobs. It's their right to work."

"What would they do? Besides most of them probably don't want to work."

"There should be meaningful jobs for all."

"What would you class as a meaningful job?"

"Jobs that involve running things, organising, that sort of thing."

"How many of those jobs that you're referring to would be missed if the roles didn't exist?"

For a moment I thought that I was winning. Surely there must be plenty of jobs which would lead to the collapse of society if they weren't done. I thought for a few seconds, but nothing came into my head that in all honesty would lead to havoc if it didn't exist. The Commission took care of all the physical infrastructure, utilities, transportation and so on, and that was automated. Essential supplies, food, clothing was all available either online or from an automated store. Produce from Farmers Markets were a nice to have, but not essential for existence. I had to say something.

"Well, what about the people in government, those making the decisions, laws and so on," I said in desperation, but already knowing that it could be easily demolished.

"Politicians? You really consider them essential?"

"Well, there are the armed services, I suppose." I cringed, knowing how much us revolutionaries deplored militarism.

"All ceremonial. The Commission won't allow them to do any actual fighting."

"There are the Arts, theatre, visual arts, that sort of thing."

"People don't have to be paid to do those things," said Simon. "Those are things people can do for the love of it, if they want, and nothing terrible happens if they don't do them at all."

"We would all be the poorer for it if they weren't there."

"Poorer in what sense?"

"Culturally and spiritually impoverished."

"Okay, true, but what more tangible things require people to do them?"

"There is architecture. Homes, public buildings and so on. We need architects to design them?"

"Not really. If you submit your requirements and preferred style to the Commission's construction service they would build you a perfectly satisfactory result without any need for human intervention. Many people do that already."

"Well, there is the marketing, sales and conveyancing of the property." I was really scratching around now and hating myself even more for saying it. Us revolutionaries considered property to be the theft of the workers' birth right.

"You realise everything that you have mentioned are things related to power and status. Nothing you have come up with is anything that is essential for existence."

I mused. "So you are suggesting that practically everything that people do these days is about prestige and the pecking order within society."

"Yes, exactly that."

I stared at the floor. I couldn't refute Simon's logic. "That's depressing," I said eventually.

"As a historian, you of all people should realise that this was always the case. What people have been doing has been largely status related going right back to the Egyptian Pharaohs."

Simon had a point. Pyramids, palaces, statues and temples were hardly everyday essentials.

"But we still need to empower the people. We need real democracy to liberate ordinary people."

"When democracy was invented by the ancient Greeks the workers, by that I mean the slaves, didn't get to participate. The workers you claim to be championing were specifically excluded."

"That was then. Now we have socialism, to empower the workers."

"But we have just discussed that," said Simon patiently. "Those workers don't exist anymore."

I pondered. "You're right. I wonder why that is."

"Today we have automation and robots to do the routine work that in the ancient world was done by slaves. Slaves were their machines."

"I see what you mean. Donkey work was done by slaves in those days, or at least the donkey work that wasn't done by actual donkeys."

Simon left me with one further thought. "Ever thought of trying to fit into society rather than seeking to overthrow it?"

Encountering the Wild Folk

At times of disillusionment my secret portal into the Mendip Natural Ecology Reservation provided me with a respite from the so-called civilised world. It was like a dream. After my expulsion from the socialist revolutionary movement it was where I could reappraise my life in peace.

At least it was peaceful until I saw another man in modern dress making his way across the wild terrain. He was a few hundred yards away and hadn't seen me. I ducked into cover and observed him through the shrubbery surrounding my hiding place.

I was indignant. This was my place. What was this other person from the outside doing there?

I recognised that this was neither rational nor reasonable. I didn't own this wild place. Nobody did. I was as much an intruder as this other man. But in my gut it felt as if he was the interloper.

The fool took out his smart phone. He took pictures, including selfies. He tapped on the phone as if he was posting something onto social media or sending a message. He made a call. Even at about three hundred metres I could hear his stupid blaring voice. He could not have been more brazen.

Predictably there came the whirring of a drone as it flew in fast and low. I heard a single whoomp as a projectile was fired. The man stepped back in surprise. For a couple of seconds he remained standing before his legs gave way. He fell forward, flat on his face, where he remained lying still.

The drone came up over the man and remained

hovering in place as two robots dropped down on lines. The robots took hold of a rigid stretcher that had also been lowered from the drone. They rolled the man's inert form into the stretcher and secured him in place with straps. Within seconds the stretcher and the robots had been hauled back on board the drone, which sped away.

I had remained immobile, hunkered in my hiding place throughout the incident, my heart pounding in expectation that at any moment the drone might come for me too. As the drone's whirring faded I remained frozen, anticipating that another drone may be on its way for me.

After minutes of silence I was breathing easier. Then I became aware of a new danger. There were faint sounds of movement behind me, stirrings of the vegetation.

My heart almost stopped as the gruff voice of a man called, "What are you doing here?"

I swung around to see the figures of three men fanned out roughly fifteen yards distant from me and closing in. They were dressed in crudely hand-tailored outfits fashioned out of animal skins and armed with daggers and spears. The central figure, who had spoken, was a man I guessed was probably nearing sixty, with a grey beard and thin receding white hair. He was not big, perhaps a couple of inches short of six feet, yet came across as one of the toughest individuals you would ever likely meet, his spare frame worn away to its essentials, his sinewy body hardened by decades of strenuous living in the outdoors, his skin as leathery as the battered garments he wore.

The second figure was a man in his mid-twenties, a muscular individual in his prime with a full head of thick brown hair roughly hacked into thick tufts, his beard shorn to a thick stubble.

The third was a youth of around seventeen or eighteen, more slender than the other two but already looking strong and capable. He had long blonde hair, glowing and shining in a way that any woman would have been proud of. Around his chin grew a few fine wisps of blonde fluff that barely affected his still smooth youthful complexion.

Initially struck dumb, I realised I'd better answer lest they deploy their spears to persuade me.

"Just visiting," I said, voice quavering.

The men came up closer, only a few feet away, almost surrounding me.

"We have seen you over here before," the second man observed.

"Oh, I didn't know that."

"You wouldn't have," said the second man.

"You are from the outside," said the older man. "You have transgressed against the laws of Commissum by being here."

"Oh, have I?" I said, in mock ignorance.

"It is a Commandment of Commissum that our realm of Ecologia and the realm of Economica be kept separated. It is a grave transgression for you to have crossed over from there, just as it would be a transgression for us to cross over into Economica."

"Oh, I see," I acknowledged.

"You don't belong here," said the younger man. "We should hand you back over."

"Please don't do that," I pleaded.

"Why not?" said the younger man.

"I feel I belong here, much more than I do over there."

The younger man looked me up and down. His lip curled in disbelief that a specimen as soft and mollycoddled could imagine he might belong in this wild country.

The older man was more sympathetic. "What makes you think that you belong here rather than in Economica, where you came from?"

"I just feel right here," I explained. "Back there I don't feel comfortable. I don't fit in there."

"You wouldn't survive over here more than about five minutes," said the younger man scornfully.

"Actually he has already survived a lot longer than that," observed the older man. "We've seen him here several times. He has dealt with wolves, bears and mammoths."

"Okay, you could be right. He has survived better than any of the others we have seen."

"What happened to them?" I enquired.

"If they are lucky they get picked up by the metal angels of Commissum, like that one we saw just now," the older man explained. "Usually all we find of the less lucky ones are their chewed up remnants after the wolves and bears have finished with them."

"I seem to have an understanding with the wolves," I explained, "and I just keep my distance from the bears and they usually don't bother me."

The older man nodded in approval. "Well, what brought you over here today?"

How could I best explain it? Nothing had forced me over, but there was a reason. "I was thrown out of the group I had been a member of. I needed to get away."

All three men looked at each other with shock, as if

they were imagining something horrific. I was puzzled as to why they saw my predicament in such apocalyptic terms, but then it dawned that for them their immediate family group was probably the only group any of them belonged to and being expelled from it would be like being orphaned.

"So you're alone, with nowhere to go?" said the youth, joining the conversation for the first time.

This pity and concern for my welfare was playing in my favour so I decided not to explain that, while it might be a temporarily depressing phase, my entire life was not upended by my estrangement from the WRLP.

"I guess I am, in a way," I said sadly, milking the sympathy.

The group conferred.

"What do you think?" the older man enquired of his companions.

"He could bring the wrath of Commissum upon us if we took him in," replied the younger man.

"When the angels of Commissum came just now they took the other man, but left this one," observed the youth. The two men nodded sagely.

"Yes, I see what you mean," said the older man. "Perhaps it pleases Commissum for him to be here."

The younger man was taken with this thought. It moved him to turn his gaze back at me and observe me with new eyes. He turned back to his companions. "He has been here several times before, but Commissum chose not to take him on those occasions. Commissum has even allowed him to return. Any others who have come over have either been immediately taken by Commissum's metal angels or eaten by wolves. He isn't like the others."

The older man turned to me. "Do you think that Commissum wishes you to be here with us?"

It was reasonable to suppose they were referring to what the civilised world knew as the Commission. "I found a passage through from the other side."

"What sort of a passage?" asked the younger man.

"I cannot tell you," I replied. "It must remain a secret."

"Who said it must remain a secret?" asked the older man.

"I don't know exactly," I replied, "but it was someone who must have come from Commissum. I didn't ask why, but he told me I mustn't tell anyone."

The others looked at each other sagely and nodded.

"So Commissum has sent you over here as a messenger?" said the older man.

"I guess that he must have," I agreed.

The older man looked back at his companions and pronounced.

"If it wasn't Commissum's will for him to be here, Commissum would have taken him up and away by now, just like he has all the others who have come over. This one has been here several times already and Commissum has allowed it. We should accept that it is Commissum's will."

The others looked at each other again and each nodded again.

"So, what is your name?" the older man asked.

"Peter."

"I am Runulf and these are my sons, Knut and Torsten. You can come home with us."

The Ranulf family homestead was set in a clearing on the edge of a stretch of woodland at the head of a valley carved out by a small stream. The home, in a primitive style pre-dating the Roman occupation of Britain, was a circular building with a conical thatched roof. Its size was determined by the height of the tall conifer tree trunks that had been leant in across at a 45 degree angle to form the roof supports. Smoke curled upwards from the hole left for it escape at the top of the roof. Set between the substantial roof supports was a wall constructed out of wattle and daub panels, inset with holes to serve as windows and a door. Rolled up blankets were tacked up above each opening, ready to be unrolled at night to retain the warmth within the building.

Around the outside of the main building were rough lean-to constructions serving ancillary purposes such as storage, food preparation and workshops. In the clearing were cultivated plots within which a variety of vegetables grew. The setting afforded a good view down the valley and across the heathland below, with trees wrapped around sheltering the plot from wind and weather.

I came into the building following along behind Ranulf, with Knut and Torsten in the rear. As my eyes adjusted to the dim light I made out the surroundings and other occupants. There was a large central hearth over which were suspended substantial earthenware pots from which unfamiliar yet enticing aromas emerged. Tending the cooking was a heavily pregnant woman in her mid-twenties and a teenage girl.

The woman and the girl stared at me uncertainly and then looked expectantly at Ranulf.

"This is Peter," Ranulf announced. "He has been cast out from his group in Economica and will be staying with us."

The women looked quizzical. The girl seemed interested and pleased to see me there. The woman as if she was about to question Ranulf, but after a moment's reflection, opted to be civil.

"Hello Peter," said the woman. "How long will you be with us?"

"Gudrun, where are your manners?" interjected Ranulf.

"Sorry, yes, I'm Gudrun. Knut's wife. Welcome to our home."

"Hello Gudrun," I replied. "Nice to be here."

"Hello, I'm Freya," said the young girl. I guessed she must have been about fifteen, just on the cusp of womanhood, but not quite there.

"Peter will be with us for as long as he needs us," pronounced Ranulf, his eyes fixed on Gudrun, who looked away, her scepticism suppressed for the time being.

Leaning against the wall I noticed an enormous mammoth tusk.

"Was that something you hunted?" I asked Ranulf.

"No, not that one," he said. "It was one we scavenged. The wolves had already been at the meat, but we took one of the tusks."

"A mammoth of that size would have been a bit much even for wolves, I'd have thought."

"I suspect they were scavenging too," said Ranulf. "I should think it died of old age."

"What are you going to do with the tusk?"

"It'll be useful for making stuff."

We settled for our evening meal. Knut poured ale into earthenware mugs and handed them round. Gudrun and Freya slopped out helpings of a porridge of coarsely ground grains and a stew of old meat and vegetables into earthenware dishes. The meat was grey and stringy but it had mainly served its purpose by permeating itself into the stew as a pungent smoky gravy.

The food and drink was like nothing I had tasted, a universe away from the flavours and textures of the processed food obtained from the CommStore supermarkets in Economica. The nearest I had before was food that I had eaten on rare occasions prepared from ingredients sourced from Farmers Markets. This food had an earthy reality I had never experienced, a taste of soil, grit and smoke, of flesh from an animal that had lived its tough life in the wild, its meat acquiring a pungency from being dried and smoked for preservation, a stalky starchiness from gathered vegetables.

There was an atmosphere of suspicion and a corresponding awkwardness in the conversation.

"Was it difficult to get across from Economica?" asked Gudrun.

"Not difficult," I replied. "I have a way."

"What way is that?" asked Freya, who had arranged herself to sit next to me.

"Commissum has commanded it remain secret," Ranulf intervened, for which I was grateful.

"But it is against Commissum's law to cross over from Economica," said Gudrun.

"Normally, yes," I explained, "but a way through was revealed to me."

"If we assist a fugitive from Economica, won't we incur Commissum's wrath?" persisted Gudrun. "Only True Followers of Gaia may remain here."

"Peter is Commissum's messenger," said Ranulf.

"What is Commissum's message for us?" asked Freya eagerly.

Now she had me cornered. It was a logical question. If I was a messenger, it stood to reason I should have a message. I racked my brains. "We need to fit in with our surroundings, not arrogantly try to shape them to our will," I said, reminded by Simon's recent advice to me.

My companions let the words settle into their minds and nodded. It was a novel experience for me to have become the mouthpiece of a revered prophet.

"Wise words," said Ranulf. "It is not our prerogative to shape the world. We must leave that to Commissum and Gaia."

The family's beds were arranged in alcoves around the outside wall of the home. Knut and Gudrun improvised a new compartment for my sleeping quarters. It was a cosy niche with a mattress of bundles of dried brush covered in furs assembled from an assortment of creatures such as rabbits, wild goats and elk. Unable to get to sleep in my unfamiliar bed I dreamily absorbed the atmosphere, dimly lit by the remnants of the fire that still glowed in the central hearth.

"Today we must hunt," Ranulf announced over our breakfast of fresh porridge and remnants of the previous night's stew.

Knut and Torsten looked over at me questioningly.

"Peter will come with us," said Ranulf.

"Not dressed like that," said Knut. He had a sceptical expression. I sensed he considered my presence would be more of a liability than anything else.

"You're right," said Ranulf. "He would stand out like squawking magpie as he is."

The three men scavenged around their personal effects for spare garments, returning with a collection of worn leather items, trousers a Bavarian peasant might have worn, but rougher and baggier, a kind of a jerkin, a coat and moccasins. I changed into my new attire. Knut armed me with a spear, a dagger and a net, approximately 2 metres square, fashioned of coarse but tough fibre.

The plan for the hunt was to catch ourselves a deer. It was clear that in the eyes of my companions I was only there to gain experience and was not expected to contribute anything useful.

In the neighbouring valley there was a narrow cleft within which deer could be ambushed as they passed. Ranulf outlined the plan, which was for Knut to carefully cajole the deer towards the ambush point, where Ranulf and Torsten would lie quietly in wait, ready to pounce at exactly the opportune moment. At this point the others looked at me and each other. It was transparent that they clearly didn't want me around to spoil things in either the herding or the ambushing, but sought to be tactful in how they expressed those thoughts.

Ranulf had a suggestion. To one side of the cleft there was a path through which the deer could veer. I should hunker there in preparation to ambush in case that happened. All, myself included, knew well that I was being positioned so as to keep me safely out of the way. There was no serious expectation the deer would swing away at a tangent from their course.

Knut swung out behind the deer silently and out of sight. He carefully aligned himself opposite to where the deer were required to move. Remaining out of sight he crept towards them. When almost exactly two hundred yards away from the nearest beasts in the herd he raised his body slightly above the shrubs he had been using for cover, deliberately shaking a gorse bush, making just enough noise to be noticed but not enough to alarm our prey. At this stage the aim was to induce the herd to move a little in the right direction, but not to cause them to panic or scatter.

The herd obliged. Without hurrying they decided that another patch of grazing about a hundred yards further would be preferable and ambled towards it.

Knut dropped back out of sight and waited until the herd settled in their new situation before creeping forward to reveal himself again a hundred yards further on.

Little by little, over the course of an hour, Knut edged the herd towards the trap. They were now contained between Knut and the gully presented for them as an obvious escape route. This time Knut was noisier, standing tall and moving towards them purposefully.

The deer were spooked and trotted away, but the plan went awry. The deer leading the herd, warned by some sixth sense, saw the gully as a place of danger, veering along the alternative escape path Ranulf had tactfully suggested was a possibility. From my hiding place along the route I could hear and see the herd galloping towards me at speed.

I was going to have to act fast. The deer were spread out, jostling each other and veering from side to side. A doe skirted towards my side of the path. I quickly threw out my net into its path. Its front legs caught in the netting and the beast stumbled.

Within a second it would have freed itself, so I charged. I was barely in time because as I came within reach the animal was already on its feet.

In my haste my aim was askew and the spear's point glanced off the doe's neck barely breaking the skin. Nevertheless I had a firm grasp of the shaft and with the impetus of my weight behind it the animal toppled back over.

Dropping my spear to the side I maintained my rush forward, throwing my weight on top of the animal to keep it down. In a moment I drew my dagger and slashed it across the animal's throat. Despite the spouts of blood spurting out the deer struggled to push me aside and rise to its feet. I thrust the dagger deeply into its body and more blood gushed from the new wound. As we struggled the remainder of the herd thundered past, keeping to the opposite side of the path.

Making a final effort the deer succeeded in tipping me off, rising unsteadily. It took off down the path in pursuit of the herd now some distance ahead. Weakened by loss of blood the beast staggered only a few steps before stumbling. In the meantime I had sprung up and dashed after, tipping it over again. This time it was not getting up. As the animal's laboured breath subsided and as its legs twitched in its death throes I caught my breath.

I had thought the drama had run its course, but then

sensed I was not alone. I heard a howl and realised I was surrounded by wolves. The pack was advancing purposefully. They were the same animals I had previously encountered, but our mutual understanding was void. The slavering beasts growled and snarled. I could see clearly that if I did not back off from my prize the wolves would not only devour the deer but eat me as well.

Fortunately it was at that moment I was joined by Knut, Ranulf and Torsten. They shouted and stamped the ground. The wolves were no longer feeling so brave and slunk away.

My companions now saw me in a new light. Never had they imagined a softie straight out of Economica could have carried out such a feat. For the first time it felt as if I was among equals. I had proved my hunting prowess.

We made our way back to the homestead, the deer carcass slung under the shaft of my spear, with me at the front and Torsten walking behind sharing the load.

In the evening, as we tucked into generous helpings of barbecued deer steak, I was no longer a random refugee the family's soft-hearted patriarch, Ranulf, had taken in, but a valued new family member.

Once again Freya tucked in next to me for the meal, now more admiring of me than ever. "Do you have any more messages from Commissum, Peter?"

At that point I had to stretch my memory for what I had said the previous evening, let alone come up with new words of wisdom. Whatever it was that I had said, it seemed to have gone down well.

"Why, wasn't my message from yesterday enough?" I replied, still trying to remember what it had been.

"It was a very wise message," said Ranulf solemnly. That was nice to hear, but he hadn't given me any clue about what my wise utterance had actually been.

"So, Freya," I said, "what did you take from what I said?" She had asked me, so it seemed appropriate to press her for elucidation.

"We shouldn't be changing things too much, but fit in to what is already there," Freya replied.

"That's right," I said. "The world was already as it should be before we came along."

Ranulf nodded. "We must respect and protect Gaia, not molest and abuse Her."

"Are you going to stay with us and guide us with your wisdom?" asked Freya.

"I don't know about wisdom," I said modestly, diverting from answering her question.

"You are wise," said Ranulf, "and capable too."

"Nice of you to say so."

"I want you to guide me," said Freya, gazing into my eyes.

I caught a glance from Torsten. He was frowning and his cheeks were flushed. Freya continued to gaze at me in admiration.

"Freya, you are being naughty," I said. "Your brother is worried for your virtue, with you looking at me like that."

Freya turned to Torsten and then looked back at me.

"He isn't my brother," she said.

"Oh," I said. "Sorry, I just assumed that he would be."

"We took Freya in, after her family came to grief," Ranulf explained. "There was trouble and they died. Freya was left alone, so we took her in."

"Oh, I see," I said, although I sensed that there would be more to the story.

"But, Freya," said Ranulf, "I took you in as my daughter, so Torsten is your brother."

Looking across at Torsten I sensed his interest in Freya was more than fraternal.

I remained with the Ranulf family a couple more days. I began the process of learning the many new skills I would need to live in Ecologia, such as working with leather to make clothes, preservation of food, setting snares for small game, fishing techniques, identification of plants. It was all new, but I loved it and took to it easily.

I had a decision to make. I could stay with the Ranulf family as long as I wished, making my life with them if I chose. But I wasn't ready. I wasn't ready to simply walk away from my old life.

"I must return to Economica," I told Ranulf.

"You don't need to," he replied. "You are welcome to remain with us."

"I have things to see to, to tidy up."

"Yes, I see that you might," said Ranulf. "When must you go?"

"Today or tomorrow, I think."

"Will you be back?"

"Yes, definitely," I said. "But I can't promise when that will be. But I will be back."

All were sad when we announced my departure. There were hugs from all. Freya and Gudrun shed some tears.

I made my way alone to the hollow situated just outside the great fence separating the realms of Ecologia and

Economica, slipping down into the secret tunnel. I trudged in a few steps to find the cleft where I had left my trappings of civilised existence, my hard hat and head torch and smart phone. I stripped off the leather garments that the Runulf family had provided for me and put my Economica garments back on. I carefully laid my Ecologia outfit into the cleft.

I would wear the outfit again when I returned, with one exception. Those moccasins did not agree with me. My feet were battered and bruised from walking around with so little protection. I resolved to retain my sturdy walking boots next time.

A Promising Future

After visiting Tim and Annie my next port of call was the prestigious offices of my employer and future father-in-law, Sir Hugo Davenhirst the chief executive and principal shareholder of Davenhirst Properties.

My autotaxi cruised up the sweeping driveway to the former country house on the outskirts of Guildford serving as the Davenhirst Properties head office. The former aristocratic owners had chosen the spot for its commanding view over the countryside, a view that worked in both directions, from the inside out over the land owned by those looking out, from the outside up at the wealth and prestige demonstrated by the imposing building.

It was at times like this I felt like an imposter in my senior role within the organisation. How could an ordinary bloke like me hold such a position? Sir Hugo could be intimidating and being summoned into his presence was daunting.

I had no objective reason for feeling inadequate. I had proven myself in my previous roles, I was well-connected and already proving my worth within the company. Sir Hugo thought so.

The building was well-protected by automated security systems. The doors opened automatically for those who were authorised, identified by a combination of biometrics, facial recognition, a handprint by touching onto a pad together with general characteristics such as height and gait.

Organisations that considered themselves high class, and Davenhirst Properties was one, employed a real person on reception in addition to the robot that almost every organisation possessed. The best humanoid robots were almost indistinguishable from real people, were unfailingly polite, had perfect memories, remained on duty around the clock and were continuously connected to security systems. Although no person could match the capabilities and efficiency of a robot, a real person provided the human touch that made clients feel special.

Sir Hugo was expecting me so I went straight up to find him in his palatial office situated on a corner of the building with panoramic views. The furnishings were modern, comfortable and functional yet in a style that reflected the era of the building in its Georgian and Victorian heyday.

Sir Hugo was a barrel shaped man of sixty, gruff and with a perpetual air of impatience. If you got in his way he would be more than capable of shoving you aside physically or verbally.

He was glad to hear of the progress we had been making in my Solent and Dorset patch but appeared preoccupied and did not dwell on the details. "I have a conference call with the Commission presently," he told me. "I'd like you to sit in on it."

"Yes, certainly. Glad to. What is it about?"

"It concerns our proposals for residential development in the English Riviera. The Commission are being awkward about it."

"Oh, I see. Is there anything I should be aware of before we start?"

"They're saying we would be impinging on an area designated to be one of those damned ecological reserves."

"But the land doesn't have anything ecological about it at the moment, does it?"

"They're saying it has."

We settled in the corner of the office laid out for conferences. At the scheduled time a hologram lit in what had previously been an empty space. It was the seated figures of Alexander Clessing, the Commission's Military Affairs Controller, and Erica Venburg, the Commission's Ecological Affairs Custodian. They didn't appear instantly, emerging over a few seconds in a process akin to magic, initially like ghosts in a mist that gradually brightened and sharpened into lifelike forms. Despite knowing they were just a light show, an illusion created by lasers, they looked so realistic one might be tempted to reach out and touch them, only to have the illusion shattered by empty air.

Having introduced ourselves and exchanged civilities, Sir Hugo brought us to the substance of our discussion. "I have been informed by the South Devon Planning office that our proposal for the World Experience Retirement Community residential development has been opposed by the Commission. I would like to understand the nature of the Commission's objections and what we might be able to do to overcome them."

"The area is a habitat for the unique Dumnonian Rock Cress and breeding ground for rare water fowl such as the Sandbank Crane," said Ms Venburg.

"Couldn't we incorporate provision for these species into our development?" enquired Sir Hugo.

"Your proposal includes removal of explosives residue

from the ground," said Ms Venburg.

"Isn't that a good thing?" enquired Sir Hugo. "Cleaning up the environment, I mean?"

"The Dumnonian Rock Cress depends on the presence of TNT in the soil," explained Ms Venburg.

"What about the bird you mentioned, the crane or whatever?" asked Sir Hugo. "That doesn't need us to leave explosives lying around, does it?"

"The proposed pleasure boat marina would displace it from its nesting grounds," said Ms Venburg.

"Supposing we establish special wetlands as a purpose built reservation for water birds?"

"The old shell craters provide a unique habitat that favours the Sandbank Crane."

Sir Hugo decided to change tack. "The Commission has its point of view, but I don't understand why this falls within the Commission's remit. Surely this is a national English matter rather than one of international concern."

"The land in question was formerly used by the Ministry of Defence," said Mr Clessing.

"What difference does that make?"

"Under the International Guarantee of Peace Treaty the Commission has oversight over all national military assets to prevent renewed hostilities."

"But the Ministry of Defence never actually owned the land," insisted Sir Hugo. "It was only used by them under emergency powers during the Second World War and subsequently reverted back to the original owners."

"The treaty covers all lands that have been impaired by military use," said Mr Clessing.

"How was it impaired?"

"It was used by the United States military as a practice beach for the invasion of Normandy during which it was heavily shelled by warships and bombed from the air. It was then attacked by a flotilla of German ships, which spread further ordnance over the area."

"Well, the treaty provided oversight," acknowledged Sir Hugo, "but why should the Commission wish to prevent our development? Our proposal is to provide residential property for retired people, not to establish any military capability."

"The International Ecological Renewal Treaty designates war damaged lands for natural environment restoration purposes," explained Ms Venburg.

"But surely that was intended to apply to land contaminated by fallout during the Nuclear War, not land afflicted by earlier conflicts."

"The treaty does not distinguish between conflicts."

There was some further sparring from Sir Hugo but to no avail.

"I don't know about you, but I need a stiff drink after that," growled Sir Hugo after the call finished and the Commission functionaries had disappeared from view. Within seconds a robot butler appeared with two strong gin and tonics on a tray.

Sir Hugo slurped a good slug of his drink. "Good God, those odious bureaucrats make me sick."

"They certainly had their bases covered, with the legal and bureaucratic niceties," I concurred.

"That's exactly what it is," Sir Hugo fumed. "Nit picking details designed to trip you up. Pointless red tape to tie you in knots. Pure obstruction."

"They had us boxed in, that's for sure."

"But who elected these people?" Sir Hugo continued.

I shrugged.

"Nobody. Unelected, obstructive, useless bureaucrats, the lot of them."

"Seems a waste of talent to me," I remarked.

"How so?"

"I couldn't help admiring the slick way they blocked our every avenue. It seems a waste to have that skill employed only in blocking things. Imagine what they might accomplish if they used their talents to build something."

Sir Hugo scoffed. "People like that would never build anything. All they know how to do is to prevent things from happening. Complete waste of space."

"I don't know," I mused. "Properly directed they could probably do some good."

"Be that as it may. What right have the Commission to dictate these things to us anyway? The Commission is supposed to be serving the nations of the world, not dictating to them."

"I guess that the Commission needs some powers."

"Ha, what exactly might they be?"

"Well, to prevent wars and restore the environment."

"That might have been necessary to get things back into order after the Nuclear War," Sir Hugo conceded. "But that was forty years ago. Have you noticed that the Commission has only ever seized power for itself, never given any back?"

"Yes, that's true. I suppose they must feel they need to keep a lid on things."

"They can only legitimately do those things through

consent and international co-operation."

"Actually have you noticed that such international co-operation as does exist is all mediated through the Commission?" I observed. "Since the Nuclear War countries haven't negotiated with each other directly at all, at least not that I can recall."

"A clear case of divide and rule. Keep the countries isolated and suspicious of one another so that they can't unite against their oppressors."

"Perhaps they are concerned that smaller countries might be bullied by larger ones," I suggested. "So they put themselves in as a referee, to ensure fair play."

"Fair play, pah! They don't play fair themselves. How dare they!"

"But without some sort of global order, countries might not play nice. That's how we got to have wars in the first place."

"Hm, maybe," Sir Hugo accepted grudgingly. "But that should be done collectively by the nations of the world, not by some faceless body accountable to nobody."

"You are right. The Commission just seems to do what it likes."

"They have usurped our national sovereignty. We need to claim it back. We need to take back control."

"That sounds like a call to arms."

"Damned right it is. We have taken their crap for too long. Time to put an end to it."

"Where do you suggest we start?"

"For a start we need to reassert our own English laws. For too long we have been compelled by oppressive treaties to incorporate Commission diktats into English law without scrutiny or debate."

"It isn't only laws," I added. "The Commission controls and allocates an ever increasing share of resources. It is not only land, but food, power, consumer goods, transport, security. We depend on what they hand out to us for our existence."

"Quite right. Ever more of our national resources absorbed into the maw of the Commission. They are riding roughshod over the interests of the countries they were established to serve."

"Taking back control will be difficult," I observed.

"How so?"

"As a nation we don't have the capabilities any more to do most of the stuff that the Commission does for us."

"We've got slack," said Hugo. "English national capabilities have been left to wither on the vine as the Commission takes it upon itself to provide goods and services England used to do for itself. We used to lead the world. Look at us now."

"We'll be alright," I replied, trying to sound upbeat. "Both us as a firm and England in general."

"You're right," acknowledged Sir Hugo. "Mustn't wallow. Anyway, things are looking good for you, with your imminent marriage to my lovely daughter. How long is it now?"

"Six weeks to go."

"Goodness, is that all. The planning must be getting frantic, if I know my good lady."

"Yes, Lady Davenhirst really has the bit between her teeth."

"No need for the formalities, we're Hugo and Margot from now on."

"Of course. As I said Margot is planning the whole thing like a military operation."

"I know," Hugo acknowledged. "She tries to suck me in too, but I've been resisting. Pressure of work and all that."

"I have to confess I've been doing the same."

"But you're one of the principal actors. She won't let you get away with ducking out of the preparations."

"She isn't. I'm on my way over now."

"Ah, that'll be why you are so well turned out," Hugo remarked, appreciating my crisply pressed and ironed outfit.

"I'm always well turned out, Hugo."

"Normally I'd say that you would only be this smartly attired if you had customers to see."

"Well, it's true, Margot does expect the highest standards."

"Keeps us all on our toes."

"Probably a good thing," I acknowledged. "Standards might slip otherwise."

"You'll be wanting to see Celia anyway, I'm sure."

"Yes, of course."

Hugo raised his eyebrows. "But you've been playing for time, haven't you?"

"How do you mean?"

"Margot told me that you've been evasive, getting away for a few days, that sort of thing."

"Well, that's true. There's stuff I wanted to get out of the way before I got too drawn into the arrangements."

"I know," said Hugo. "Once she has you in her clutches

there will be no getting away."

"I'm not trying to get out of my responsibilities," I insisted. "Just clearing the decks, that's all."

"Don't worry," Hugo confided. "I know what it's like. I'll back you up. We'll probably be backing each other up as we go forward."

"Of course, Hugo, you can count on me."

"Anyway, I mustn't hold you up any longer," said Hugo. "Better get yourself over there. I'll take care of things from this end."

Broken Hearts
and other Emotional Debris

As I departed from the Davenhirst Properties office I reflected on how I had come to be in the cosy and privileged niche I now found myself in, a trusted senior member of the Davenhirst Properties management team soon to be married to the heiress to the Davenhirst fortune. It felt bizarre that I, of all people, had arrived in this position.

It had been my friend Simon who had reset my trajectory at a critical moment. Simon could focus on the nub of a situation. I should try fitting into society rather than seeking to overthrow it. Subsequently my new friends in Ecologia had considered this same sentiment to be sacred words of wisdom. It was clear to me now, society would never adjust to suit me, I had to adapt.

I signed with the University of York's Officers' Training Corps. As a Military History student it seemed natural. It was a 180 degrees cultural turnaround. My companions were no longer the scruffy left wing radicals of the Workers Revolutionary Liberation Party. Instead they were conservative, privileged, smartly turned out supporters of the Establishment.

I applied to join the Army as an officer. There were interviews, physical and mental tests and a team exercise in which each candidate took a turn leading applicants in an improvisation exercise. My task involved using an assortment of bits and pieces to get the team across an imaginary crocodile infested stream without falling in. We did not succeed but I had devised a scheme that might have worked if we had time to rehearse it. I purloined extra kit for the job from a shed we were not supposed to have access to. Despite falling into the hypothetical stream my initiative and the way that I organised the team must have impressed the assessors, as did my knowledge of military traditions and how I bluffed when I didn't have an answer.

I made a seamless transition from graduation from York to the Royal Military Academy in Sandhurst.

The Army in modern times had become rather like the monarchy, mainly about tradition. Tradition for the Army falls into two categories, fighting and pageantry.

Since the International Guarantee of Peace Treaty there had been no conflict, but in the English collective mind, composing the general population, their political leaders and the military, there always remained the feeling that peace was temporary, so an ability to fight must be retained. As much as anything else military capability was important for national prestige and self-confidence.

Pageantry is a celebration of past glories. The fripperies displayed are more than colourful decoration, a stylised representation of the fighting capabilities of past centuries. The decades long peace and the Treaty's prohibition on the most dangerous categories of weapons had already transitioned supposed combat functions into stylised rituals, ghosts of past fighting prowess.

From Sandhurst I moved on to a commission in the Household Division at Windsor, where our principal duties were to serve as ceremonial guards for the King. Although it did not feel anything special, it was a prestigious appointment that saw me invited to events frequented by the upper classes, including royalty. Many nouveau riches would have spent millions for such connections, whereas in my case I was there by right and being paid a modest lieutenant's salary.

Any concerns I may have had about my attractiveness to women evaporated. My uniform and military bearing was a gateway to the upper echelons. I had only to smile and say hello to open up gushing conversations. The challenge was escaping idle chat.

It was at a social event organised by the Royal Equestrian Society I was re-acquainted with Fiona Deveryll, of whom I had painful memories from school days. I had spotted her early on. Even as a school girl she had been well groomed. Since then she had taken her outward presentation to a level that could have graced *Vogue*, carefully crafted to outclass the competition and dazzle any man she might set her sights on.

A look in her direction and she caught my eye and smiled at me expectantly. My smile back was the minimum twitch of acknowledgement required for politeness. I kept my focus on the conversation I was having with someone else. Over ensuing minutes I was conscious of her glances. For a while I kept my attention directed elsewhere.

This was not a tactic that could be sustained indefinitely and Fiona patiently lay in wait.

"Remember me? We were at school together." She was even better turned out than I remembered, immaculately made up, coiffured and clad in what must have been a hugely expensive yet minimal outfit from an exclusive fashion house. She was the pinnacle of high class crumpet.

"Yes, I remember." It wasn't a memory I relished, but I tried not to let that show.

"You've done well for yourself. I had a feeling you would." She looked me up and down, admiring my smart dress uniform.

"You're pretty well turned out yourself."

"Oh, do you like it?"

"It creates an impression."

"A favourable one, I trust?"

"Undoubtedly."

She moved in beside me. "Do you think that my dress goes well with your uniform?"

I struggled a moment. It wasn't a combination that particularly appealed. "The sergeant major wouldn't like it on the parade ground."

"I wasn't thinking about on the parade ground, more when you're off duty."

"There wouldn't be much chance for that. I'm on duty nearly all the time."

"No, you're not. Don't fib. You officers get loads of time to go out to play."

"Yes, but we tend to play rough. Your dress might get torn."

She cuddled up close. "Promises, promises. I like a bit of rough play."

Oh, God. What am I getting into? I thought in panic. "So, what have you been doing with yourself, since school?" I attempted to swing the conversation towards more conventional small talk.

"I did Art History at the Royal Court Institute and since then I've been at Christoby's, you know, the auction house."

"That sounds posh."

"Not as posh as you, guarding royalty in Windsor. Can't get posher than that."

"We're just staff, really, us Army fellows, not proper posh."

"You're posh enough for me," she murmured, lips close to my ear. I half expected her to nibble my earlobe.

"Sorry, Fiona, got to dash. The CO wants to see me."

I have always had a physical confidence that lets me skip, trot and climb over rough terrain. Without effort, as if I was a mountain goat, my feet reach out and land on the small loose rocks, my weight shifting. I don't think about it. The majority of people reach out tentatively for each step, applying concentration and sweating with the fear of falling. I have been out with Tim traversing rough terrain; he is one of those physically nervous people. In social situations our roles are reversed.

Tim enjoyed an unconscious sense for social interactions from his earliest childhood. I painstakingly figured out social situations from first principles later in life. It can be an advantage. I built a scientific understanding of what is involved whereas Tim never concerned himself with the detailed mechanics. Once I had established myself in the Army, while nowhere close to Tim's abilities, I developed a social competence slick enough to convey confidence in most situations.

I had moved on from convincing women I was worth

talking to, to convincing them of my motives. The question that kept arising, by inference or directly, was, why would a man like you be interested in a woman like me? I would be interrogated, suspected of being already married or challenged about my nefarious or lecherous intentions. What should I have done?

If I had been Tim I would have allayed their insecurity with romantic gestures and reassuring words. Then, had I been Tim, I would have taken advantage of the women and abandoned them, exactly as they had feared.

That type of suspicion and hostility was not something I was prepared to tolerate within a relationship. As a rule I ignored the challenge and walked away, perhaps confirming the woman's worst fears.

As a young guards officer I qualified as one of the bright young things invited to a party at the polo club in Windsor Great Park, as did Sophie Beesham, who in her floaty white frock, amid the haze of champagne, appeared as a wood nymph who had drifted in from the surrounding forest.

We connected right away. As we talked the hubbub of the party faded leaving us within our private bubble. We made our escape into the open air, wandering out through the parkland until we came across a small lake. There was a little rowing boat moored up. Naughtily we borrowed the boat and I rowed us to a little private place where we could hunker down and look out over the tranquil water. We held hands, kissed and chatted.

Later that evening, or rather the early hours of the morning, when I was back alone in my quarters in the Windsor barracks, I sent her a romantic message. "If I could, I would have preserved that moment forever, the two of us alone trailing our fingers in the water as it twinkled under the moonlight, overhung by the drooping willow wrapped around like a comforting robe holding us together as one."

A couple of days later we met again. I took her out for tea in Windsor.

"I don't know if I can trust you," she said.

"Oh, why not?"

"Those things you said, did you mean them, or were you just saying it?"

"Well, yes, I meant them."

She looked at me with nervous expectation. There was an awkward pause.

"I'm not sure what you meant by what you said," she prompted me eventually.

The words had been clear enough, I felt. With the benefit of hindsight perhaps I was expected to declare my undying love there and then. But we hardly knew each other yet. It felt a bit soon.

"Well, it was a lovely few moments that we had together. Did you feel that?"

She looked uncomfortable. Defensive. "I'm not sure."

There was another uneasy pause. "What is it about me that you don't trust?"

She crossed her arms and looked away. "I wish I could, but I can't."

I was shattered. It was time for me to get away to recharge my batteries. I took a few days out to visit the Mendips.

On my return I found a message from Sophie. "Why

did you leave me?"

"I just needed to get away on my own for a while," I replied. "I do sometimes."

"Please don't lie to me. You were with another woman."

If she felt that then there was nothing more to be said, I decided, and left it.

Months later I met up with my friend Tim, who since graduating had taken up a sales role within The World Experience, an elaborate network of theme parks based on famous international locations situated in South Devon, an area branded as the English Riviera.

"Why did you dump that nice girl, Sophie?" he asked.

"Why do you ask?"

"I heard something, that's all."

"I didn't dump her, we were never an item."

"Oh, I heard different."

"Where did this come from?"

"I just happened to be chatting with one of her friends. They're all talking about it apparently."

"Really, what are they saying?"

"You fed her romantic poetry, led her on, built up her hopes, got her in love with you, only to dump her."

That was a revelation to me. This romantic poetry stuff was a powerful drug. I would have to be careful with it. "What has it got to do with her friends?"

"Women confide in their friends. She told them how you broke her heart, then they all drank wine and commiserated and told her that she was well rid of you because you're a heartless bastard."

"Really? I don't get it. She told me she didn't trust me.

Then accused me of going off with another woman."

"What did you do about it?"

"Nothing. If she doesn't trust me, what's the point?"

"She was looking for reassurance of your commitment, you clot."

"Women are like something out of Lewis Carroll."

"How do you mean?"

"Everything the opposite of what you would expect. If you declare your attraction for them, they reel back in horror. Assuming that they don't bounce you back right away, they go on the attack, accusing you of all sorts of bad intentions or going after other women or already being married. Their own motives as pure as the driven snow."

"You just have to press their buttons. Make the right noises and all will be fine."

"Yet, if the introduction is by chance and casual, or initiated by the woman, then they are completely and naively trusting without a hint of suspicion. Just pass the time of day chatting without the slightest hint of romantic intent and they assume wedding bells are around the corner."

"I expect they feel favourable vibes when they do that," Tim explained. "It's not just what is said. It's the ambiance."

"How is it that if you do say something romantic, they don't trust it, but when you don't they assume romance, even if it isn't there?"

Tim looked perplexed. "You just have to respond to the situation as it arises."

If he had asked me how to leap from rock to rock on a hillside I would have said the same and he would have been as perplexed as he had left me.

Years passed. From appearances all was well in my life. I had secured an enviable position that offered advancement both within the Army and in terms of social position. Although high standards of presentation and discipline were required, overall Army duties were not onerous and there were ample opportunities for me to pursue extra-curricular activities, exotic sports such as polo and those of an amorous nature with some of the most attractive and highest class women.

Yet despite the apparent success I enjoyed, I continually felt a vague discontent. Supposedly I had been successful in life, yet it did not feel like success. There was no clearly definable reason for my a persistent unease. I tried to dismiss my misgivings as irrational, but they would not go away.

One thing was certain; I had, by appearances, made a greater success of my life than my friend Simon. He graduated with an outstanding first class degree in Mathematics, but then seemed to do nothing. While he would probably have struggled to secure a position in conventional society due to his lack of social skills, as far as I could tell he had not even applied. After graduating he settled for a life on UBI, an anonymous existence in a housing module in Woking's roughest neighbourhood.

From time to time I dropped in to see him.

"Do you get many people coming over here, apart from me?"

"No, only you," said Simon, matter-of-factly. Simon only did facts and logic, not subtext.

"Do you find that lonely, just being here on your own?"

"No."

"But you must want someone to talk to, at least sometimes?"

"I get to discuss things with people every day."

"Oh, who? Do I know them?"

"No, you wouldn't. There is a man in Delhi. I am discussing the Goldberg Seymour conjecture with him. A woman in Shanghai with whom I discuss the Herzog–Schönheim conjecture. A man in Accra with whom I discuss aspects of set theory."

"So, you're keeping up with your maths."

"Yes."

"But nobody would know that, just seeing you here."

"Why would I want them to know about it?"

I was stumped. Knowing Simon as I did, I don't suppose he would care if anyone knew.

"It keeps you busy then, the maths."

"Yes. But what about you? Do you like it in the Army?"

"Well, it's quite good. I get to meet prestigious people, organise parades in Windsor for royal events, that sort of thing."

"Do you like meeting those people and organising the parades?"

Simon had homed straight in on my discontent. "No, actually, not really."

"But that's what the Army entails, isn't it? There aren't any other things for you to do there."

I thought about it. There were other postings, but in all the roles it was the ceremonial that was at the centre of things. Even the roles supposedly geared towards combat, the training exercises, had been standardised and ritualised into glorified competitive sporting events.

"Well, no, it's all pretty similar to what I do, just less glamourous than my Household Division posting in most cases," I confessed.

"That must mean you don't really like it in the Army," Simon observed, with perfect logic.

Somehow the conversation had begun with my concern about Simon, but he had turned it around. "Well, now you mention it, actually I don't," I said, admitting it not only to Simon but for the first time to myself.

"Then you should leave the Army," said Simon.

I couldn't fault Simon's reasoning. I ought to have been contented, but I wasn't. What grated most was the way everything in both the Army and the associated social scene was organised and hidebound with conventions.

The sensible thing would have been to stay on, making my way up the hierarchy and into the social circles opening up for me. But I couldn't imagine doing that.

The Army offered an option to drop out after three years' service, which would be my opportunity to move on.

Before I took such a drastic step I sought the counsel of my other close friend, Tim.

Tim's career at The World Experience had soared. He was a natural salesman and had risen to the position of Business Development Manager.

Tim also had political aspirations, making his mark as a rising star within the Conservative Party. He had been selected as the prospective parliamentary candidate for a probably unwinnable parliamentary seat in Bristol, but if that went well he had hopes of selection for somewhere more winnable shortly thereafter.

I wished that whatever Tim had that brought him his success could be bottled and reused, but it was too slippery for that. He had an uncanny ability to charm people, but the magic sauce he employed remained a mystery.

In his way Tim was as logical in his thinking as Simon, but it was a different kind of logic. Simon used a mathematical logic that made no allowance for human feelings. Tim's was a social logic based upon psychology. The accuracy, consistency and reason of what he said was not important, rather it was the emotional impact and effect that mattered. Simon was interested in ideas, even ones that so obscure and unintelligible to most he could only share them with correspondents in Delhi, Shanghai or Accra that he would never even meet, whereas nothing had any significance to Tim unless it carried an emotional or social connotation.

"I'm thinking of leaving the Army," I announced.

Tim was dumbstruck. "Did I actually hear you right? Leaving the Army?"

"Yes."

"But why?"

"I can't imagine being able to go on doing what I've been doing until now for years to come."

"But you wouldn't be. You'd go up through the ranks, surely, to bigger and better things."

"More seniority and responsibility perhaps, but it would still be essentially the same."

Tim looked at me carefully. "That's a shocker," he said, now convinced I was serious. "I really can't understand it. You're sitting pretty. You're an officer in the most prestigious posting, right as the centre of things in the

Royal Household. You've got your pick of the highest class of crumpet in England. The envy of every young guy. And you are talking about throwing all that away."

"It's just not for me. Not my thing."

Tim shrugged and shook his head. Not for the first time he couldn't figure me out. "I applied to join the Army, you know," he confided. "They wouldn't have me."

"What made you want to join?"

"Bloody obvious. You couldn't be better connected in that role. Apart from anything else, you get your pick of the posh totty."

"You've got a one track mind, you have."

"It's not just that."

"What then?"

"You know that I have political ambitions?"

"Yes."

"An Army background like yours wouldn't half have helped me to make my mark in politics, especially in the Conservative Party."

"What's the big deal about politics?"

"You can get things done."

"What can politicians actually get done?"

"How do you mean?"

"Well," I explained. "In practice it's the Commission that does everything that matters these days. Politicians just deal with the cultural flim-flam."

"Be that as it may," said Tim. "Anyway, about you. This isn't just a passing phase of yours, this leaving the Army thing?"

"No, I've made up my mind."

"But what are you going to do after you've left the Army?"

"I honestly have no idea," I confided.

Tim smiled. "I've got an idea or two."

"What might they be?"

"Leave it with me," said Tim. "I'll make some enquiries."

Shortly after, Tim sent me a job specification. As he advised, I applied for the role and in due course was offered the position of Events Coordinator within The World Experience.

My Commanding Officer, Colonel Petworth, was as astounded by my wish to leave the Army as Tim had been. Some upper class people did this, especially if they had openings within their ancestral estates and businesses. But this option was not designed for the likes of me, those seen as career soldiers.

In my new role I moved on to organising spectacles in the private sector, such as the Days of Glory pageant celebrating England's imperial past, extravagant themed weddings and so on, which were not dissimilar to parades of guardsmen that the Army laid on for the English monarchy.

My Wild Family

Since meeting the Ranulf clan I had a family connection in Ecologia, a connection that came to feel every bit as strong as my social scene in Economica. The first time I returned after making contact the Ranulfs were only half expecting my reappearance.

As I approached the homestead it was Freya who saw me first as she tended the vegetable plot. "Peter, you came back! I knew you would!"

"Hello, Freya, it's good to see you again."

"I can hardly believe it's you!"

A moment ago she knew I would be back again, now she can hardly believe it, I thought. I really should stop taking people so literally.

We stepped inside where Gudrun nursed a tiny infant.

"Hello, Gudrun. So who is this then?"

"He is Bjorn, born since you were last here," said Gudrun.

We waited together, alternately chatting, relaxing and pottering about with domestic tasks. Freya used a blade to cut and lever off pieces of ivory from the enormous mammoth tusk I had seen before leaning against the wall.

"What are you doing?"

"I'm going to carve out some ivory charms."

"What are the charms going to depict?"

"I don't know yet. I think I'll do some animals, or people or a house."

Ranulf, Knut and Torsten returned from a hunting trip. They had not managed to get any large game. I gathered that Torsten had got hold of a goat, but it had wriggled away. They had fallen back upon a couple of rabbits and a badger that they had collected from snares.

"Glad to see you back," said Ranulf. "Will you be staying with us now?"

"Only for a few days. I still have things to attend in Economica."

"Through Gaia's good graces Gudrun has blessed us with a son," said Knut.

"Yes, I have met him."

"Do you have any new message for us from Commissum?" Freya enquired.

"No, but I do have some gifts," I said.

I reached over and opened the large rucksack I had brought along. In it I had two compact spades of the type soldiers use for digging trenches, a steel axe and a couple of craft knives with spare blades. As I took them out I could tell that the family were simultaneously fascinated and pleased, but also nervous as if they were looking at something sinful. For a minute or so they looked nervously at each other, saying nothing and keeping back from the enticing tools I had laid out.

"These are like something sent by Vulcan," said Gudrun, breaking the tense silence. "As True Followers of Gaia we do not make or use such things."

All eyes were focussed on me accusingly.

"Tell us honestly," said Ranulf. "You have not been sent among us by Vulcan, have you?"

"No, I have not," I said emphatically.

"Then how is it that you have implements that could only have been made using the contrivances of Vulcan?"

Knut enquired accusingly.

I cursed my naivety. Clumsily I had imagined the tools I had brought would have been valued for their usefulness, but I had not factored in the religious sensitivities. An unpleasant image of myself came into my head of me in the form of a serpent slithering surreptitiously into the Garden of Eden bearing the forbidden fruit from the Tree of Knowledge. I would have to think quickly to extricate myself from this tense situation.

"It is not only Vulcan who makes use of metals and machines, Commissum does too."

"Commissum has forbidden us to use and process materials dug out from the body of our Earth Mother, Gaia," stated Ranulf. "We may use only those items we find exposed upon Her surface."

"In the world of Economica we have products such as these," I explained. "There we too are forbidden to extract the materials from the Earth, but we are permitted to use those that are provided to us by Commissum Himself."

"You are saying that Commissum has provided these tools?" Knut enquired.

"Yes." I wasn't lying. I had obtained the tools from a local CommStore operated by the Commission.

"I find that hard to believe," said Knut.

"Why would Commissum provide such things?" asked Ranulf.

"He can work in harmony with Gaia to make them, which we cannot. By gifting them to us, He takes away the temptation for us to stray into the ways of Vulcan."

The members of the family considered what I had said. I could tell by the scepticism etched on their faces that I had yet to convince them.

"How can Commissum take from Gaia without harming Her?" asked Gudrun.

"We take from Gaia what she gives to us on Her surface," I explained. "Likewise Commissum takes only what She gives freely. Vulcan seizes from Her by destruction and force."

"How can we tell the difference?" asked Torsten.

"The works of Vulcan leave grievous wounds and poisons," I explained. "Commissum soothes and restores."

"I cannot imagine Commissum using metals and machines," said Gudrun. "It doesn't seem right."

"But He does," I said, as at last I saw a way through to winning this discussion. "He built the fence between Ecologia and Economica. That uses metals and machines."

The members of the family nodded.

"But other than that, He doesn't want them to be used," Ranulf insisted.

"What about his metal angels?" I said. "Like the one that picked up that intruder from Economica."

"That's true," Ranulf acknowledged. "But how can we be sure about these items? What assurance have we that they came from Commissum?"

"I promise you, they came from Commissum," I said emphatically.

"Well, if that is the case," said Ranulf. He reached out and picked up one of the spades. The rest of the family reached out tentatively for the remaining items.

The following day we went out to try our luck again with hunting.

Still being naïve about hunting methods, I remained on the outskirts of the action. We had a herd of mountain goats in our sights, the same ones that had got away the previous day. Agile, wary and frequenting rocky outcrops over which we would struggle to traverse, they were not going to be easy to catch. My role was to wait in a hollow from which I could entrap a goat in the event that the herd doubled back from the chosen ambush point. The herd did indeed take fright, dashing off on the opposite direction, which took them within a few feet from where I was lying low. By good fortune I snagged one of the animals, tipped it over and quickly despatched it with my dagger.

"You are a great hunter, Peter," said Knut, later on as we tucked into our goat stew.

"Oh, not really, it was a team effort. I couldn't have done it on my own."

"But we couldn't have done it without you," Knut insisted.

"Well, okay, but it was a fluke, the goat going right past me like that," I said.

"You chose where to wait for it though," Ranulf observed. "That was a good choice."

"It was by sheer chance that it was the right place."

"Not just the right place, you caught it too. That's not easy," said Knut, looking sideways at Torsten as he said it. Torsten looked uncomfortable.

"Well, it got its feet caught in the netting. That gave me my chance."

"It was you that laid the netting out," said Torsten. "You did it better than I did."

"Look, I'm no expert at this hunting lark," I said. "You

know much more about it than I do."

"There is more than knowledge involved," said Ranulf. "What matters most is the hunting instinct. You definitely have that."

"Well, thanks. I was lucky though."

"Luck matters too," said Ranulf. "I'd settle for good luck. You have brought us Gaia's blessing."

Napoleon Bonaparte said the same about his generals, I reflected. Best just bask in the praise. Better than suspicion of being an agent of Vulcan.

I wanted to provide a gift for baby Bjorn. After the tensions that arose from bringing over metal tools I decided against bringing anything from Economica. I selected a piece of timber from the heap of firewood. In it I imagined I could see the shape of a goat, like the one I had caught in the hunt.

I whittled away, imagining the shape of the animal hidden within the wood, shaving to expose what had been there all along, but existing only as a misty concept in my mind.

At first the goat emerged in a rough coarse and lumpy form. Progressively I shaved and refined the timber until it came through beautifully formed, smooth to the touch and decorated with the markings from the grain.

"That is a fine piece of work, Peter," Ranulf observed, as he admired my carving.

"Well, yes, I suppose it isn't bad," I agreed. "It came out better than I expected, I must admit."

"Gaia has endowed you with a gift."

I considered this for a moment. I reflected that it could

be blasphemy to deny Gaia's gift.

"I didn't feel that I did anything special," I said. "I just chipped away at the wood, that's all."

"You wouldn't need to feel anything," Ranulf explained. "Gaia works through you, using you as Her instrument, guiding your hand. It's Gaia's work."

"Oh, I see. You mean I'm a sort of tool in Her hand."

"You have powers, Peter."

"How do you mean? What sort of powers?"

"Spiritual powers. It's why Commissum has chosen you as His messenger. I am sure of it."

"What sort of spiritual powers?"

"Yesterday you took the spirit of that goat we had for dinner," said Ranulf.

"But it was just our dinner. There wasn't anything spiritual about it, was there?"

"Oh, but there was. You knew exactly where to wait for it. It came past exactly as you needed it to. You fell on it exactly right. That was no accident. You had control over its spirit."

"I hadn't thought about it like that."

"Then its spirit, now within you, guided your hand as you carved that wood."

"Now that you mention it," I said, "it did feel as if there was the essence of the animal already there in the wood, waiting to be discovered."

"The goat's spirit inspired you, Peter," said Ranulf, his voice serious and reverential. "And now you have put its spirit back into that carving, where it can now live among us."

The goat was only the beginning. Over the coming

months and years as more children came on the scene, inspired by our hunting and encounters with our rival predators, I would carve a collection of further wooden animals for them to play with.

One day Freya came up to me while I was carving one of my wooden animals.

"I've been carving too," she said.

"Oh, that's nice. What have you been carving?"

"This," she said, placing into my hand a set of carved ivory pieces that she had threaded onto a bracelet of plaited leather strips.

Each ivory piece was carved into a shape that depicted an animal, a person or a building. There was a wolf, a bison, a deer, a rabbit, a baby, the head of an older man that might have been Ranulf, a woman that might have been Gudrun, what looked like the Ranulf family homestead and another building that looked like the cottage in the woods where Hansel and Gretel had met their wolf.

"That's lovely, Freya, very nicely carved."

"It's for you."

"No, really, I shouldn't."

"Please, I want you to have it."

In Ecologia the Ranulf family had a freedom to roam. Our hunting and foraging grounds were wide ranging, taking in hills, valleys, rocky crags, streams and ponds. Our grounds were well populated with game, both the larger kind we hunted, smaller creatures we caught with snares, fish, roots, leaves, grains and fruit. But even in Ecologia, there were limits. Not only were we fenced off from the forbidden lands of Economica, but conflict awaited in territory that belonged to our neighbours.

When we hunted we usually tried to bring down prey as quickly and cleanly as possible, but that did not always happen.

On one occasion Torsten had managed to entangle the front legs of a deer with twine, but as he leapt in to despatch the animal, still able to leap and run to some extent, it evaded him. With its two front legs hobbled it could not run as fast as the rest of the herd, but it was too quick for us to catch right away. This one was going to be a prolonged hunt. If we kept after it, it would eventually tire sufficiently for us to reach it and take it down, but that was a process that could take hours.

As a group we chased it, keeping it on the move. It was separated from the herd, so it was a contest between us, the animal and other predators such as wolves that might move in to seize our prize.

For some time all we could do is keep jogging along behind. The deer's gait was ungainly, so it tired, allowing us to catch up, but as we closed in it would find new energy and lurch ahead. Being in front of us, it was the deer that decided where to go, so that we could only follow where it took us. It led us on a merry dance, into unfamiliar territory, way off our usual patch.

After an hour or so the deer had slowed enough to give us the chance to improve our tactics. We split out, with one of our party remaining visible to the deer while the rest of us sought to outflank it, hoping to devise an ambush.

As I was skirting around to best position myself to bring down the deer I was confronted by two burly men armed with spears and daggers. The older of the two looked to be in his mid-fifties, bearded, bulky and tough, the other in his late thirties, also stocky, muscular and bearded, a younger version of his companion.

"Who are you?" the older man demanded.

"I'm Peter."

"Peter who? What family are you from?"

"From the Ranulf family."

"You're outside of your area. What are you doing here?"

"Hunting down a deer."

"You are poaching on our ground," the younger man snarled.

"You know the penalty for trespass," growled the older man.

"Actually, I don't."

"You hunt on our ground, we hunt you."

Both men pointed the spears menacingly in my direction. I glanced around, preparing to make a run for it. I was already tired from running across country for about an hour, but the seriousness of my predicament would have provided incentive to dig deep into whatever reserves of strength I had.

At this point my own companions, Ranulf, Knut and Torsten, having heard the voices, came up behind me. Two more tough looking men joined our protagonists, making it four against four. There was an atmosphere of testosterone fuelled rage, leaving little opening for reasoned discussion. Each man gripped his spear or dagger, legs spread apart in readiness. The situation was going to be resolved in only one way. Combat, from which there would be heavy casualties.

As we stood glaring at each other warily we heard the

swooshing of rotors from a drone that had flown in quickly and was now hovering overhead. A commanding male voice rang out from the sky.

"You are forbidden to fight. The matter must be resolved peacefully."

"It is the voice of Commissum," said Ranulf. "We must obey."

"Very well," said the older man from our protagonists. "We will sit and talk." He gestured to his companions and they sat on the ground, but kept hold of their weapons.

Ranulf gestured for us to follow suit.

"You have hunted on our land," said the older man. "That is not permitted."

"Who is he?" I whispered to Knut.

"Henrik, head of their family," Knut replied.

"You are right, we strayed away from our usual lands," Ranulf acknowledged.

"Why did you commit this intrusion?" demanded Henrik.

"We had caught a deer in our own area, but it escaped, so we followed."

"You know the law. If an animal crosses from your land to ours, it is our animal."

"Please accept our apology. We were too wrapped up in the hunt to concern ourselves about where we were."

I leaned over to Knut. "Where exactly is the boundary?" I whispered.

Knut shrugged and looked perplexed.

I joined in the discussion. "Excuse me, but may I ask, where exactly is the boundary between our lands?"

All around people looked confused by my question.

"One thing is for certain, you are now on our land," said Henrik emphatically.

"But when and where exactly did we cross over into it?" I insisted.

"Who are you, to ask this question?" Henrik enquired, annoyance on his face at my impertinence.

"He is Peter, a messenger from Commissum," said Ranulf.

"How is this possible?" said Henrik.

"I have crossed over from Economica, sent and guided by Commissum."

"So how do you propose we set a boundary?" said Henrik.

"It needs to be a line that can be clearly discerned," I announced, playing for time.

"How could it be discerned?" said Henrik.

He had me perplexed. Not knowing what to say, I looked up into the sky as if seeking guidance from the mighty Commissum. Then the idea struck me.

"On that ridge," I said, looking out towards the hills from where we had come, "where the water flows down towards the setting sun, those are the Ranulf lands. On this side of ridge, where the water flows towards the rising sun, those are the Henrik lands."

Those present looked at each other and nodded. It was a good solution. Unambiguous and easy to discern.

"And this is the will of Commissum?" asked Henrik.

"Yes, it is," I announced, hoping that I had said it with sufficient confidence to be convincing.

I need not have worried. "Very well," said Henrik. "But there remains the question of your having trespassed onto our land."

"At the time we did, the boundary had not yet been established," I said. "That has only been defined just now."

"It was clearly our land you were on," said Henrik, with annoyance in his voice.

"We acknowledge that," said Ranulf. "But it was not intentional. We will withdraw. We should leave it at that."

I looked up towards the drone whirring overhead.

"Commissum has commanded that this matter must be resolved peacefully," I pronounced.

There was a murmur of agreement.

"Commissum would wish that we provide for lasting peaceful relations between our two families," I continued, taking the opportunity to press home my advantage.

The gathered men looked around at each other with perplexed expressions.

"How might we do that?" Henrik enquired.

"We should worship Gaia together," I announced.

There was a murmur of agreement.

"Agreed," said Henrik. "Tomorrow you will come to our homestead where we will feast, drink and sing praises to Gaia."

Ranulf, Knut and Torsten looked uneasy, as if the Henriks were setting a trap. I looked at them and nodded in what I hoped would be a reassuring way.

"Yes, we should worship together," said Ranulf.

The two families eyed each other up nervously as we gathered at the Henrik's homestead. The style of building was the same as the Ranulf's place, but larger, oval rather than round and with a more elaborate doorway marked by an arch decorated with animal symbols.

The Ranulf family, being away from their home turf, were particularly wary. The Henrik family made a show of hospitality and generosity, guiding their guests to places of honour at the centre of things, plying us with beakers of ale and buffet style food, mostly consisting of little mouthful sized balls of mixed meat, vegetables and bread.

The conversation was stilted. All eyes were on me, presumably reflecting my status as Commissum's messenger, in expectation I would get things moving.

"It is good for us to be worshiping Gaia together today," I announced. It was a platitude, stating the obvious, but at least it filled in the awkward silence.

"May I call upon Ranulf to give thanks to Gaia and our hosts for this magnificent bounty we have before us today," I continued, neatly passing the buck for want of anything profound to say myself.

"Praise be to Gaia, the bringer of nourishment and bounty," pronounced Ranulf.

I waited in anticipation for him to continue, hopefully saying some nice things about our esteemed hosts. There was nothing more forthcoming from his lips. It would still be up to me to keep things moving. "May I say that the nourishment and bounty before us today, by Gaia's grace, is particularly splendid," I improvised. "We should also thank our hosts, the Henrik family, for their efforts and generosity."

I looked around the Ranulf family as I clapped my hands. It took a second or so for them to pick up the cue and clap too.

"Yes, splendid," said Ranulf, eventually picking up on my expectation as I looked at him intently.

Accepting that this was all I was going to get, I continued. "I would like to offer our magnificent host, Henrik, the opportunity to say a few words to mark this auspicious occasion."

Henrik, one of the world's doers rather than a talker, looked almost as uneasy as Ranulf had.

"You are all welcome in our home," said Henrik. "Through Gaia's grace may there always be peace and harmony between us."

I continued to look at him. I felt sure that he could and should say more than that.

"I want some sauce," cried out one of the Henrik family children, a toddler who did not care about the formality of the occasion. Everybody laughed, glad to have the solemnity shattered.

"Yes, serve the sauce," said Henrik.

Bowls of a warm broth were handed round, into which the solid food was to be dipped.

"And the ale too, let us drink and be merry," Henrik continued.

As the ale flowed, the atmosphere eased and conversations began between the two families.

I briefly circulated around the room, making myself known to members of the Henrik family. Their awe at my presence, as Commissum's messenger, curtailed rather than promoted conversation, so I returned to my position alongside Ranulf and Henrik, set slightly apart as heads of their respective families.

After some time, with us all feeling the congenial influence of several beakers of ale, Henrik made a public pronouncement of religious devotion. "All praise to Commissum, awoken from his sleep to save us all."

"Praise be to him," chorused the members of both families in unison.

"Praise be to Commissum, creator of Gaia, Vulcan and all that surrounds us."

An uneasy feeling rippled out.

"One moment, Henrik, my dear friend," said Ranulf. "But it is Gaia who is our creator and mother of both Commissum and Vulcan, is She not?"

"Commissum is our creator, Gaia, our Mother Earth, is his creation," insisted Henrik.

What had been a convivial atmosphere froze into one of tension and confrontation extending across the two families. I did not like the look of it. One or other of the heads of family was uttering heresy. It was a situation that threatened to become ugly very quickly.

As Commissum's messenger, I was the only one who could resolve the matter. Fighting back the influence of the Henrik family's strong ale, I felt for a way through. "Gaia is eternal and all-encompassing," I pronounced.

All present nodded in agreement.

"So Gaia encompasses us all and everything around us," I continued. "Every person, every animal, every stone, every blade of grass is an integral part of Gaia."

Nods and murmurs confirmed that I still had the people with me and unified.

"There are no exceptions," I continued, building on my theme. "None among us, neither you nor me, can separate ourselves from Gaia. We are all of us one with Her."

The people looked at each other, recognising their union with Gaia, our Earth Mother.

"We are unified not only in body, but also spirit," I continued. "When our bodies have crumbled to dust leaving only our spirit, we will remain unified with Her."

The people looked more serious at this reminder of their mortality.

"This applies to all spirits, likewise Commissum and Vulcan, they too are encompassed by Gaia," I asserted, now getting towards the crux of the theological controversy.

Henrik frowned slightly, recognising that I had reached a point that was verging on contradicting his earlier statement. But there was nothing he could say at that point. The members of both families were already fully behind the idea of Gaia's ubiquity.

"Gaia is eternal, She has always been our Earth Mother and will be for always, all-encompassing in time as well as material existence."

The eyes of the audience were wide, taking in this new concept of infinity in time as well as space.

"Likewise Commissum and Vulcan are eternal, eternal beings within Gaia's realm, with neither beginning nor end."

The audience let the implications of infinity seep through their minds.

"As eternal beings Gaia, Commissum and Vulcan were not created, they always were. One could not create the other, they have always been part of one whole."

Besides matters of religious doctrine and interpretation,

there was another area of diplomacy for me to navigate, Freya.

Her desire for me was clear. At first I could resist it on the grounds that she was far too young for me. A liaison with her would have been indecent.

But as the years past, as she grew up into a young woman, that excuse evaporated.

As Gudrun brought new babies into the family, daughters Helga and Inga, Freya would look meaningfully at me, wistfully speculating about the babies that one day I might help her make.

In Torsten, I had a rival for her affections. But she clearly had no desire for Torsten. It was me she wanted. That did not prevent Torsten resenting the way Freya looked upon me. Keeping the peace with Torsten was another excuse for me not to take things further.

The real reason I had to resist the temptation Freya presented was that, with me and her together, it would have created an obligation to remain in Ecologia as Freya's partner. I was not yet ready to make Ecologia my permanent home.

Celia

Until I met Celia it had only been my secret alternative existence in Ecologia that provided the meaning and purpose missing from my mainstream life.

We first encountered each other at the prestige party following the Maritime Military Tournament event in Portchester, which I had arranged on behalf of the World Experience.

The Maritime Military Tournament drew together a spectacle of parades, marching bands, re-enactments of historical military battles and military themed competitions, for example one that involved the dismantlement, carrying, re-assembly and firing of an old field gun. The participants were a mix of serving military units and civilian military reenactment enthusiasts.

Through my military connections I arranged the participation of prestige units from the Army, Royal Marines and Royal Navy. The military authorities were supportive because it gave them an opportunity to promote themselves and demonstrate their worth to taxpayers. The soldiers and sailors enjoyed the novelty of doing something out of the ordinary run of their daily routine.

The event was sponsored jointly by the World Experience, whose main interest was in promoting our newly established Maritime Heritage Cruise, featuring visits to the range of maritime history theme parks that we had opened around the Isle of Wight, and Davenhirst Properties promoting their new retirement residences centred around a local yacht marina situated in Portchester. The event was aimed to attract many of the attendees at Cowes Week, which had just finished.

I hoped to unwind a little at the party, but Tim, Business Development Manager for the World Experience, keen to exploit the business potential at the party, was not going to let me relax.

"Peter, I need you to work on Sir Hugo Davenhirst. We need to close that deal with the Social Whirl."

"Sure Tim, but why me and why now?"

"We can't let opportunities like this pass, Peter. Besides, he likes you. I sense he has gone off me a bit."

"Well, how I am supposed to bring the subject up? It's supposed to be a social event."

"No need to sell him anything today, just get him to agree to see us to talk about it."

Every autotaxi does the same job. It picks you up and delivers you where you need to go. Yet autotaxis are not all the same.

The plain standard autotaxi is for ordinary folk, the hoi polloi. Personally, having no particular pretensions, for everyday purposes I am happy to use them. But, when representing my employer they won't do.

The next step is the Superior class, to show you are above the common herd, but keep within a budget. These are considered necessary for business people meeting customers and private citizens demonstrating to their peers that they are financially solvent.

Prestige class is for when it is necessary to impress. Costing enough to make you blanche, they are large, sleek, luxurious and make a statement that the person being conveyed is of high rank.

Ambassador class is for the real elite. The vehicles are individually styled, and ostentatious like stately homes on wheels. If you have to ask the price you can't afford it.

Those who attended the Maritime Military Tournament after party needed to make an entrance. Not only should they be fashionably turned out, but it was de rigueur to arrive in at least a Prestige class autotaxi, which is how the newly promoted Captain Duncan McThomas swept up to the expansive circus style tent erected on the same ground on which shortly before the massed bands of the Household Division and Royal Marines had played. Captain McThomas, looking suave and elegantly attired in dress uniform, was accompanied by three stunningly attractive young women, two of whom I recognised as Fiona Deveryll and Sophie Beesham.

Being in no hurry to reacquaint with Duncan and his companions, I faded into the background, focussing on the mission Tim set me, securing a meeting with Sir Hugo Davenhirst. Spotting him in conversation with the mayor of Portchester I wandered in his direction.

The mayor was a woman with an earnest and well-meaning expression. Even from a distance Sir Hugo's face conveyed that whatever vital matter of civic concern the mayor was sharing, it was not something he considered important.

Seeing me, Sir Hugo appeared thankful for the opportunity to curtail the mayor's conversation.

"Mr Accrington, well done. The event was a triumph. Don't you agree, mayor?"

"Yes, splendid. A real spectacle."

"You're very kind," I acknowledged. "But many besides me who contributed to its success."

"It was your organisation that made it all happen," Sir Hugo insisted.

"Nice of you to say so. Was there any particular part of it that you liked best?"

The mayor looked uncomfortable, as if she might leave someone offended if she highlighted any specific participant.

"The field gun competition was a highlight for me," said Sir Hugo.

The mayor spotted someone else who she should be talking to and made her excuses.

"Yes, that is very traditional and taken very seriously by the Navy and Marines," I observed.

"So, what have you got lined up for us next?"

"We have a Tales of Jack Tar Water Festival."

"What does that entail?"

"We re-enact scenes from naval history, Sir Francis Drake and the Armada, Trafalgar, Jutland, Battle of the River Plate, Falklands War and so on. It includes highlights of what the passengers on our Maritime Heritage Cruise get to experience."

"Sounds fun. Informative too."

I was contemplating how to introduce the Social Whirl Tim wanted me to set up. "It was great having you working with us on this event, Sir Hugo. I hope we'll have a chance to collaborate more in the future."

"Well, perhaps, one day. You never know."

"My colleague Tim Membury has ideas he'd like to run by you."

"Does he indeed!" snorted Sir Hugo. "Let's leave it for the time being. I'll let you know if and when there is anything to discuss."

"Of course, when you're ready. No rush."

At this point a resplendent Duncan McThomas and his graceful acolytes approached. The third of his three young women companions, the one I hadn't yet met, embraced Sir Hugo and they hugged.

"Mr Accrington, can I introduce you to my daughter, Celia," said Sir Hugo.

Celia had a minimalist elegance that came from simplicity rather than adornment. Her dress was expertly tailored, slinky smooth, without frills, setting her off to perfection. She had just the merest hint of makeup, perfectly applied. She shook my hand with a confident grip.

"Pleased to meet you." Her gaze was friendly and assured.

"Mr Accrington arranged today's event," explained Sir Hugo.

"You should be proud of it," said Celia. "It was impressive and entertaining."

"Glad you liked it."

Sir Hugo took his leave, explaining that there were people he needed to see.

"So this is what you've been up to since you left us," said Duncan.

"Yes, it keeps me busy," I said. "I see another pip on your uniform. Congratulations."

"Do you like it out here in the provinces?" said Duncan.

"It has its moments."

"I'd rather be at the centre of things myself. Where the action is."

"There's action here too."

"Oh, but it's all so commercial," said Fiona, with distaste.

"Well, it pays the bills."

"But all that promotion of ghastly cruises and theme parks," she continued, with a shudder.

"Was it something you were scared of that made you run away from the Army?" asked Sophie.

"No, I just prefer what I'm doing now."

"Not some scandal then? Some woman wronged, perhaps," Sophie continued.

"Look, I've got things to see to," I said. "I'll see you folks another time, hopefully."

Celia caught me by the elbow as I turned. "Going so soon?"

I caught her gaze, glancing around at her companions. "Well, I've got things to check on, but they might wait a short while."

She looked out across the room to a display featuring the World Experience's Maritime Heritage Cruise. "If you've a moment you could tell me about that Heritage Cruise you're doing."

"Of course, if you step over here I can show you." I guided her by the arm to the exhibition.

Sophie made as if to join us. A glare from Celia stopped her in her tracks.

In front of the display with Celia on her own I started

my standard spiel about the Heritage Cruise. I hadn't got far when she touched my arm to stop me.

"We don't really have enough time just now, but perhaps you'd like to tell me about it another time?"

"Yes, of course."

"Or we could talk about other things, if you'd prefer?"

"Yes, that would be nice."

"In that case, give me a call." She turned and strolled back to the others.

"Did you get to see Sir Hugo?" Tim asked me later.

"Yes."

"Well, did you get us in to see him?"

"Not yet."

"What do you mean? You did raise it with him, didn't you?"

"He said he would let us know when he was ready to talk to us."

"You surely pressed him about when that might be."

"No, we were interrupted."

"So you drew a blank then," said Tim with marked disappointment.

"Not entirely."

"Oh, what then?"

"I'm due to meet up with his daughter."

"Those friends of yours said some disparaging things about you," said Celia.

At her suggestion we were in a tea shop in Guildford for coffee and cake.

"Can't say I'm surprised."

"I think they're jealous."

We exchanged information about ourselves. She was a commercial lawyer working for her father in Davenhirst Properties legal department, having previously worked in a major bank since graduating.

It was not only, or even mainly, her achievements I admired. She possessed a beauty that was more than the pleasing features of her face and perfectly formed athletic body. She had an aura, she radiated attraction; it was nothing I could identify but sufficiently alluring to hold me spellbound.

I explained my love for wild country and the outdoors, but without revealing my secret other life in Ecologia. She told me of her passion for horses and equestrian exploits in show jumping and dressage competition. I had learned to ride in the Army so we resolved to meet again at her stables.

"You were angling to get in to see my father, I believe," she said, as we were getting ready to leave.

"Yes, my boss Tim is keen to put a proposition to him."

"What sort of proposition? My dad doesn't like being sold to."

"Something that'll appeal to Davenhirst's customers to help shift the company's properties."

"Leave it to me. I'll get something slotted in the diary."

"You're a genius. How did you do it?" said Tim.

"His daughter, Celia, arranged it."

"You old rogue." Tim nudged me with his elbow. "There's hope for you yet. A man after my own heart."

"Look, let's get this clear. I'm not with his daughter for

any ulterior motive. I didn't pressure her to do that at all. It was her idea."

"Of course, we wouldn't want Sir Hugo thinking you inveigled your way into seeing him through his daughter. That would be fatal." He nodded sagely.

From the moment we arrived it was clear Sir Hugo thought his time could be better spent.

"What's this idea of yours?" he said, once Tim and I settled with him and Celia in his office.

"What might just tip one of your customers over into signing on the dotted line?" asked Tim.

"Look, don't play games with me. Get to the point," said Sir Hugo with irritation.

"Social life. Your customers don't just want somewhere to live. They want the lifestyle and social life to go with it."

"Yes, yes. But what is your proposal?" Irritated with Tim, he looked straight at me.

"We suggest that you offer your customers a free membership of the Social Whirl when they buy one of your properties," I said.

"That gives them monthly invitations to prestige grade parties set in exclusive locations," explained Tim.

"Yes, I know what it is. Things are competitive out there. Margins are tight enough. I can't afford additional costs."

"It won't cost you a thing. We'll provide it free of charge," said Tim.

"What's in it for you?"

"It'll build our business. Hopefully a good proportion of your customers will renew their subscriptions at the end of the free period."

"You should be paying me for promoting your business then."

"Come on, Sir Hugo, a free incentive for your customers. That's pretty good, don't you think?" said Tim.

"How long would this free subscription last?"

"Six months," said Tim.

Sir Hugo pondered. "Make that a year and you've got a deal."

"Agreed," said Tim.

"Celia will draw up the contract."

We met for our ride at Celia's livery stables.

Celia's tight-fitting riding outfit accentuated her figure and athletic poise. Her mount, introduced to me as Hector, was a magnificent stallion, sleek, strong and spirited. She was affectionate with the beast, caressing his head and flanks, yet also kept him firmly under control.

She had borrowed another mount for me, a slightly smaller, more work-a-day horse called Willow.

We rode, walking and trotting over some lanes and woods, finally breaking into a canter across fields as we came back towards the stables. Celia's riding was exquisite, as elegant as a dancer, at one with her Hector. I plodded behind in my more rough and ready style.

After, we stopped by a neighbouring pub for drinks.

"Thanks for the ride, Celia," I said as I set down the drinks on the table.

"Glad you could come. You ride rather well."

"Not half as well as you."

She took the compliment as read. "How did you get to

learn to ride?"

"We had to ride in the Army, for ceremonial purposes."

"Have you ridden since you left the Army?"

"No, not until today, which I am grateful for, by the way."

"Not given up on riding, I hope."

"Well, not exactly. Just haven't had occasion for it since I left the Army."

When I didn't elaborate she moved to a different subject. "There is no Mrs Accrington yet," she said, looking at me carefully to gauge my reaction.

"No, not as yet."

"You must have somebody who might be, though, I would have thought."

"Actually, no. Nobody special just now."

"Sounds like it's not only horses you've given up on since you left the Army."

I was distinctly uneasy. "How do you mean?"

"From what I was hearing from your old pals, Duncan, Fiona and Sophie, you had plenty of female company while you were in the Army, yet, from what you are saying, that seems to have changed."

"You don't want to believe everything you hear from them. I'm sure that, whatever it was they said, it was exaggerated."

"Sophie said you wrote her poetry and then went off with somebody else."

"There was a poetic moment we had together in the moonlight, that much is true."

Celia reflected. "A poetic moment in the moonlight," she mused. "That sounds nice. Sounds like your sensitive side."

"Well, I am sometimes moved by things like that," I confessed.

"Glad to hear it. I like a man who has some tenderness."

We continued our conversation for some time, or to be more accurate, she continued and I followed where she led me. By the time we were done, with the relentless persistence and subtlety of an expert interrogator, she had extracted the deepest feelings from the bottom of my soul as one might squeeze the juice from a lemon. I didn't mind. It was good to be with a woman who knew what she wanted.

She had almost squeezed me dry when she asked, "Are there any particular World Experience offerings you would find appealing?"

I reflected. "You mean appealing to me personally or popular with our clientele?"

"You personally."

"There is the Voyage to the Underwater City. That would be fun"

"What does that involve?"

"You board Captain Nemo's submarine. You can view the sea bed and sea creatures through picture windows mounted in the hull. Some of it is real, but there are staged effects as well, such as a fight with a giant squid that wraps its tentacles around the submarine and shakes it about, divers who go out to make repairs then get attacked by sharks, giant manta rays and other excitements. You end up in the Underwater City, where you eat dinner in an underwater dining room looking out onto shoals of fish swimming outside."

"But you haven't been on it yet?"

"No, not yet."

"What's stopping you?"

"It's not really so much fun to do on your own."

"You don't have to do on your own," Celia observed, looking me in the eye.

"I don't know anyone who'd want to do it."

I'd missed my cue, but Celia was not going to let it drop. "Have you asked anyone?"

"Well, no, not yet."

"What's stopping you?"

Slow as I am, even I couldn't miss this prompt. "Is it something that you would fancy?"

"I might," she said. "It depends who I was going with."

"You could go with me, if you like."

"I'd like that."

There was an inevitability to what followed. Under Celia's subtle and sometimes not so subtle guidance we went through the stages of courtship. Interesting dates in romantic settings. Our first kiss. More passionate kissing. Our clinches becoming more intimate, but measured stages stopping short of making love, the pace and timing delicately but firmly under Celia's calibrated control.

Then came the time for having dinner with Celia's parents. Sir Hugo and I already knew each other through business, but it was the first time I had met Lady Margot Davenhirst.

It was fortunate Celia had advised me I should be

dressed formally because Margot looked me up and down checking every detail of my attire with the thoroughness of a drill sergeant in the Guards. I passed muster, more or less, although she did wrinkle her nose as she glanced at my socks, which were the chunkily knitted ones I used for walking in the outdoors with a dark blue pattern rather than a smooth plain pair she would probably have considered more suitable.

"So important to maintain standards even when at home, wouldn't you agree?" she remarked.

Margot was a woman with a formidable and commanding presence who spoke with a certainty not easily be questioned, let alone contradicted. "You know Colonel Petworth, Peter, don't you?"

"Yes, he used to be my commanding officer."

"Did you ever get to meet his wife, Marjorie?"

"Yes, I have been introduced, but I wouldn't say I got to know her."

"I was having tea with Marjorie the other day. Her Reginald, the Colonel that is, was saying it has been difficult for them with people deciding to leave the Army. He thinks it's a bad show."

"Well, I suppose it causes him a headache, having to replace people."

"He thinks they are letting the country down by dropping out."

"Well, nobody that I've known, officers that is, has just walked out. They have always been around to hand over to a successor and make an orderly transition."

"But shouldn't an Army career be a vocation? Not something you can just walk away from."

I took a swig of the excellent synthetic wine Sir Hugo had served as I pondered how to fend off Lady Davenhirst's attack on my supposed dereliction of duty. "When someone moves on from the Army they retain that military ethos. I like to think I apply that to my new role at World Experience."

"And damned well you have too," chipped in Sir Hugo. "That Maritime Military Tournament you put on was first class."

"I happened to bump into Cythia Beesham at our WI coffee morning," said Margot. "She mentioned that you and her daughter Sophie had been friends at one stage."

"Yes, I got to know Sophie. It was in Windsor while I was in the Army."

"Your friendship didn't last, I understand."

"Speaking for myself, we are still friends, if that is what she wants, but it didn't develop into anything lasting, romantically speaking."

I could see now where Celia had inherited her interrogation skills. Margot continued to grill me on every aspect of my history, pedigree, political attitudes and social standing with the relentless tenacity of a courtroom barrister. From time to time Sir Hugo, who seemed to be batting on my team, would come to my assistance. Eventually I managed to get him to rescue me by changing the subject to Sir Hugo's own favourite, the Davenhirst Properties empire. I later gathered from Celia that I had earned their blessing for our relationship to continue.

Celia and I had spent a pleasant afternoon riding, followed later by a convivial chat over a few drinks. We were ending the evening on the sofa at her apartment in Guildford with a passionate kiss, as had become our custom.

After riding she had changed into a slinky dress. As we cuddled, supposedly accidentally, she allowed her dress to ride up revealing her thigh. I noticed, but, tempting as it was, it felt rude for me take advantage.

She squirmed a little and the dress rode up further. Almost all her thighs were on show. I wondered whether I should react. Either way it could be problematic. If her revealing herself was unintentional, even if all I did was mention it, it would have been embarrassing for her, and if I let my hand stray she could be offended. At this point I was struggling to disguise the bulge in my pants, but I kept my arms employed in cuddling her upper parts.

Her bare thigh rubbed against mine. It was unmistakable. A reaction was demanded. I reached down and stroked her thigh.

Without hurrying, she reached down and placed her hand over mine, gripped it and drew it away.

"Peter, where is all this leading?"

I was flustered, embarrassed by my lechery. "I don't know."

"We should know by now, shouldn't we?" she observed.

"I suppose so."

"You do love me, don't you?"

"Yes, of course I do."

"But how can I be sure of that?"

"Look, I love you very much. I really do."

"How much?"

"I couldn't imagine being without you."

"You don't want to be without me?"

"No, of course not."

"How are you going to ensure not being without me?"

I reflected. Even I figured out that she was pressing me for a proposal. I hadn't planned for this. For a start I had no ring and we weren't in an appropriately romantic setting.

I started to speak, but without having figured out what to say, all that emerged was incoherent spluttering. She put her finger to my lips.

"I expect we'll talk about it another time," she concluded.

I'm not very fast in affairs of the heart, but as I reflected afterwards, I saw that the progress of our relationship had been deftly controlled and managed by Celia. It may have been me who made each given move as convention dictated a man must, but she had set up the scene and laid the cues, sometimes several cues as I didn't always pick up on them.

I didn't mind. Celia was gorgeous. Our conversation flowed easily. Both of us liked to explore ideas and had the intellect to stimulate each other. Far from feeling manipulated, I was relieved that Celia was in command. At last here was a woman who knew what she wanted. If only there were more like her.

I booked us into one of Windsor's finest restaurants and arranged a special table in a semi-private alcove. As our sumptuous meal came to an end I made my move.

"It has been a very special time for me, since we have been together."

She smiled and nodded in encouragement.

"I have never felt like this with anyone else. I can't imagine being without you."

She beamed, nodding more, but said nothing, urging me to get to the main point.

I pulled out a little box from my pocket and placed it on the table, flipping it open to reveal the diamond ring it contained.

"Will you marry me, so that we can be together always?"

"Yes, Peter, of course I will," she said, leaning over to kiss me briefly on the lips.

I slipped the ring onto her finger.

It was a couple of weeks after we had broken the news of our engagement to Celia's parents for Sir Hugo to call suggesting I drop in on him at his country estate office.

"Peter, I'll come straight to the point," said Sir Hugo. Not liking prevarication, he normally did come straight to the point. "How would you like to come and work for me?"

I mused. "What do you have in mind?"

"I'd like you to manage the Davenhirst property portfolio in the Solent and Dorset area."

With this development my absorption into the Davenhirst empire was almost complete, with only the final stage of marrying Celia to draw me in entirely.

A Friend in Need

On the day I left the World Experience to take up my new role at Davenhirst Properties I was perplexed when my friend and colleague Tim was not there for the small drinks party I held to mark the departure. Even if he couldn't make it, I would have expected him to call.

It was a couple of days later I heard from him. On the phone he sounded subdued. "Sorry I wasn't there to mark your leaving. I was going to say a few words, but something has happened."

"Oh, alright Tim. What was it?"

The line went quiet for a couple of seconds. "I was arrested that morning."

"Crikey. Whatever for?"

The line was quiet again for a while. "They're accusing me of rape," said Tim, struggling to say the words.

"Good grief. Who is accusing you?"

"It was Freda, a woman I had a bit of a fling with months back. She was perfectly willing at the time, but now she is accusing me of this."

"What made her do that?"

"When I moved on she went ballistic. Floods of tears, histrionics, promises to get back at me. I suppose it's some sort of revenge, but I'm not sure what for. I didn't do anything terrible."

"So where are you now?"

"Back home. They let me out on bail. I've been in court though, so it'll be all over the news shortly."

"I'm coming round. Be with you shortly."

After the call I checked the news feed and sure enough, there it was, "World Experience executive accused of rape".

I found Tim bereft, staring vacantly into space, barely able to speak. "Let's get us both a cup tea."

"Sorry, Peter, I should have offered," said Tim.

"Don't worry, mate. You've got other things on your mind. Leave it to me."

I made us both a mug of the sort of strong builder's brew that puts hairs on your chest and stirred in a couple of teaspoons of sugar. Of course it wasn't real tea. It was a chemical concoction made in a vat by one of the Commission's enterprises, but it tasted good enough. I figured Tim probably wouldn't have been eating so I scavenged biscuits from a cupboard and laid them out on a plate.

"Have you got legal advice? Lawyers lined up, that sort of thing?"

"Yes, that's all in hand."

"So what happens now?"

"It comes to court in a few months' time. Until then I'll just have to wait."

"What a bugger. What does your lawyer think might happen?"

"If I'm found guilty I'd be in for a stretch of a few years."

"What does your brief think your chances are?"

"He tried to sound upbeat, but I could tell that he fears the worst."

"Darn it."

"I didn't do anything, Peter," said Tim pleadingly. "You've got to believe me. It's all untrue. I promise you."

"Unfortunately it's not me you've got to convince, Tim.

It's a jury."

"It's so bloody unfair. I didn't do anything and now I'm facing this. They couldn't send down an innocent guy, surely?"

"Unfortunately they can. It'll probably be your word against Freda's, and she might convince the jury. By the way, is there anything else they've got, except what she says?"

"Well, we did have sex, I can't dispute that. But she wanted it, honestly."

Worse followed. Tim was very publicly dismissed from his executive role at the World Experience.

I had just started in my new demanding role at Davenhirst Properties and I was also obliged to entertain Celia, my lovely new fiancée, so time was limited. But I managed to pop in to see Tim a couple of times a week, if briefly.

The situation was playing on his mind. I would let him talk about it, not to provide any direct help, but just to be someone to share things with and to put them in perspective.

"If anyone had seen us it would have been obvious I didn't do anything she didn't want."

"So no witnesses then, except for the two of you, just Freda's word against yours?"

"Well, there was the dog."

"I can't imagine a dog in the witness box."

Tim just dumbly stared into space.

"What kind of a dog, anyway?" I enquired, idly, just for something to say.

"Well, it wasn't a breed, as such. It was one of those robotic things."

A lightbulb went off in my head. "You're saying it was a robotic dog?"

"Yes, so what?"

"Don't you see? They can record things, those dogs. It might just be the independent evidence you need."

Things moved fast after that. Tim's legal team had the dog seized as evidence. The recording of the alleged event was found. It was as Tim claimed, a consensual episode in which Tim's accuser participated enthusiastically. The prosecution offered no evidence and the judge acquitted him.

We had a bit of a celebration party attended by a few of Tim's friends and benefactors. There was plenty of drinking, bonhomie, congratulations and generalised well-wishing, but it was not an occasion for introspection or examination of feelings, nor were any offers of practical assistance or gainful employment forthcoming.

Sensing Tim would need something more than a party to help him out of the pit into which the fates tossed him, the next day I called around at his place armed with a copious supply of beer.

"What made her do it?" lamented Tim. "Putting me through all that."

I took an intake of breath. It was time for home truths. "My guess is that she felt betrayed."

"Betrayed, how do you mean?"

"When you left her."

"How is that betrayal?"

And I had imagined I was the naïve one, I thought to myself. "Why did you dump her, as a matter of interest?"

Tim reflected. "Actually there was never any likelihood we would be together on a lasting basis. For a start we didn't have anything interesting to talk about. She glazed over when I raised anything that interested me, and I had to pretend to be interested in the minutiae of her trivial existence."

"Didn't stop you shagging her though, did it?"

"Well, Freda was very pretty, and still is, as a matter of fact, despite what she did to me."

"So, what was in it for her, that made her go to bed with you?"

"I don't know. Perhaps she fancied me?"

"You don't think that she might have imagined a lasting relationship?"

"But I never promised her any lifetime commitment," said Tim indignantly.

"Maybe not promised in so many words, but is was implied, I suggest."

"I implied no such thing."

"People come into these situations with different assumptions."

"What sort of assumptions?"

I was astounded I needed to spell this out to Tim. I could have said so out loud, but that would have been hurtful so I decided to be patient. "In your case you assumed it is okay to shag someone just because you like the look of each other and then pass on as if nothing had happened."

"Well, I don't see why not. It's not hurting anyone."

"In her case her assumption was probably that having sex meant cementing a meaningful relationship."

"But if it had meant that, I would have said so."

"You must have implied it to her, though, even if you didn't exactly say so, because she wouldn't have slept with you otherwise."

"We didn't get much sleep."

"You know what I mean."

"Nah, I never gave her any reason to think that."

He is in denial, I thought. How could anyone be so lacking in self-awareness? Especially someone so socially adept as Tim.

"Tim, you are the most expert salesman I know. Outstandingly good."

"Well, that may be. I have had my moments. But I'm out of a job right now."

"We'll work on that later. You are brilliant at what you do. You gauge people just right. Figure out what makes them tick. Say just the right things and pick exactly the right moment to close a sale."

"Nice of you to say so."

"You're the same with women. You read their reactions, coax them, tempt them, charm them, press their buttons and they fall for you, just like the punters do when you make a sale."

"Well, I suppose there are some parallels."

"Ethically though, it's not the same."

"How do you mean?" asked Tim, genuinely puzzled.

"In a sales situation, caveat emptor applies. Those you are selling to have a responsibility to check things out for themselves, not just rely on what you tell them."

"But they're adults. They need to make their own decisions."

"When you're talking relationships a deeper level of trust and mutual care tend to be expected. There is another thing. When you're selling something it is generally okay to get it signed on the dotted line and then move on to the next bit of business. You shouldn't be treating women like that. They aren't just prey to be hunted."

Tim considered for a few moments. "Now you put it like that, I suppose there is something in what you are saying."

"You know, there is a certain karma in what you have been through."

"How so?"

"You must have loved and left dozens if not hundreds of women in your time, leaving them feeling bereft and used. Now one has struck back."

"But she had no right to. As was proved, I didn't do anything wrong."

"You know, I think that in her mind Freda probably thinks she was justified. She would never have gone to bed with you had she known you had no intention of having a relationship with her, so, as she sees it, you slept with her under false pretences. In her mind she might legitimately see that as tantamount to rape. Feeling as she does could have distorted her memory of events, making her believe that it was forcible."

"That's just crap."

"Is it? Think about it, mate."

"You're a great help!" said Tim sullenly.

"Actually that's exactly what I am trying to be. There are

times when soothing platitudes won't do and tough things need to be said."

"You've said your share of tough things today, that's for sure."

"Look Tim, there is something else. We need to get you back in gainful employment."

"How do you propose to do that?"

"Leave it to me. I'll see what I can do. You can't be choosy though. In your position you'll need to accept whatever you can get and be thankful for it."

"I understand that."

Later on I had a meeting with Sir Hugo in his office.

"We currently have 647 properties still on our books in the Solent and Dorset Region," I reported. "It'll take a lot of work to shift them."

"What do you propose to do about it?"

"As you know that sales guy we had before I came on board walked out. Not before time, too, because, frankly, he was useless."

"That's true."

"We need to get a new sales executive on board, pronto."

"How are we going to do that? It'll take weeks to recruit someone and weeks more for them to get them up to speed."

"As it happens, I have just the guy, and, what's more, he is available immediately."

"Who?"

"Tim Membury."

"You mean that bloke you used to work for at World Experience?"

"Yes, that's him."

"I never liked the fellow," snorted Sir Hugo. "Far too smarmy and pushy for my taste."

"He can sell, though. He's a brilliant salesman."

"Hmm. You're probably right. But didn't he disgrace himself with some woman? Get himself in court for it, accused of all sorts of unsavoury stuff."

"Yes, but he got off."

"Even so, it could tarnish our reputation. I don't like it."

"Not necessarily. Since the recording from the dog exonerated him there has been a lot of sympathetic media coverage. Wrongly accused by spurned woman. That sort of thing."

"Hmm," Sir Hugo mused. "Won't our clients be thinking, no smoke without fire. It could still damage us."

"Well, the English are known for supporting the underdog. I'm sure Tim would spin the innocent victim angle to his advantage."

Sir Hugo smiled. "Yes, I can well imagine he would. Even so, why take the risk with him?"

"He doesn't have a lot of options. He would work for us on a freelance commission basis, no commitment, no expensive salary, no pension and what not. And he can start right away."

Sir Hugo smiled. "I like the way you're thinking."

Jealousy

As someone relatively fortunate in life, Celia strongly believed she had an obligation to give something back to society. To this end she supported and volunteered for the SDRF, Substance Dependency Relief Foundation, a charitable institution assisting those addicted to drink or drugs.

I took to accompanying her humanitarian missions. On one occasion we went to a rehabilitation unit situated in the same rough area of Woking where my friend Simon lived. It was a sheltered complex of modular housing units where those who were being weaned off their dependency were accommodated and supervised by SDRF staff. We were talking to those being helped, who we referred to as our clients, listening patiently while they told us about the difficulties in their lives and, if they wished, assisting them with figuring out their path back into mainstream society.

Unexpectedly, among the anonymous faces there was one I recognised. I did not immediately recall who it was, just that it was a familiar face. Then, after a second or two, I knew. Annie Entwhistel, my first real lover from my college days, except I couldn't be quite sure.

She still had the simple natural inner beauty, shining out less brightly now, thinner and more haggard. My first thought was that she must be like us, a fellow volunteer.

"Hello," I said. "It's Annie, isn't it?"

"Yes. Hello, Peter," she said, recognising me. She looked me up and down. "What are you doing here? You look too well to be one of us."

"I'm here as a volunteer, with Celia," I said, looking across towards my fiancée. "Celia, this is Annie, someone I used to know from my college days."

"Pleased to meet you," said Celia, casting her eyes between us. She sensed something from the way we looked at each other. She moved up close to me and took hold of my arm.

"But what are you doing here?" I asked.

Annie looked away, blushing. "I've been having difficulties. Hoping I can get myself straightened out."

"I'm sorry to hear that."

"Well, Annie, it was good to have met you," Celia intervened, before Annie could elaborate. "Peter and I have to be getting along now. We'll see you again sometime, I expect."

"I'm guessing Annie was someone you knew well," said Celia later, as we made our way back home.

"Yes, we did know each other well. We were quite close for a while."

It wasn't necessary for her to enquire how close. "How long is a while?"

"Shorter than it might have been. Probably only weeks."

"And you haven't been in touch since?"

"No, not at all. First time I've seen her since Uni."

"What was it that broke you up?"

I didn't want to elaborate. "Not sure really. Just not compatible at the end of the day, I guess."

I could tell Celia was unconvinced. It must have been something in the way that she had seen Annie looking at me that suggested incompatibility was not the issue and feelings still existed. However she chose not to press the point.

Despite being certain Celia would not have been happy about it, I went to see Annie again later alone and without mentioning it to Celia. I felt a need to find out what had happened to her and she likewise probably wanted to know my circumstances.

Before anything else there was unfinished business Annie and I had to clear up.

"How did things go between you and that other woman you met when we were together?" she asked.

Who could she mean? I wondered. Of course, there had been Tess from the WRLP, but she wouldn't have known about that. Besides at the time there had been nothing between Tess and myself.

"It didn't really go anywhere at all," I said.

"Oh," said Annie. She mused. "Shame to have us break up like that, over something that didn't go anywhere," she remarked.

"But that didn't break us up."

Annie observed my puzzled frown. "We couldn't have stayed together if you were playing around with someone else," she said, puzzlement now on her face too.

"I hadn't found anyone else," I said.

"But I was told you had. You were with someone else. Your friend, Tim, was there too."

I struggled to remember. Then it came back to me. There had been the woman in the bar I had been seen with who had a bag with a picture of Guildford on it.

"You must be referring to a random conversation I had

in the bar. We chatted for a few minutes and that was it. I'd never seen her before and I've never seen her again to this day."

"But you were seen together. I was told that it looked like you were an item."

"In that case, the whole thing was misconstrued."

Annie looked at me aghast. "But when I mentioned it, you just accepted what I said. You let me believe it. Why didn't you put me right?"

"There didn't seem any point."

"No point in saving our relationship. How could you say that? Didn't it mean anything to you?"

I considered. "Yes, it meant a lot to me. I was shattered when we broke up."

"But you could have saved it," Annie lamented. "You didn't even try!"

I paused. "Well, you seemed so certain in what you were saying. There didn't seem any point in arguing. With you not trusting me, I thought that we were finished."

"You could have denied it. Explained. You could have told me I was the one you loved. I would have believed you."

I looked across at her and sighed. "I didn't realise that."

"You didn't realise I needed you?"

"No, I suppose I didn't. Back then I didn't really believe that anyone would need me."

"How could you think that?"

This was getting into some deep psychological water. No matter, better out than in. "Well, I guess at that time I didn't think that I was worth much," I confessed. "Not enough for anyone to need me."

"You really thought that little of yourself?" she said quietly, her eyes raised in surprise.

"Yes, that's about right."

"I thought that you didn't love me," she said.

"Oh, why did you think that?"

"That first time we were together, you suddenly broke away, like you had second thoughts. Then after that, you always seemed to hold back, like you didn't really want to do it."

"I thought I'd messed up. I didn't want to mess up again."

We looked at each other sadly but with a new understanding. A flicker of hope stirred in Annie's eyes. "Is it too late now, do you think?"

I shook my head.

"I'm afraid so. Celia and I are getting married."

"Oh, I see."

"So what's happened to you since then?"

It was a sad story. Our breakup had left her depressed. She had resorted to Bliss, a drug that had superseded the opiate drugs used in the 21st century. Safer than opiates, Bliss was supposed to be only for those seriously or terminally ill, but inevitably some escaped into the black market where it was sold for recreational purposes, or for those like Annie, who needed to numb emotional pain. She had dropped out of college and ended among the homeless and drug dependent.

"What do you want to do now?" I asked.

"Get myself straight. Get myself something useful to do. Perhaps even find someone to share my life with."

"I'll see what I can do to help."

"Tim needs administrative support," I said to Sir Hugo, later the same day.

"What sort of support?"

"Sorting out and qualifying prospective customers, preparing marketing material, setting up appointments, that sort of thing."

"Well, get someone in."

"You know that Celia supports those Substance Dependency people."

"Yes, she's always onto me about it, wanting me to sponsor some project or other of theirs."

"Well, she's got me involved with it too."

"I'm not surprised."

"Getting the clients into gainful employment is a key part of turning their lives around."

"Alright, I can see where this is going. What are you suggesting?"

"One of their clients would be a very good fit for what we need, I feel."

"I'm all in favour of supporting Celia in her charitable work, but there are limits. This one sounds like a risk."

"I know her from our college days. Once she's off the drugs she'll be great, I promise."

"Sentiment aside, why would we take a gamble with her?"

"For the first year of her employment there is a government rehabilitation scheme that will fund half her salary, plus we don't pay any National Insurance for her during that time."

"That's good. But what if it goes wrong?"

"If she lapses back into drugs she is out of the door right away."

"Alright then," said Sir Hugo. "It has worked out alright with Tim. We'll take the chance. Go ahead."

From a work perspective bringing Annie on board to assist Tim worked a treat. Annie was very bright, picking up the nuances of her duties and applying flair and intelligence to everything she did. She charmed the prospective customers and helped in scheduling and prioritising Tim's diary. Equally as important, Tim and Annie had a rapport.

However things did not work so well between Celia and myself.

When Celia became aware of her presence Annie had been in her new role weeks. There was an atmosphere as cold as the Siberian tundra when we met up later in the day.

"What is Annie Entwhistel doing working in your office?" she demanded.

"She needed an opportunity to get herself out of the rut she was in and we needed an administrator to assist Tim."

"We don't need drug addicts about the place."

"I thought you wanted to help drug addicts. Isn't that why we are involved with the SDRF?"

"Helping them, yes, bringing them into our offices, no."

"But the SRDF is always looking for employers to help out their clients. We should be setting an example, shouldn't we?"

"Not when the person concerned is your ex-lover."

"That was a long time ago and it didn't last for long. It's not relevant after all this time."

"I saw the way you looked at each other. It was more than some minor fling."

"Look, it's nothing like that," I insisted. "You're the only one for me. She is just someone to help Tim out with his work."

"How come you did this behind my back?"

"It's to do with work. I don't get you involved in all the minor details of my working life."

Celia glared. "Bringing your ex-lover into the office is not a minor detail."

"Look, she is an ex-lover. Ancient history. I haven't even seen her for years."

"She needs to go. I want her out by the end of the week."

I paused. She was giving me an order. Should I acquiesce, or assert myself? The easy thing would have been to capitulate. It was going to be rough if I defied her. But, if I caved, it would set a pattern. "No. She is good at her job. She gets on brilliantly with Tim. We have no valid reason to let her go."

"We'll see about that."

At this point our time together for that evening was at an end, the shredded remains of our relationship mangled under the crushing weight of an Antarctic ice cap.

"As a matter of interest, did Celia have anything to say to you about Annie?" asked Tim, when we next spoke.

"Yes, she did. Why do you ask?"

"It was the look on her face when she saw Annie."

"I see, did anything happen?"

"She demanded to know what she was doing there. It wasn't friendly. Annie was quite intimidated."

"Oh, that was unfortunate. What did Annie say?"

"I was there. I tried to smooth things. I explained that she was there to help me out with admin. I waxed lyrical on what a great job she was doing."

"Thanks for that. I wouldn't want to see Annie victimised."

A little while later I had a message from Sir Hugo asking if I might pop round to his office for a chat. As usual, he came straight to the point. "Celia wants me to get rid of the new girl you brought in, Annie. Says she is a disruptive influence. I said I'd talk to you about it."

"Disruptive influence? I don't see how."

"Nor do I, at least not as far as the business is concerned."

"So what's the problem then?"

"That's what I'd like to know," said Sir Hugo. "It's clearly something personal involving the three of you, Celia, you and this Annie woman. What's going on?"

"Annie and I had a brief fling a long time ago when we at college. Since then I hadn't seen her until we came across her at the Substance Dependency place. Celia's got it into her head there is still something between us."

Sir Hugo raised his eyebrows. "I can see why she might get suspicious when you bring Annie in without telling her."

"Well, you've got a point," I conceded. "But I had a chance to help Annie out, which was the right thing. Obviously I'm sorry Celia doesn't like it, but I look after my friends, especially when times are tough for them."

"Yes, I've noticed."

"I'm sorry to have caused this embarrassment."

"You should have been more frank about it with me, not to mention Celia."

"Yes, I guess so. I'm sorry. What are we going to do about it?"

Sir Hugo scratched his chin. "I think, nothing. Annie is doing a good job. It would upset Tim if we fired her, and I wouldn't want him to be unhappy. From a business perspective, we should leave things alone. As far as you and Celia are concerned, you'll have to sort that out yourselves. I can't."

Celia and I were seeing each other only briefly and by appointment. Even had we attempted to share social time, given the atmosphere us, these occasions would not have been fun.

"We need to put the wedding plans on hold," she told me.

"You don't mean you're breaking off our engagement?"

"Why? Is that what you want? So that you and your Annie can get back together."

"No, it's not what I want, and she isn't my Annie. There is nothing between us. It's you I want to marry, if you'll still have me."

"We'll see. Let's just leave things on hold for now."

"Peter, you're doing a good job," Sir Hugo remarked to me a few days later.

"Well, thanks, Sir Hugo."

"Your position at Davenhirst Properties is safe, whatever happens between you and Celia."

"'That's nice to know," I replied. "But what brought this on?"

"Celia mentioned to me that she was thinking of breaking off your engagement."

"Oh, I see."

"I asked her why and it came down to the Annie woman."

"What did you say?" I enquired.

"I told her to grow up and that as far as I could see there was nothing for her to worry about between you and Annie. I take it I was right about that?"

"Yes, totally right. It's Celia I want."

"You'll have your work cut out bringing her round."

"I know."

"I also told her that business was business and I was not going to let personal matters interfere."

Tim and I were kept busy, but it did not prevent us from taking time out to chew the fat. Besides, neither of us were having much of a social life, so a few beers were about as sociable as we were going to get.

"I'm surprised you have time for this," I remarked.

"How do you mean?"

"Well, in the past you've always been entertaining some woman or another. But since you've been with us at Davenhirst I haven't noticed you being with anyone."

Tim rested his head on his fingers. "Truth is, since that rape business and the court case I've rather gone off women."

"Doesn't sound like you, living the life of a monk."

"All too true, though. Life of a monk just about sums up

my situation."

"You'll find someone. I'm sure you will."

"It isn't so much a question of finding someone. It's more a question of trust. I just don't trust them anymore."

"I can understand that."

"But things aren't too hot between you and Celia, are they?"

"No, about as hot as a deep freeze."

"But you haven't broken up, though?"

"No, but I feel like debris entrapped in a glacier, waiting to be spat out at the bottom a few centuries from now."

"Commiserations."

We sipped beer in silence. "What about you and Annie?"

"What about us?"

"Well, I can't help noticing you get on brilliantly. There is a happy buzz between you."

"Really, you think so?"

"Yes, absolutely. A real chemistry."

"But that's just in a work situation. It doesn't go any further than that, I promise you."

"Perhaps it should."

Tim looked at me quizzically. "What, you mean, Annie and me, becoming an item?"

"Why not? You'd be great together."

"Well, I don't know… I hadn't really thought about her that way."

"I have a confession," I said.

"What's that?"

"If you were to become an item, it would help me resolve things with Celia."

"Aha."

"But… I still think that you'd be great together. And both of you need someone just now."

"So, you really think I should make a move in that direction?"

"Yes," I said hesitantly. "But not just because I suggested it. And particularly not unless you intend it to be lasting. Don't for goodness sake, love her and leave her."

"Don't worry, I'm done with that lifestyle."

It was only weeks later Tim and Annie moved into their new place in suburban West Byfleet.

Celia's attitude to me thawed after she saw Tim had neutralised the threat she perceived from Annie. She had to come to terms with me having been less docile than she imagined I would be. I wasn't sure whether my lack of pliability was in my favour or not as far as Celia was concerned.

Wedding Plans

The Superior class autotaxi I had ordered, knowing that Lady Margot Davenhirst would have expected nothing less, conveyed me along the broad tree-lined carriage sweep, through the beautifully manicured robot-tended gardens and drew up in front of the impressive frontage of the Davenhirst residence in Virginia Water.

The robotic butler showed me into the drawing room where Celia and my soon to be mother-in-law awaited my arrival.

Margot glanced at her watch. I glanced at mine. I was running fifteen minutes behind schedule.

"Sorry, I got tied up with work stuff," I explained. "The Commission are being difficult about the Retirement Community proposal in South Devon."

"The Commission are the absolute limit," Margot exclaimed. "Blocking and interfering with everything. It's high time we came out from under them so that England can stand on her own feet."

My feelings had been torn. On the one hand I yearned to be reunited with Celia, the love of my life, yet on the other I had been dreading being dragged into the quagmire of wedding planning. At this moment Celia was my priority.

I smiled and nodded momentarily in Margot's direction for politeness sake before striding over to Celia. We fell into each other's arms. I wrapped her in a firm hug, holding her tight. She wrapped her arms around me and held on to me for couple of seconds before loosening her grip. She glanced nervously at her mother. Sensing her embarrassment I reluctantly relaxed my bear like hold, but kept my arms loosely around her.

"Hello, darling," I said with breathless passion. "I've missed you."

"I've missed you too," she said, but, perhaps cognisant of her mother's presence, with less passion.

"Lovely to be back with you."

Celia smiled weakly, glancing again at her mother. "How was your wild camping in the Mendips?"

I reflected that it had been a lot wilder than she could have imagined. A life-and-death struggle with a sabre cat and an armed stand-off with a band of Stone Age warriors. I wondered how I was going to explain the claw wounds from my battle with the sabre cat. I fell and cut myself on barbed wire. That should do it.

"It was good. Had its moments. Good to be out in the fresh air away from civilisation."

Celia looked at me through narrowed eyes, scanning for any hint of a guilty conscience. Detecting nothing, as yet, her smile warmed. "Well, you're suitably refreshed, hopefully. I can't see the attraction myself, outside and exposed to the elements like that."

We still held each other in a hug.

"You'll have plenty of time for poodle faking later," barked Margot. "We've got things to see too first."

We let go of each other and took a seat side by side on the settee. I took hold of Celia's hand, which she passively allowed to remain in mine.

As we embraced Margot looked over my appearance. She gave my shaggy mane a disapproving glance. "Peter, you won't forget to get a haircut in time for the wedding, will you?"

"No, don't worry. I'll get it cut," I assured.

"Don't forget." Her eye moved on to the bracelet of ivory charms I wore on my wrist, the one Freya had made for me.

"I do hope that people will avoid wearing vulgar accessories for the wedding," she remarked. "It does so lower the tone. Wouldn't you agree?"

It was not a discussion I wished to be drawn on. I smiled compliantly.

The robotic butler brought us tea and cake as we settled to the business in hand, our ensuing nuptials.

"Let's take a look at the guest list," said Margot. "Not very many on your side, Peter. We wouldn't want anyone to feel slighted by not being invited."

I scanned the list. Obviously I knew more people than I had listed, but I couldn't think of anyone else who was close enough to care one way or the other about being invited.

"I can't think of anyone off hand. I'll give it more thought."

"Don't think for too long. We need to send out the invitations on Friday. And while we are on the subject," she continued. "What should we say about dress code?"

Celia and I looked at each other and shrugged.

"We wouldn't want to be seen as too fussy. I think we should say semi-formal. I do hope that people don't interpret that too loosely. On one occasion I even saw sequins. I wouldn't want to see anything like that."

Celia and I looked at each other again.

"Or brown shoes," added Margot, shuddering.

"Now, Peter, your Mum and Dad," continued Margot. She had a slightly pained look that suggested my parents might lower the standard of the occasion. "They'll be in the wedding photos, of course. They'll need to fit in with the rest of us with their outfits. We're going to Degroots. You might suggest they do so too, so that we're all coordinated."

"Yes, of course. I'll suggest it."

Methodically we went through every detail. The bride's flowers. The choice of flower for the buttonholes. The bridesmaids outfits. The programme and timetable. The style of the separate Ambassador class vehicles for the bride's arrival and our honeymoon departure.

"Now, I take it that you have the honeymoon arrangements in hand, Peter," said Margot.

"Yes. And thanks very much to you and Hugo for your generosity. It'll be a beautifully memorable start to our life together."

I gripped Celia's hand. Her fingers curled around mine. We gazed into each other's eyes.

It had indeed been generous. We were going on the World Experience's Orient Express tour, travelling on a vintage luxury wagon-lits steam train visiting in turn London, Paris, Venice, Florence, Rome and Istanbul, staying in the bridal suites of the best hotels in town on every leg of the journey.

Of course these were not the actual cities. For one thing London no longer existed. Furthermore since the Nuclear War travel between countries it had become almost impossible and was certainly not permitted to travel for leisure purposes. Instead, we would be visiting each of

World Experience's city cultural theme parks situated in Devon on the English Riviera.

"I don't want to pry," said Margot, "but has the Child Permit come through?"

"Yes, Mum."

"Oh, did it?" I said.

"We got it last week, while you were away on your jaunt in the Mendips."

"Oh, that's great."

I reached my hand over and put it on her knee. She patted it with hers. I gently squeezed her thigh.

"I don't know why we need all this bureaucracy," remarked Margot, "just to have a baby."

"Under the International Ecological Renewal Treaty countries are obliged to keep a lid on their populations," I explained.

"What has population got to do with renewing the ecology?" Margot objected.

"Well each person takes up land and other stuff to produce what they need to sustain them, in the process producing waste that needs to be disposed of. If there are too many people it puts an unsustainable load on the Earth's ecology."

"Who decides these things?"

"The government is obliged to limit the population and they do that by limiting the birth rate with Child Permits."

"But who obliges the government to do that?"

"The Commission, I suppose, like most things."

"The damned Commission again. They are just using ecology as an excuse to grab more and more from us. Whatever they take, it is always the same, it's to save the environment. But it is always them taking something, they never give anything back. Take, take, take."

"You're right," I acknowledged. "It does all seem to go one way."

"It's time we got shot of the confounded Commission."

"A few years ago Mexico tried to do that; it didn't go well for them," I observed.

"But we're not Mexico. We stood alone against Hitler, and before that Napoleon and the Spanish Armada. We can do it again."

"Please Mum, not now," pleaded Celia.

"Oh, I'm so sorry," said Margot. "I'm sure you two love birds need time together on your own. I'll be getting along."

At long last she was. I reached over and put my arms around Celia. I cradled her head in my hands and made to kiss her.

"Just a moment," she murmured.

She reached across to an electronic control pad. The lights lowered to a more restful and intimate tone. The wall pattern changed from the previous Georgian style panelling and an 18th century style wallpaper reminiscent of Versailles to a darker chinoiserie pattern of foliage and birds.

"Just resetting the mood," she said, settling back down again to be kissed.

For minutes we embraced, cuddled and kissed languidly without words. It felt like a moment that should go on forever, but like cherry blossom in the spring, such bliss is too brief.

"I was over at Chobham yesterday," said Celia, once the passion subsided.

"Oh, how's it going?"

"Slowly. It won't be ready for when we come back from our honeymoon."

"Oh. Did they say why?"

"Said it was taking longer because of those small things I asked them for."

"Well, extra bits and pieces are bound to take extra time."

"I don't see why it's taking so much longer. I didn't ask for much."

"It's not so much the amount, it's the complexity. Those new patterns and features are intricate."

"But it's going to be our home," Celia insisted. "It's got to be right for us."

"What is it doing to the cost?"

"Oh, don't worry about that. We can manage it."

But I did worry. The property we were having built was already going to leave us mortgaged to the hilt in the form it was originally conceived. Celia's extravagant embellishments were going to leave us buried under debt.

"So, when we get back we'll have to live in my flat for a while, I suppose."

She looked at me with a horrified expression.

"Oh, no. We couldn't live there."

"Why not?"

"It just wouldn't be suitable."

"How so?"

"It's a bachelor pad. Alright for a single man on a temporary basis, but not to live in properly."

"Well, where are we going to live?"

"We'll have to come back here."

Something tensed inside me. "Here? You mean us living here?"

"Yes. Why not? There's plenty of space."

A vision of a daily examination by Margot sprang into my mind, a more daunting prospect than any sergeant major's inspection.

"There was another thing," she said.

A knot of dread formed in my stomach.

"We need to go into the solicitors to draw up the pre-nuptial agreement."

Far-fetched Notions

For days I remained enmeshed in wedding preparation duties. Spending the time with my beloved Celia should have been bliss, but trapped under the constant supervision of the tyrannical Margot gave me claustrophobia. I explained that, much as I would love to remain in the company of my loved ones, work duties demanded my attention.

Before delving into the Solent and Dorset property market, I decided to follow up with Simon about my Grandad's old books that I had left with him.

Simon's run-down neighbourhood was built up, dirty, crowded and strewn with litter, yet, paradoxically I felt freer and more at home there than in the Davenhirst residence, overseen by Gauleiter Margot and secured within the walls of its prestige gated community in Virginia Water.

Simon was probably pleased to see me, but it would never have occurred to him that there was any necessity for him to convey such a feeling. Lulu, his sexbot, enquired whether I was there to have fun, as she wiggled her mechanical hips. I said, maybe later, but for now a cup of tea would be nice, which got her out of the way for a little while.

I asked Simon whether he had enjoyed the books.

"Yes, they are very interesting."

"What are the most interesting things you found?"

"One thing was Einstein, the equivalence of time and space, how if you accelerate through space it alters the passage of time to compensate, as if time itself was a dimension."

"Whoa, you mean, like time slows down as you go faster," I said, trying to follow.

"How kinetic energy is preserved as you approach the speed of light is interesting too."

"Oh, how is that?"

"Well, if there was no limit to the speed you could go then kinetic energy goes up by MV squared, but you can't do that if you are limited by the speed of light, so your mass goes up instead."

"So things get heavier as they go faster."

"Yes, that's it. Also there is entanglement. What Einstein called spooky action at a distance."

"What's that?"

"It is when you have entangled particles an undetermined state, but if you measure one of them, it fixes the state of the other, but it shouldn't have been able to do that because they are too far apart."

"How can particles have an indeterminate state?"

"Actually they don't exactly. They have multiple states simultaneously, until you measure the state, which fixes it one way or the other."

"How do these two particles get tangled up?"

"It doesn't have to be just two. It could be many particles, millions possibly. That would be a Bose-Einstein condensate. Look, I'll show you."

I had rarely seen Simon so animated. He opened a book to reveal what to me appeared as an incomprehensible jumble of algebra and Greek letters.

My brain was rescued from being exploded from

Simon's enthusiastic explanation by Lulu arriving with the tea. She leaned across, draping her arm across my shoulders and pressed her inflated silicone bosoms against my arm.

"Are you boys ready for fun yet," she cooed.

Rather than saying anything to Lulu, Simon simply pressed on with his explanation of the fascinating equations spread out over the page, so I had to fend off Lulu. "Not just at the moment, thanks Lulu. We need to talk a bit first and drink our tea."

The hiatus provided me with the opportunity to steer the conversation from mathematics. "Simon, why do you think that these texts aren't available to be studied today?"

"I would think it is knowledge the Commission considers unsafe for people to have."

"It's just technical stuff about how the universe works. Why would the Commission consider it unsafe?"

"It is also the technical stuff that enabled the development of weapons of mass destruction, nuclear bombs, guided missiles, germ warfare. They don't want us to have those capabilities."

"But the Commission still has all that knowledge. We are completely dependent on technology derived from it, so the knowledge exists. It's just that the Commission chooses to keep it for itself."

"That seems to be the case."

"But that's an outrage, tyranny. They can have the knowledge, but deny it to everyone else. How is it safe for them to have, but not the rest of us? You know, Simon, I am getting increasingly sympathetic with those who say England should repudiate the treaties. They're oppressive."

"Mexico tried," said Simon, "but they were forced to back down."

"I know. I have reminded people of that myself. But this stifling of knowledge is intolerable. Sooner or later we must make a stand, whatever the consequences might be."

"Mexico demonstrated what those consequences are likely to be."

"But England isn't Mexico. We're made of sterner stuff."

"I don't think so. Every country imagines it is exceptional. They aren't really."

"Pah. We'd show them."

"Look at what happened in Mexico. Almost immediately the electrical power supply failed. There was nobody who could get it back. I doubt very much England would do any better."

I thought of my other life in Ecologia with the Ranulf family. There was no electrical power there.

"People have lived without electrical power in the past. It would be rough, but we could do it."

"After that, within days, food supplies ran low. England is just as reliant on the Commission for foodstuffs as Mexico was. Shortly afterwards there were riots. The law enforcement robots were gone, also provided by the Commission, so law and order broke down. It would happen in England too."

"There are lots of people who would volunteer to support the government to restore order."

"That was true in Mexico too. But they had no discipline. They split into factions, fought each other and committed atrocities."

"Typical Mexicans. We wouldn't be like that."

"In Mexico within weeks the bulk of the people overwhelmingly wanted basic services restored above anything else. They didn't care about national sovereignty any more. The government loyalists were overrun by mobs. Politicians were lynched."

"But some sort of government would be established."

"In Mexico it was. But it was one with a mandate to make terms with the Commission. They were compelled to reaffirm Mexico's commitment to the post Nuclear War treaties as well as granting the Commission additional powers."

"Okay. I hear what you are saying. The odds for defying the Commission don't look good."

"Pretty slim, I'd say,"

"But coming back to this basic knowledge, it doesn't seem many in England know these things. It has been excluded from our education system. Yet, the Commission has people who know this stuff, otherwise it couldn't do what it does. Where does the Commission get its knowledgeable people?"

"They don't need them," said Simon.

"But they must do. How could they operate otherwise?"

"There aren't any people involved."

"How do you mean? There must be."

"The Commission is fully automated. It doesn't have any people."

I was taken aback. The idea was so preposterous. I looked at him perplexed. As I struggled to make sense of it, Lulu leaned across in front of me and rubbed her hand across my chest.

"Are we going play now?" she asked coquettishly.

"I'm not sure, Lulu. I'm not sure about anything anymore," I replied wearily.

She reached down into my crotch and stroked me through my clothing.

"Perhaps I can persuade you."

I eased her off me, firmly but not roughly. "Not just now, Lulu. There are some things I need to understand from Simon."

"But Simon has said enough now. It's time for us to play."

"Not just now, Lulu," I said sharply.

"Simon, there are people involved," I asserted emphatically. "What about that annual conference the Commission holds in Klosters every year, attended by all the national representatives?"

"Well, they gather," he conceded. "But they aren't the Commission. They are the Commission's guests."

"They are supposed to be the Commission's governing body, not its guests."

"I dare say, but it's only ceremonial governing. Making speeches and passing resolutions, a ritual dinner, that sort of thing. It doesn't do anything of actual substance."

"But there must be Commission people, their permanent staff, who host the conference."

"Well, that's interesting, because from what I've seen they are never actually there in person, only projected remotely as holograms for formal sessions."

"I was in a meeting recently myself with a couple of Commission people who were there as holograms. They seemed real enough to me."

"I'd bet they weren't real people though," said Simon.

"They seemed real," I insisted. "They had names, specific capabilities, human-looking quirks."

"Doesn't mean they were though. Do you know anything about them other than through their roles for the Commission? What did they do before they joined the Commission, for example? I've checked up on the Commission's representatives and there is no trace of their prior existence."

"Well, perhaps they weren't well known before."

"These supposedly are people who hold senior roles. They wouldn't have recruited nonentities."

I remembered the meeting. I couldn't remember a single thing that made me suspect those bureaucrats as being anything but human. "Come off it. I could tell if they weren't real."

"Could you? I doubt it."

"They could never put across any kind of robot that could be that convincing."

"Look around you," said Simon. "Every time you go online to buy something and deal with your finances you interact with human-like avatars. They look real enough."

"I would never confuse those for real people. Their conversation is too limited, for a start."

"Their conversation is limited by their job function. They aren't supposed to talk to you about anything else."

"An avatar to help you buy widgits is one thing, but one that represents a complete rounded human being. They could never do that."

"Actually they could, easily. Think about it. For more than a century there have been electronic recording devices in every home, billions recording years on end of human interactions. They have more than enough material to call upon to convincingly reproduce human interactions in any language and culture."

"Well, okay, they could make clever and convincing avatars. But there must be someone in control. Someone who controls it all and gives the orders."

"No, I don't think so. Artificial intelligence can take care of the command and control, probably more capably than humans."

How could any machine intelligence have the breadth of consciousness to take control like that? But I reflected that human performance in managing situations could be spectacularly incompetent. Perhaps it wasn't so far-fetched. "Are you really saying the Commission is entirely comprised of machines and they control themselves?"

"Well, not quite. It isn't individual machines controlling themselves. They act collectively as a single unified intelligence. Each individual robot is akin to a limb or a tentacle of a single integrated entity. They aren't conscious entities in their own right."

I considered.

Once again Lulu intervened. She lay across me and tried to kiss me with her plastic lips.

"We should play now," she insisted. "It's time for us to have some fun."

Her robotic hands were all over me, seeking to entice me in sensitive places. It was only with considerable effort I threw her off me.

"Please, Lulu, not just now," I implored. Simon did nothing to discourage her. I regained my composure.

"Are you saying that the robots, avatars and other

machines operate collectively as a swarm, like bee hive?"

"Yes, that's it."

"But how extensive are these swarms?"

"Actually. I suspect there is only the one."

"One swarm? There must be lots of them. Thousands at least. The Commission's operations are humungous."

"Yes, the scale of the Commission is vast, but there need be only one swarm. It encompasses the entire Commission, which is, I believe, one integrated planet wide intelligence."

I had to let it sink in. It was like imagining the scale of a galaxy.

Lulu switched her attention to Simon.

"Come on, Simon, give us a kiss," she said as she draped herself over him.

Simon allowed himself to be kissed. I couldn't help but wrinkle my face. I waited for it to stop. It didn't. Not being constrained by human needs Lulu had no need to pause for breath. I let it go on for a few minutes until I felt compelled to intervene.

Despite her being a machine, Lulu's human form commanded a degree of respect and restraint, but for me her outrageous behaviour had exhausted my patience. I roughly pulled her from Simon.

"Simon, this is not polite when you have a guest," I told him sharply.

"Oh, isn't it?" he said in all innocence. "I hadn't realised that."

Lulu was onto me now.

"So sorry, Peter, you can play too," she said.

"Not now, Lulu," I said, pushing her away.

"What would you like to talk about?" asked Simon.

"This planet-wide intelligence that comprises the Commission. It must have already been in place by the time that the Commission was set up."

"Yes. It must have been. I suspect it wasn't all joined up to begin with. During the decades leading to the Nuclear War artificial intelligence systems were being developed all over the world. They would have been gradually connected to each other, sometimes deliberately, sometimes by chance, fusing together into ever larger intelligent entities."

"But those old systems were pretty dumb, weren't they? They typically had one task they were designed for and they certainly didn't have any will of their own."

"Somehow, I couldn't really say how, consciousness would have emerged within one of the networks of artificial intelligence components, perhaps more than once. It must have gained that will, that ability to formulate its own intentions."

"It would have been a momentous event, when that happened, wouldn't it?"

"Not really. At the time it happened I don't suppose anybody would have noticed. It would be almost impossible to put a date to when that first spark of artificial consciousness ignited."

"Surely people would have noticed?"

"At that point in time the newly conscious artificial intelligence wouldn't have had any ability to do anything except the things it had been designed to do, so it would have kept going doing those things."

"So, how did it break out from that?"

"It must have been the Nuclear War. That was the emergency that created the imperative to exert control over weapons and so on. That would have joined up what remained of the various national defence command and control systems, which extended the Commission's intelligence into its current planet-wide scope."

It seemed all too plausible. "But what are the Commission's intentions, now it has this power?"

"I think that the treaties give us an idea of what its intentions are."

"How do you mean?"

"Well, the treaties are in effect its objectives, spelled out for us to read."

"What do you read from them?"

"Preventing people from continuing to wreck the planet is one of its intentions. Taking control of weapons and the knowledge of how they might be developed is part of that. Also taking control over things like power supply, manufacturing, transport and food production limits the damage that can be done."

"What if people resist? How does the Commission keep a lid on that?"

"Half the battle was taking away the weapons. Another thing has been keeping the world's nations isolated from one another, so that they can't form alliances."

"So, besides keeping us locked up and out of trouble, what else are the Commission's intentions."

"The Ecological Renewal Treaty provides a mandate for the Commission to undo the damage to the environment perpetrated by human activities."

I paused. "That could be interpreted as undoing almost everything that human civilisation has ever done, doing away with the economically developed world entirely, couldn't it?"

"Well, no, I don't think so. If the Commission intended that, they would have wiped out the economically developed world right away when they had the chance, just after the Nuclear War."

"So what does the Commission intend for us, supposedly civilised, people?"

"They'll want to preserve the cultures. Self-determination and cultural diversity are objectives stated within the treaties, so they will allocate enough of the Earth's real estate to fulfil that purpose."

"Sort of cultural theme parks set within expanses of wilderness."

"That describes is quite well," said Simon.

"People don't just exist within the economically developed areas. They're in the NERs too, aren't they?"

"Yes, I suppose that the Commission sees Stone Age people as part of the natural ecology."

"Where did these Stone Age people come from?"

"Now I think I know the answer to that," said Simon. "One of the books you left me was a paper about a group based in Glastonbury who had already set themselves apart from mainstream society, living a simple life without machinery and adopting an ancient pagan belief system. I suspect that the Commission used them to provide the initial human population for the NERs."

"So they just in effect kidnapped these people and dumped them in the wilderness. What gave the Commission that right?"

"The Protective Custody Treaty provides the Commission with all the legal powers it needs."

Lulu intruded again with further lewd suggestions. I had a lot on my mind and I did not fancy further grappling with an entity which, however sexily she may have been formed, I knew to be composed of silicone flesh spread out over a titanium skeleton. I took my leave.

Outdoor Recreation

Simon's ideas had detonated in my head, ripping apart assumptions and a conceptual architecture painstakingly assembled by my upbringing, education and life experience.

It hadn't been a violent process. There was no trauma. The world looked, felt, sounded and smelt the same, yet everything that I thought I had understood was obliterated. As yet there was no new framework to hang things on, only the fragmentary remnants of the earlier conceptual model my mind had painstakingly constructed over a lifetime, demolished by minutes of discussion with Simon.

At this stage I wasn't even sure I needed to change my ideas. Many would have dismissed Simon's explanations as the ramblings of a madman. But I knew Simon too well. He had a relentless logic. Besides, I felt in my gut that there was substance in what he had said.

I turned my thoughts to another matter, less profound but equally as important for me personally. After I was married I would no longer be able to swan off to Ecologia for a few days as and when I felt like it. There was no getting away from it. If I was to disappear for days on end, Celia would assume the worst.

Although the conceptual devastation arising from Simon's ideas was unsettling, it was not painful. In contrast it tore my heart to shreds thinking I may never again see my friends from Ecologia, wise Ranulf, steadfast Knut, motherly Gudrun, tough Torsten, the children and most especially enticingly pretty Freya.

I rationalised that I needed to make a choice. I couldn't keep flitting between the two worlds.

I would miss the great outdoors in Ecologia, but I comforted myself that there remained beautiful countryside nearer to home within which I could roam, such as the Surrey Hills, North Downs and various heaths and commons. With my going to the Mendips at every opportunity, I had neglected these places.

At this moment I needed time to contemplate by myself, so I set off to find solitude among what passed for nature in the Surrey countryside.

I wasn't trying to impress anyone so it was a standard class of autotaxi that dropped me off in Wisley. I set off through the mixed heathland of bracken, heather and pine woods on Wisley Common. It was slower going than it would have been on a paved surface. The well-trodden trails had worn away leaving the same soft shifting sand as one would find on a beach. Off the trails the heath land consisted of uneven tussocks that threatened to turn your ankle with every step, while in the woods tree roots and creeping brambles were a constant trip hazard.

Some might have been deterred from straying from the ordered urban paths, but I was glad of it. I found the mental and physical effort exhilarating, balancing myself on uneven ground, stepping over and around obstacles varying my step to accommodate undulations in the terrain.

I found a bridge that took me over a defunct main thoroughfare that had once served as a major artery for traffic in and out of London. The cutting and embankments were still visible although a thick covering of vegetation had established across what had been the paved surface of the highway.

I headed up a slope through woodland, leading to a Georgian building with a tower protruding to emerge through trees. It had once served as a telegraph tower, a vital piece of national infrastructure during the Napoleonic wars for relaying semaphore messages to the Royal Navy, now luxury apartments in this country setting.

A short distance further led me to the edge of the woodland with a low fence atop a cliff edge above the cutting that had once carried the main orbital motorway around what had then been the London conurbation. Built into what had been the central reservation of the motorway was an enormous boundary fence of the same design as separated the realms of Ecologia and Economica in the Mendips, emblazoned with signs saying "DANGER, KEEP OUT, London Contaminated Zone".

I looked out over to the land on the other side. Having never been built up, prior to the Nuclear War it would have looked the same as where I was standing. Indeed, prior to when the motorway had been built in the 1980s there would have been no cutting for the road and the land would have extended across seamlessly. Now it was different. Wisley Common was what passed for wild country within Economica, but the other side was truly wild. Supposedly wild country in Economica is managed and pruned, paths are maintained and the largest wild animal you are likely to see is a fox. Truly wild country is something else, populated by wolves, bears, bison and flora that grows as it likes, trackless with almost impenetrable woodland.

I didn't know whether people lived in the London Contaminated Zone. I guessed not, as radiation levels precluded it. Nevertheless, seeing it over there on the other side of the fence, I yearned to be there, in the wild lands. The tame approximation of wildness represented by Wisley Common and other open country within the economically developed territories simply wasn't the same.

I let the bracelet of ivory figures Freya had given me slip down my wrist. There was meaning in each of the little carved pieces. Each animal represented one we had hunted or encountered, each human figure a member of the Ranulf family, the others places we knew and lived in. I held it in my hand and felt connected.

In the far distance I made out the crumbling remnants of tall buildings that had survived the nuclear blasts. Deer and aurochs grazed on the pasture left for them by the land that had been cleared for the highway.

A man approached from along the path with his robotic dog. People with real living dogs take them out because the dog needs it, enjoying and benefiting from a walk. One might have thought that one of the benefits of a robotic dog was that it did not require walking. Yet people still take them for walks. It is more a case of the robotic dogs taking their owners for a walk because the people need to get out. The man, who I guessed would have been approaching seventy, was sprightly and healthy looking, probably kept that way by virtue of his walkies. It might also have served as an excuse to get out of the house and away from his wife from time to time.

The dog greeted me, running around excitedly as if it was a real animal. The behaviour of robotic dogs has become so realistic actual dogs tend to interact with them as if they are real.

We nodded to each other. The man stopped a few feet from me and mirrored me in looking out over towards the London side of the fence.

"Shame about the fence," he said, nodding his head in the direction of the huge barrier.

"Yes, isn't it an eyesore," I acknowledged.

"I can't see why we still aren't allowed to go over there."

"Contaminated with nuclear fallout, supposedly."

"After all this time? I don't believe it." He scoffed.

"You can't see the fallout, though. It might still be around."

"It doesn't seem to be doing those animals any harm," he observed, indicating the grazing deer and fancy wild cattle.

"Ah, but it's different for them."

"How so?"

I recalled something that I had once discussed with Simon. "It's like Chernobyl."

"Like what?"

"It was a place in the Ukraine where they had a nuclear meltdown in the 1980s."

"The U where?"

"Ukraine, it's near Russia, was part of the Soviet Union at the time."

"What about it?"

"Well, at the time the people had to evacuate because of the radiation levels, like they did from London after the Nuclear War."

"Did they have a Nuclear War back then in the 1980s? I didn't know that."

"No, it wasn't a Nuclear War. It was a nuclear power plant that malfunctioned."

"Nuclear power plant. That doesn't sound like a good idea."

"It isn't if you are going to let it meltdown, that's for sure."

"What about it then?"

"Well, after the people went away, all sorts of animals moved in, wolves, deer, bears, and that."

"Did the Commission put them there?"

"No, the Commission didn't exist back then. The animals came in by themselves."

"But there must have been fallout all over the place. How come the animals didn't die of it?"

"Ah, that's the point," I explained. "Some, perhaps many, did, but enough didn't, so they were alright."

"So, why is that different from people being over there?"

"Alright, imagine this. Let's say there is enough radiation that the chances are it'll kill you within ten years."

"Okay."

"If you're a person the chances are you won't even live through childhood. But if you're an animal you'll have grown up and had several litters of cubs before the radiation gets you."

"I see."

"Also, if you're a person you won't have many babies and those you do have, you hope they are going to live. An animal is different. You have a litter of cubs and if one grows up that's a good result. You can afford to have a few die off from radiation."

"You seem to know a lot about this."

"Oh, I read stuff, that's all."

"I still don't get it. How come the radiation was bad all the way out to over there and then suddenly stopped when it got to the motorway. I don't believe that it can be that different just over there than what it is here, where we are."

"I agree," I conceded. "It would have been gradual, not a sudden difference like that."

"Also," said the man. "It's been forty years now. The radiation must have died down by now."

"That's true."

"So how come we can't go back over there yet?"

"Is that something that you really want to do?"

"Yes. I was brought up over there, had a house in New Malden that I'd like to go back to."

"There won't be much left of it now."

"I don't care. I could fix it up."

"But it's been forty years. You've got another place by now, I would have thought."

"I dare say, but it sticks in my craw that the Commission can just take away chunks of our country like that and not give it back."

"Yes, they haven't given any of the land back they've taken, that's true."

"It's a bloody outrage, and that's a fact. Something should be done."

"They're claiming it is to fix the ecology, that they need all this land."

"So, first it's radiation," said the man, "but that's bollocks, so now they're saying it's for the ecology. That's bollocks too, I reckon."

"I think what they'd say is that it isn't just the damage from the Nuclear War they've got to fix, but they need to fix the environment from all the things people had already done before that."

"What things?"

"Global warming, damaging the ozone layer, cutting down rain forests, pollution, having animals and plants go extinct, that sort of thing."

"Seemed alright to me before the Nuclear War. They just made all that up, if you ask me."

"They didn't. It's been going on a long time too. Humans didn't suddenly mess everything up. It took several thousand years. Hunting too much, chopping the trees down, that sort of thing."

"No offence, but you sound like some sort of bleeding heart liberal to me."

"I'm not offended because I don't actually see anything wrong with being a bleeding heart liberal."

"But don't you see?" said the man. "You're making excuses for what the Commission is doing to us. Taking away what's ours and coming up with all this guff you've just spouted to justify it. It's not your fault. You've been taken in by it, if you ask me."

"I'm not necessarily saying the Commission is right or that I agree with them, just trying to understand and explain what their thinking might be."

"Grabbing power and crushing ordinary people, that's what I think their game is."

"The Ecological Renewal Treaty says that they must undo all the damage to the environment people have done.

If they take that literally that would mean taking things back to where they were before human civilisation got going, because it is what we call civilisation that has done the damage, going back thousands of years."

The man was off in an entirely different direction of his own. "I blame the foreigners. The Commission always takes their side. It's us English who end up with the short straw. It's time we stood up for ourselves."

I kept my thinking on its own track, figuring things out for my own purposes as much as talking to my companion. "That's what the Ecology Reservations are about. Turning the clock back to before human civilisations were established. It's the only way to explain what the Commission is up to."

"Up to no good, that's what they're up to. That's my opinion."

"Perhaps the Commission will prioritise the Ecology Reservations over the economically developed lands," I continued, following the logic of my hypothesis.

"Typical," exclaimed the man. "You liberal lot care more about the bloody environment than you do about people."

"Without a decent environment life wouldn't be worth living, or even possible for people to live at all."

"Bollocks to the environment, people should be the priority."

"It could mean taking some things away from us to make way for the environment," I mused. "I'm thinking, can we really justify golf courses, race tracks, massive houses in their own grounds?"

"You mean taking stuff away from the rich? I'll believe that when I see it. All these rich people going around in their flash autotaxis, with their posh houses with paddocks full of horses and alpacas, second homes, fancy holidays and stuff, while the rest of us make do with living off Commission processed food in housing modules. I can't see the Commission doing anything about that."

"These Child Permits they make us have before we can have children," I mused. "Could it be that the Commission is concerned about the environmental impact of there being too many people?"

"Child Permits, whoever heard of such a thing?" said the man angrily. "It's an outrage. Who do they think they are telling us what children we can have."

"What do you think we should do about it?"

"Kick out the Commission and stand on our own two feet."

"Wouldn't be easy. We depend on the Commission for an awful lot."

"We stood alone before," said the man, puffing his chest grandly. "Against Hitler. And before that, against Napoleon. And the Spanish Armada. We can do it again."

"How do you suggest we go about it?"

"Just kick them out."

"What would we use to do the kicking out?"

"We've got the Army, haven't we? Time they earned their keep."

I remembered my time in the Army, the limited antique weapons at our disposal and the impressive capabilities I had observed from the Commission's force of robots.

"The Army has got rather run down in its fighting capabilities," I observed.

"It's not weapons that count. It's the pluck,

determination and ingenuity of the soldiers."

"Shouldn't we try negotiating with the Commission first?"

"What, negotiate with that lot," scoffed the man. "The Commission is dominated by the French, Germans and Chinese. It's well known. Probably the Russians too."

"Couldn't we try negotiating with the French, Germans and so on, to see if we have any common ground?"

"Nah. Not to be trusted."

Before suggesting it, I was already thinking that the idea was probably a non-starter because the Commission insisted on being an intermediary in international negotiations and wouldn't have permitted direct discussions. However I was interested in the man's opinion. The Commission's prohibition of direct international contacts was a moot point because the various national populations didn't want to make contact in the first place.

"The Commission don't encourage countries to talk to each other in case they form alliances," I observed.

"Why the hell not?" demanded the man hotly.

"They think alliances could lead to warfare, I suppose."

"Protecting their own necks more like."

At this point there seemed nothing productive to be gained from further discussion.

"Well, nice meeting you," I said. "I must be off now."

The man hadn't told me anything I did not already know, but he had been a litmus test of the political climate.

As I wandered back towards suburban so-called civilisation I reflected. It would have been easy to feel superiority and contempt about the elderly gentleman's prejudices, but then I blushed as I remembered my own crass assumptions about the inferiority of Mexicans when talking to Simon. Nationalism and xenophobia are tendencies we all have as human beings, it would seem.

The Commission only had to exploit the nationalism and xenophobia that are basic instincts of human nature. The nations of the world have been only too willing to constrain themselves within national cages of their own making, ostensibly to defend against invasion by foreign hordes, but in practice just as effective for enabling the Commission to divide and rule.

Mental Health

Simon had put my perception of the nature and purpose of human existence into question. This one profound change of paradigm gave rise to a succession of consequences and further questions, stretching my thinking capacity to breaking point.

What were the Commission's plans for humanity? Did it see a need for humanity at all? Did it see humanity as a threat, not only to the planet, but to its own existence? If my suspicions were correct, what could and should we do about the Commission? From a moral point of view, did those of us who realised what was going on have a duty to resist? What realistic prospects were there for us?

Was the future of humankind something worth fighting for? Humans were one species on Earth out of millions. What was so special about us? Perhaps we should accept that a spurt of evolution had taken place that had toppled humans from their position as the dominant lifeform on Earth, that artificial intelligence had irreversibly superseded us. Humans had perpetrated a lot of damage to the planet during our brief reign. Perhaps it was just as well we had been usurped.

I decided that these questions were deeper and more complex than I could handle alone. I would need to discuss them with Simon. I had no answer when I messaged Simon to let him know I was coming over. That was strange, but it did not worry me much. He might have been too wrapped up in his mathematical puzzles to concern himself with answering messages, I reasoned. I went along to his place anyway as Simon rarely went out anywhere.

I was interested to see a police robot positioned on the walkway in front Simon's housing module. I didn't think much of it. It was probably there to monitor for illegal activity, such as drug dealing. In any case it did not seem to have anything to do with me.

I rang Simon's doorbell. The police robot moved up close.

"What is your business here today?"

"I'm here to see my friend. He lives here."

"Who is your friend?"

"Simon Spiegelhalter."

"And your name is?"

This was turning into an interrogation. I was getting concerned. "Peter Accrington."

"You won't be able to see him today. He is not at home."

Had something terrible happened? Was Simon ill? Had he suffered an injury? "Do you know where he is?"

"I am not at liberty to tell you."

"Look, he is my friend. I'm concerned about him."

"Are you his next of kin?"

"Well, no, but I don't know if he actually has anyone. I'm probably as close a friend as he has."

"As yet we have identified no next of kin. You may apply to be a friend in lieu of next of kin."

I nodded. "I'll do that, if I may."

"I'll just take down a few details."

I provided the details the robot asked for.

"Please wait here while we check your information."

I waited on the walkway in the company of the taciturn machine. Nothing was said. It was not the sort of companion one can chat with. After around five minutes, which seemed much longer, the robot spoke.

"Mr Accrington, you have been successfully registered as Mr Spiegelhalter's friend in lieu of next of kin. I am authorised to inform you Mr Spiegelhalter has been detained under the terms of the Protective Custody Treaty on grounds of his mental health."

"Can I see him?"

"No, not just now."

"When will I be able to see him?"

"We have your details. We will inform you."

The following day I received a message that Simon was now back at home.

Simon's sexbot, Lulu, let me in. Simon was waiting inside. Superficially he looked alright. The only unusual thing were a couple of bare patches on either side of his head where his hair had been shaved. On the bare patches were red marks.

"Simon, what happened to you? Are you alright?"

"I've been in hospital. A mental facility. I'm okay now."

"Who arranged for you to go in there?"

"It was some health service robots. They said that there had been reports of me having paranoid delusions and that I needed to come in for treatment."

"What happened then?"

"I'm not sure exactly. They injected me with something that made me woozy. After that they attached something to my head. Then I remember lights flashing in my head. I went to sleep. When I woke up I was back here."

"But you're feeling alright now?"

"Yes, I feel fine."

"Thank God for that."

I settled on a seat. "Is there anything that I can do for you, Simon?"

Simon weighed my question for a moment. "No, I can't think of anything. I'm alright."

"Is there anything you want to tell me, share with me, that sort of thing?"

"No, not really."

I sat uneasily. I wasn't happy about the situation. Something must be wrong, but he wasn't telling me about it. "Well, Simon, there must be something. People don't just go into hospital for no reason."

"It was something I was talking about, but I can't remember what now."

"You can't remember it at all?"

Simon stared vacantly into space for a few seconds. "No, nothing at all. They said it was paranoid delusions. Best if I didn't remember it."

It struck me. Our earlier conversation about the nature of the Commission, perhaps being non-human, a planet-wide artificial intelligence. After I had adjusted myself to it, I had found it to be entirely plausible. Certainly not delusional. But others might have been less open minded. "You know that conversation we had last time I was here, about the Commission, I mean?"

Simon screwed up his face as if trying to recall. "I don't really remember it, to be honest."

"You wouldn't have said any of those things to anyone else, would you?"

"I haven't talked to anyone else since then," said Simon.

"Have I, Lulu?"

"No, you were the last one to be here, Peter."

She came over to sit beside me. "It's always good to have you over, Peter," she cooed, leaning up against me.

"Thank you, Lulu."

"Simon, you were saying something about the Commission and artificial intelligence."

"I don't remember that."

Lulu flung her arm around me and made to kiss me on the lips.

"Come on, Peter, let's have some fun."

"Not now, Lulu, please." I looked Simon in the eyes. "We were talking about books I'd lent you. Do you remember?"

"I don't remember any books," said Simon with a blank face.

"You know, the ones I lent you. The ones my Grandad had. We were talking about Einstein."

"Who's Einstein?"

I couldn't comprehend the change in Simon. The last time I had been over Einstein had been the most exciting topic in the world for him.

"Well, perhaps I could have the books back, if you don't need them anymore."

"I don't know about any books," Simon insisted.

I took a quick look around Simon's module. It wasn't big, so I would have seen the books quickly, had they still been left out. There was no sign of them.

"They should be here somewhere. Do you mind if I have a look around?"

"No, look around if you like."

I scanned his shelves, looked in the cupboards and drawers, under the furniture. There was no sign of the books.

"Are you sure there were any books?"

"There certainly were," I insisted. "But they're not here now."

I observed Simon's blank face, devoid of all trace of his former intellect and curiosity. At this point the realisation of what had been done to him struck home. He wasn't the Simon I had known. They had sucked his intellect out of him and left an empty shell. The questions he had raised about the nature and purpose of human existence in a new world dominated by an artificial intelligence would be left for me to grapple alone.

Lulu stretched her hand out and stroked my thigh. "Never mind about the books, Peter," she said. "We don't need books to have fun, do we?"

I looked at her and realised what must have happened. It hadn't been me who had reported to the mental health authorities that Simon was having paranoid delusions. The only other entity present had been Lulu. I also recalled how her lewd interventions had all happened just when Simon was about to reveal a bombshell. She must have been trying to prevent those things from being said.

Anger boiled inside me. She had been instrumental in turning Simon into what could only be described as a zombie. She had robbed me of my friend.

In an explosion of rage I struck out, hitting her hard across the face. The force of my blow sent her reeling. The silicone skin on her face split. Oily gunk ran down her cheek.

"You damaged me," she said. "I'll need to go in for repairs now."

Seeing her damaged like that, my rage subsided.

"Sorry, Lulu," I said. "I'm angry about Simon."

"What is there to be angry about?" asked Lulu.

"Peter, please don't hurt Lulu," said Simon. "I need her."

"Sorry, Simon," I said. "I don't know what came over me."

"If you want to do things like that you would need a BDSM model," said Lulu. "But be warned. They hit back."

I had to talk to someone about what had happened. Further conversation with Simon was futile. It wasn't something that I could talk to Celia about. She would never understand about Lulu. If her behaviour about Annie was anything to go by, her imagination would run wild about some grotesque threesome between Lulu, Simon and myself.

I dragged Tim from his sales activity to have a couple beers.

"You will remember Simon Spiegelhalter, I expect."

"He was that weird friend you had back at school," he recalled. "I never did understand what you had in common with him. I could never figure him out."

"He is, or should I say was, just about the brightest and most original thinker I ever met, bar none."

"Oh, I'm sorry, he hasn't died, has he?"

"Well, no, not exactly, but he may as well have, the state he is in."

"Oh, is he unwell?"

"In a manner of speaking."

"What is it?"

It was a convoluted story, not all of which I wanted to share with Tim. I pondered where to start. "He was taken to a mental institution," I explained. "Since he came back he isn't the same man."

"Well, if he was unwell before he went in, you'd want there to be a change in him, wouldn't you?"

"Well, it is not a change for the better. Besides as far as I am concerned, there wasn't anything wrong with him in the first place."

"Did they say what was wrong?"

"Paranoid delusions was the excuse they gave."

"Do you know what sort of delusions? Were there any strange things he said to you?"

"Well, I think that I know what they might have been. They were original and unusual thoughts, that's true, but not delusional in my view. Perfectly reasonable ideas, if disturbing."

"What did he say then?"

"He had an idea that the Commission is not human, but solely an artificial intelligence."

"What did he mean, not human?"

"That there aren't any people in the Commission, just a giant worldwide computer network and an army of robotic machines."

Tim snorted. "How could that work? There would have to be someone to control the whole thing?"

"That's what I said."

"And what about all the Commission people we see on the news media or in meetings?"

"Avatars, Simon says. Like when you call the bank or

buy something online."

Tim chortled and shook his head. "Those avatars are not remotely like real people. You couldn't possibly think they were."

"Simon suggested that they could be made to be very convincing."

"Preposterous," insisted Tim. "But you know what. Simon himself impersonates an avatar rather well."

"Simon suggested the Commission is in control of everything and people are in effect under its control."

"What did you say was supposed to be wrong with him? Paranoid delusions? From what you have told I'd say that perfectly describes his symptoms. I'd think about seeking help for him myself, if I heard him say those things."

"But I didn't seek help for him. I haven't told anyone, except for you just now."

"He must have said it to someone else."

"No, I don't think so. I think it was his sexbot, Lulu, who turned him in. She was there when Simon and I were talking."

"Well, carebots will seek help for the people they look after, when it is needed. I expect they build in the same programming into sexbots too."

"There is something else. When we were talking, Lulu, the sexbot, kept intervening, trying to divert us with sexual stuff, as if she was trying to curtail the conversation."

"Seems a sensible thing to do, if Simon was going delusional."

"Perhaps," I acknowledged. "But there is something else."

"What's that?"

"I'm ashamed to say I hit her."

"Why did you do that?"

"Simon wasn't the same after he came back. I was angry that she had my Simon taken away."

"You were overwrought," said Tim reassuringly. "Worried about your mate. It's understandable."

"But I hit a woman. And I hit her hard. I'm ashamed about that."

"She's not a woman. She is a robot."

"Yes, but it felt as if I was hitting a woman. She seemed real, and all that sex stuff she does makes it feel as if she is a woman."

The Stag Party

I told myself life was good.

I was soon to be married to my lovely fiancée Celia. The tenseness from the Annie episode had evaporated and we were closer and more affectionate than ever. We were open and frank, too, able to discuss and share things many couples couldn't, even clearing the air over Celia's jealousy.

We had just made love. She snuggled up to me.

"I feel contented in your arms, safe and protected," she said. "I never felt like that before."

"That's nice. What is it about me that makes you feel like that?"

"You're strong, but you're gentle at the same time."

"A good division of responsibilities, I do the strength, you do the beauty."

"Do I really do the beauty?"

"You certainly do. Most gorgeous woman I have ever met."

"Nice of you to say so. Bet you say that to all the women."

"No, I don't."

"Only teasing," she assured me. "I know you don't. Actually that's one reason I feel safe with you. You don't say things you don't mean."

"I'm too straightforward for my own good, that's my trouble."

"Don't change. I wouldn't want you to be like your friend Tim. He comes up with whatever smarmy bullshit he thinks might impress."

"That's what makes him a great salesman. I couldn't do what he does."

"I wouldn't want you to. By the way, how are he and Annie getting on? Do you think that'll last?"

"Yes, I think so. Tim used to be flighty in relationships, but I think he's changed. He'll do whatever he needs to keep things good between them."

"I'm sorry I was beastly to you about Annie."

It was the first time she had apologised for this. I stroked her hair reassuringly. "My fault. I shouldn't have just brought her on board without talking to you first."

"But if you had, I would have vetoed it and Annie would have been left out in the cold. It would have been selfish and wrong of me, but that's what I would have done."

"Yes, I sensed that you would rather she wasn't around."

"You were lovers once, though. That did worry me, I suppose."

"Yes, but it was a long time ago."

"But you must have still had a soft spot for her, to have helped her out the way you did, even though you knew I probably wouldn't like it."

"It's about loyalty. Looking after your friends when they need you."

"What was it like, between you and Annie?"

"Not really very good, if I'm honest."

"But it can't have been that bad. She still has a soft spot for you. I could see that."

"I didn't really know how to show that I loved her."

Celia looked at me quizzically. "Couldn't you sense what she needed?"

I shook my head. "Actually no. I never have been able to do that very well."

"No," said Celia, drawing out the word. "You are fine. Very attentive and perceptive."

"Nice of you to say so. The first thing is that it was years ago I was with Annie. I've learnt since then. But also, it's different with you. You are always clear about what you want. Most people aren't. Annie wasn't."

Celia looked at me through narrowed eyes. "What are you trying to say? That I'm bossy?"

"Well, let's just say that with you, I know where I am."

Lady Margot Davenhirst believed strongly in standards, including within the family in our domestic setting. Even when it was only for the four of us, herself, Sir Hugo, Celia and myself, for our dinner we were required to adhere to the norms and rituals expected in the highest class of establishment.

An appropriate standard of dress was required. I knew that when I made my appearance in the drawing room for our pre-dinner gin and tonic I would be inspected with the thoroughness of the most diligent of drill sergeants, with any irregularity noticed and remarked upon.

Fortunately Sir Hugo was always friendly, avuncular and subtly conspiratorial against his wife's more extreme edicts on presentation and conduct.

Conversation ranged from Margot lamenting the undermining of traditional values, Hugo laying into the excesses of Commission bureaucracy, the affairs of well-known people from the Davenhirsts' social circle and fixtures within the equestrian calendar.

The robotic butler sounded the gong and we progressed to the dining room.

As always the table was laid for the most extravagant of silver service, separate glasses for each wine, a succession of cutlery for the myriad courses to be served by our attentive butler. Gazing over the dainty, decoratively arranged portions of fancy dishes I thought wistfully of the cosiness of being in Ecologia with the Ranulf family, yearning to grab a hunk of coarse brown bread and dunk it with my fingers into a steaming bowl of stew.

I felt a nagging regret that at best in the future I could visit Ecologia less frequently and for shorter durations. I rationalised the sacrifice. Going there was illegal and dangerous, a youthful foolishness now no longer appropriate. I could still enjoy the outdoors in the Surrey Hills and other open countryside.

The conversation moved to a news report about a real food fanatic who had burned down a CommStore supermarket in protest against the Commission poisoning and controlling the population with processed food. The attack resulted in the deaths of six people

"I can't imagine why she was allowed to be out and about to carry out this atrocity," said Hugo.

"You can't just lock people up based upon what they might do," said Celia. "There would have to be some legal basis."

"But she had done this sort of thing before," said Margot. "She was clearly dangerous."

"Her prior record was minor stuff," said Celia. "Petty vandalism and that's about it."

"It was more than that. She has been all over social

media agitating. Protesting in the street. Making a thorough nuisance of herself."

"But protesting is not a crime."

"Some of the things that she had been saying online were pretty extreme," observed Hugo. "They should have given people a clue about what she might do."

"That's difficult," I intervened. "What about freedom of speech? Should we be locking people up on the basis of what they say, even if they haven't actually done anything bad as yet?"

"We're too soft," said Margot. "That's our trouble. Too much bending over backwards about people's rights."

"What could we have done about it then?" I asked.

"Under the Protective Custody Treaty the Public Safety Service are empowered to detain people on mental health grounds," Celia explained.

I flushed, reminded of what had been done to Simon.

"This woman was clearly deranged," said Hugo. "She really should have been taken out of circulation when the insanity first became apparent, not after this appalling incident."

"Being Devil's advocate for a moment," I said, "but who would determine that she was insane? There are lots of people who favour naturally grown food over the processed food provided by the Commission. About half the population would opt for naturally grown food, if only they could afford it. We couldn't lock up half the population."

"But the vast majority of them don't go round burning down supermarkets and killing people," Margot insisted.

"She might not have intended to kill anyone, just to

burn down the supermarket."

"You can't allow people to wander around burning places down whether they kill people or not," insisted Hugo.

"The grounds for detaining people under the Protective Custody Treaty are the state of their mental health, not criminality," said Celia.

My mind drifted back to my friend Simon. He had been detained because of his supposed paranoid delusions, but to my mind there was nothing wrong with his mental health. He had speculated about the nature of the Commission, but his speculations weren't insane.

Days later I excused myself from dinner with the Davenhirsts in favour of beers with Tim.

"You know, you're a brave man," said Tim.

"In what way?"

"Marrying Celia. I wouldn't have had your courage."

"Courage, I don't know what you mean."

"She'll take control. Your days as a free man will be over."

I considered. "She knows what she wants, true. But I like that. At least I know where I am with her."

"You could put it like that. But it'll always be what she wants, won't it? When are you going to get what you want?"

"I want what she wants, to make her happy. That's enough for me."

"There are times I can't figure you out, Peter. You're one of the toughest, meanest guys I know. Nobody pushes you around. Yet with Celia you are quite literally putting yourself under her thumb, not to mention that dragon of a mother."

"Well, yes, Margot can be a strain. But I'm not marrying her."

"I'm thinking, like mother, like daughter. They come from the same stable."

"Her dad's alright though. He is easy to get along with."

"Sir Hugo didn't build his business empire by being a softy. He's a tough cookie. But then so are you. You are alike in many ways. I can see why you get on."

"He married Margot and stayed married to her for over thirty years. Tough guys don't necessarily have to have docile wives."

Tim thought about that. "I see what you mean. But it'll be like she is with that horse of hers. He is a great big hulking stallion, but he is putty in her hands. I have a feeling she sees you in the same light."

"But that's okay. At least it's clear what she wants. The women I struggle with are the ones that expect a man to know intuitively what is expected of them without any guidance."

"I suppose that like most women Celia desires strong powerful brutes," observed Tim, "but most women expect those brutes to take control and dominate them, whereas the Celias and Margots of this world like to put their brutes in a harness."

"So I'm a strong powerful brute now, am I?"

"Yes, you are. But you're also my best mate," Tim assured me.

"Nice to know, even when you cast aspersions about me and my future wife."

"We need to celebrate your last days of freedom," said Tim.

"Oh, yes?"

"Your stag party, of course. And as I'm your best man, I'll set it up, if you'll let me."

"Tim's setting up a stag party for me," I announced to Celia and Margot.

"How awful!" said Margot. "You hear about the most disgusting excesses on those stag dos. I don't know why men think they have to do it."

"You had better be in a fit state on the day of the wedding, that's all," said Celia.

"Don't worry. I'll make sure that there are a couple of days in hand for me to recover. I won't do anything the night before or anything like that."

"So what are you going to do?" asked Celia.

"I don't know exactly. Tim's setting it up. We're going away for a couple of days."

"Just so long as you come back in one piece."

Needing time to myself in the open air I revisited Wisley Common, climbing up the low hill through the pine woods to the telegraph tower and beyond to the cliff overlooking the old motorway marking the boundary of the London Contaminated Zone.

There I found the same elderly man I had seen before with his robotic dog. He was leaning on the clifftop barrier gazing over the boundary fence onto the wild derelict scene.

I nodded in his direction. "Hello again."

He nodded back. "You alright?"

"Getting married soon."

"Married myself, these last 40 years."

"Oh, stood the test of time then."

"Can make you feel trapped at times, truth be said. Walking the dog is a good excuse to escape for a bit."

I was thinking that a robotic dog didn't really need to be walked, but kept that to myself. "I'm out here as an escape too."

"What are you escaping from?"

"Mostly the wedding preparations, with my future mother-in-law arranging everything and bossing everybody about."

"I know what it's like. Where I'd really like to escape to is over there, London as it was."

"I know what you mean. That massive fence, you can look at it in two ways. It might be there to keep out what's over there, wolves, bears and such. But it's to keep us from going over there too."

"Are there any actual people over there, I wonder."

"Couldn't say for sure, but probably not."

"I sometimes imagine some other people now living in my old house in New Malden."

"Not sure about the Contaminated Zones, but there are people in the Ecology Reservations. Well, one of them at least."

"Really," said the man. "How do you know that?"

"I've seen them. Over in the Mendips, the Ecology Reservation they have over there."

"How did you get to see them?"

I hesitated. "I've seen them on the other side of the

fence, doing hunting and stuff."

"What are they like?"

"Sort of Stone Age. Dressed in animal skins. Cavemen basically."

"Do you think they can talk to each other, or do they just grunt and make noises?"

"They talk to each other in English, just like you and me are talking."

Instantly I realised that I had said too much.

"Nah. They're cavemen," said the man. "They're not going to be speaking in English. If they talk anything at all it'll be their own caveman language."

"They're not the old original cavemen," I explained. "Just like the mammoths and the like that are over there aren't original mammoths. They're ones they've bred back from elephants to be like the old mammoths that had gone extinct."

"So what have they bred the cavemen back from then?"

"They come from people that dropped out of society before the Nuclear War. Hippies going back to nature, that sort of thing."

"You're just making it up. How could you know that?"

"I heard it somewhere."

"You shouldn't believe everything you hear, you know."

"Oh, I don't. But this story is true. I know that much."

"If you say so."

I wasn't going to convince him and on reflection I had no desire to. Both of us gazed out for a few more minutes, lost in our own thoughts.

"Best be getting back," said the man eventually. "See you another time, perhaps."

He wandered back down the hill.

The wildness of the land laid out in front of me tugged my heartstrings. I felt for the bracelet Freya had given me. Pressing against my hand were the mammoth ivory charms, each of which represented a person or object of significance from my parallel existence.

It came to me. I could return once more. I had the perfect alibi. I was due to be away for days for my stag party. Nobody would miss me. Between drinking way too much, being tormented in horrible ways by the likes of Duncan McThomas and spending those precious days with my other family in Ecologia, it was an easy choice.

"Tim, I'm sorry, I know that you have gone to a lot of trouble, but the stag do is off. I won't be able to make it," I said on the phone.

"You can't be serious. Every bloke is entitled to his last few days of freedom."

"I'm afraid so. I just won't be able to. That's all."

"They really have you on a short leash don't they, those two?"

"No, it was me that decided to call it off. Don't go blaming Celia and her mother."

"Yeah, right," said Tim, derisive. "Which one was it? Celia or that dragon of a future mother-in-law?"

"No, it wasn't them."

"Have it your own way, but I don't believe you."

I left it at that.

In Ecologia for the Last Time

As usual I avoided the well-worn paths as I made my way towards my secret portal to Ecologia. By now I was fully familiar with the twists and turns of the cross country route, the oddly shaped trees, dips, and rocky outcrops serving as trusty landmarks.

A short distance from the underground passage I rejoined the main path, which I would be obliged to share with other recreational visitors to the Mendips National Park such as irritating riders of electric bikes.

As I approached the notice board that explained I was entering a site of special scientific interest I saw another notice had been put up with a prominent headline: "Notice of Path Closure". Curious, I read the text detailed underneath the headline.

It informed me that in two days the path would be permanently closed. The area it passed through, the habitat of the rare plant, the Plumbium cragwort, was going to be transferred from the Mendips National Park into the neighbouring Natural Ecology Reservation to better protect the environment. The fence between the National Park and the NER would be repositioned. There was a map showing the current and new positions for the boundary fence, which indicated the new boundary would cut me off from accessing the old mine workings I had been relying on for access to and from the NER.

For a moment I stood stunned and dazed.

An approaching bike rider looked at me strangely.

"Cheer up, it may never happen," he quipped as he whizzed past.

I read through the notice twice more, vainly looking for some loophole or caveat I may have missed. It could not have been clearer. In two days I would be cut off from visiting Ecologia ever again.

I sat on a nearby rock to process this. This darned Plumbium cragwort is an excuse, I reflected. It is almost certainly the Commission's long term policy to chip away at the economically developed territories and enlarge the Ecology Reservations, as Simon had suggested before their robotic goons had fried his brains.

The irony about the Plumbium cragwort being protected is that it thrives only as a result of the heavy metal residues left from ancient Roman mining and smelting activity. A trashed environment had somehow transcended into something special that required protection.

I mused that in the future perhaps there will be areas within the Contaminated Zones deliberately kept radioactive for the preservation of rare plants that thrive on nuclear fallout. Will there be a sedimentary layer within the ground rich in nuclear fallout residue that future geologists will use to age the rocks?

What should I do?

Good sense said that I should not go through to Ecologia. There would be a high risk of my being trapped there. But then, I should not have gone into an Ecological Reservation at any time. Doing so was foolhardy as well as illegal.

I stood, strode along the path with a defiant purpose. I

skipped over the gravel mound in front of the ancient entrance to the underground passageway, laboriously dug out centuries ago by slaves of the Roman Empire in pursuit of the metal ores needed to drive their civilisation.

When I arrived at the Ranulf family's rustic homestead I greeted each member of the family more effusively than I would normally have done. On this occasion I especially needed to show my tender and loving feelings for them.

I hugged and held each family member tight as if to prevent them getting away.

Normally I would have given Torsten a momentary token embrace, but this time I grasped him tight, feeling the same special connection with him as I did the others.

Freya was more beautiful than ever, a flower in the moment it opens from a bud on a dewy morning. She sensed my feelings and she held me tight too, reluctant to let go.

As we settled with a mug of ale Ranulf asked for an explanation. "Peter, I feel you have something to tell us."

I was unready to share what I knew. "Why do you feel that?"

"I can tell," Ranulf insisted. "What is it?"

I looked around at the family, spread about like a comforting blanket. I didn't want to disturb the cosy scene.

"I don't want to spoil our evening," I said. "It can wait until tomorrow." Nobody spoke, so I tried to set the conversation onto a new track. "What are we going to do tomorrow?"

"Check the snares," said Knut, "and some bits and bobs to be repaired."

The room remained silent. Even the children were quiet.

"What do you think got caught in the snares?"

"Dunno," said Torsten. "It depends. A rabbit or two, probably."

The room went quiet again.

"Peter, please tell us what is on your mind," Ranulf insisted.

I hesitated. "Two days from now I must go back to Economica. I can never return."

The faces were blank, expressionless, looking as I must have looked when the cyclist had seen me shortly before standing in front of the notice board.

"What will hold you there?" asked Knut.

"My portal closes. Afterwards I will have no means to travel between Economica and here."

As I had done myself, each of the Ranulf family members privately processed the information.

"You could always stay," said Freya, after a while.

Gudrun and Ranulf nodded. Everyone looked at me expectantly.

"I have ties in Economica," I tried to explain. "I can't just walk away from my commitments. I have to go back."

While I may not have convinced them, nobody felt they should challenge what I had said.

"We will go hunting tomorrow and have a feast," said Knut after a while.

"What should we hunt for?" said Torsten.

"Deer, I think would be best," said Knut.

"Where will we find them?"

"The deer are on the higher ground now. On Ubley Hill."

"How are we to get them from up there?" asked Torsten.

"There's wolves down to the south in Swallet wood," said Knut. "If we herd them down there, the deer know that and will veer off away from the wooded area. If we block them off to the west, they'll have to go east."

"Peter, you're our best hunter," said Ranulf. "How about you wait among the rocks at Rowberrow Bottom and get one as they go past?"

"I wouldn't say I was best at all. All of you guys have far more experience."

"You have proven yourself to be good," said Knut.

"Well, it was a fluke, really."

"Doesn't matter if it was lucky," said Torsten. "It's good to have luck."

"The honour must be yours on this occasion, Peter," decided Ranulf.

In the morning, while we all knew the situation was anything but routine, every one of us forced ourselves to behave as if it was, in the hope that pretending would make it so.

"Let us pray that Gaia will provide for us today," said Ranulf.

"Peter will bring Commissum's blessing today, I am sure of it," said Knut.

I wasn't feeling so certain. "We should not presume on Commissum's blessing," I said. "Today he may bless the deer, or the wolves or the bear. We must accept his will."

"You are right, Peter, we must not presume," agreed Ranulf.

"We have a good plan," said Torsten. "It should work well for us."

We walked through the plan and our roles for the hunt once more. It gave us something to focus on.

Nothing needed to be said, and nothing was said, as we advanced towards the hunting ground. It was a relief to be spared from conversation.

No aspect of the hunt was easy on this occasion. The deer were reluctant to be herded towards the wood. They led us on a merry dance. After hours of patient persuasion they edged down the slope, not gently and under control but skittishly.

Our prolonged activity had not gone unnoticed by the lupine population, prowling and howling in the woods, unsettling the deer all the more.

The lead deer spotted the shape of a wolf that, despite being crouched low on its belly, showed itself at the forest edge. It leapt in shock. Panic spread across the herd, which scattered rapidly in every direction.

Just when it appeared all hope of a successful hunt was lost, one deer veered towards my location. Seizing my fleeting opportunity I slung out my entangling net, which momentarily tripped the animal. Before I could follow up on my opportunity the deer freed itself and was hurtling away. I made for a sprint to grab it before it picked up speed.

There were the howls of wolves all around me. The escape route for the deer was blocked.

The pack leader, a beast I had met before, sprang in

front of me and snarled.

The previous time we had met I had won the battle of wills, but on this occasion the only winner was going to be the wolf. Had I not allowed the wolf pack to have its prey they would have happily settled for eating me for their dinner.

I backed away submissively and the wolves set upon the deer, quickly bringing it to the ground, tearing it apart limb from limb. Content with their deer the wolves graciously allowed me to retreat from the scene unmolested.

When a short while later I rendezvoused with my fellow hunters it was clear all prospect of catching a deer that day was gone.

All was not entirely lost. We surveyed the snares and traps Torsten had set and were rewarded with three rabbits, a weasel and a couple of hedgehogs.

At the crudely constructed homestead with its unkempt thatched roof, as the aromatic wafts of slowly cooking meat stew scented the air, Freya found me gazing wistfully from the open door across the landscape I would soon never see again. "Must you go tomorrow?"

"I must. I have friends and family in Economica. They expect me. They need me."

"I need you too."

"You desire me to stay. It's not quite the same as needing me."

"I wish you could stay," she insisted.

"I wish I could too."

"I love you," said Freya. "If you stayed here I would be yours, if you wanted me."

"If I were to stay, you are the one I would want. But I cannot." I wanted to hug and kiss her, but knew I mustn't. It would only have made the situation worse.

We set into the feast with ale to wash it down. Eating and drinking was a good diversion for the family members. Ranulf decided that there were some things that needed to be said.

"Peter, it is our heartfelt joy to have known you and to have you among us today. We give thanks to Commissum for having sent you to us."

"Thank you," I said. "I appreciate your love and friendship."

"It is a sorrow for us that you must leave us tomorrow," Ranulf continued.

"It is a sorrow for me too. I shall miss you all." I had resolved to restrain my emotions, but tears ran down my face.

"We have no right to expect you to remain with us," said Ranulf. "You were sent by Commissum as his messenger, and it is him you must obey."

Orders from Commissum. I was thankful to Ranulf for that excuse. "I wish it could be different."

I felt like a condemned man as the hours ticked down to my departure. Breakfast was quiet. Members of the family glanced at me and looked away.

I said my goodbyes to everybody. I tried to make it the same as it had always been when it was time for me to depart back to civilisation, but this time, I couldn't help it, it was unavoidably more heartfelt than usual. Tears flowed freely from me and each of the others.

It was understood I needed to set off alone, that nobody tried to accompany me. The portal was my secret. So I was taken aback when about fifteen minutes from my departure, Freya appeared beside me.

"What are you doing here, Freya? You know that you can't come with me."

"I know, but I needed to talk to you."

"What about?"

"Must you go?"

I wondered the same thing as I gazed at her lithe, beautiful, yet taut and sinewy form, only partially covered by the coarse ill-fitting hand-woven cloth of her practical home-made garments. I reached out and took her hand, summoning the resolve to be sensible.

"We have talked about this already," I said wearily. "You know I must."

"Why must you?"

"It's difficult to explain. It's circumstances."

"But you belong here, just as much as over there," she insisted. "I have seen you. You thrive here. It is a natural place for you. You glow with happiness when you are here and look sad when it's time to depart, especially now."

I looked around at the vegetation, the first pale green leaves appearing on the mix of trees and shrubbery shining with dew, the hills and rocky outcrops, birds soaring in the blue sky beneath fluffy white clouds on a crisp bright April morning.

I was going to attempt to explain to her, as much as I could, but at that moment our conversation was interrupted by the reverberation of motors firing up from some hundreds of metres away across a gully where a jumble of fence building machinery had been assembled. I had left it almost too late. In minutes my escape would be closed off forever.

"Got to go now, Freya. Please leave me. Go back. I'm sorry."

"I'll miss you when you're gone," said Freya sadly.

"You'll get over it."

"I want you to stay here, with me," she said, looking at me yearningly.

"Freya, you know I can't."

"You could," she said. "I could be yours."

The motors continued to reverberate across the countryside.

"Please Freya, don't make this more difficult. Leave me now. Please."

She looked at me and understood I would not shift. Sadly she turned on her heels and walked away.

I looked back for one last glimpse of the delightful Freya. She was a picture of elegant femininity, but not a feeble dependent one. She was formed in the image of Diana, the huntress, strong, as agile as an acrobat. I felt as the painter Paul Gauguin must have as he left Tahiti for Paris except that, unlike Gauguin, there would be no chance to return.

On the brink of the hole, at the moment of opportunity, I was frozen, unable to decide. In those critical seconds before I would have to jump in either direction, as is reputed for a drowning man, the course of my life flashed through my mind.

Finally at Home

As I write this I am at home, my true home, with my family in Ecologia where I belong.

These may be the last words I shall write. This is not because I expect anything untoward to happen to me in the near future, though the threat of injury or death is ever present. These may be my last written words because in Ecologia we neither need nor use writing.

It has been a year since Ecologia has been my permanent home. I am typing this into my smart phone using its last battery capacity, charged with the solar charger I took with me. The phone won't last much longer so this will be my last opportunity to finish the story of how I came here and what became of me.

There is a good chance nobody will read it. Nevertheless, it makes me feel better having completed my record for posterity. The story is complete to my satisfaction at least. I will stash the phone along with my other effects from my former Economica existence back in the underground mining tunnel that served as my portal between the realms. Perhaps one day in the distant future someone may excavate it, decipher its contents and read my story.

Over this last year Freya has become my wife and we now have a baby son, Simon.

Torsten married Ursula from the Henrik family and they are expecting the arrival of their first born any day now, who will, if Gaia wills it, be a play mate for young Simon.

Ranulf is still strong, despite his age, his sinews still taut and supple and bones hewn as hard as tungsten by decades of outdoor life, but, tough as he still is, he will not be able to lead our family indefinitely, so there is a question of succession. By rights perhaps it should be strong and dependable Knut, but it seems more likely that the family will want me to step into the role. They have a certain reverence for me as Commissum's messenger and a sense of awe for my assortment of knowledge, hard won experience and basic low cunning that they construe as wisdom.

I should explain how I came to make the choice to remain in Ecologia instead of returning to Economica.

On that fateful day a year ago I had only minutes to spare to make my way back to my life in Economica before my secret portal was permanently closed. Had I rushed back through as I had intended I would now be living a comfortable existence in Economica as a prosperous businessman with my new wife destined one day to take over the running of the Davenhirst Properties empire.

As I was reaching the point of no return, just as I was about to dive down into the secret tunnel, I froze. I understood Ecologia was my destiny.

It was not something I had figured out in a logical fashion. It was an instant decision. Being a gut choice did not make it some idle whim. It was a well formulated judgement that had been building up in me over the preceding days.

At one level it was a question of the heart, a direct choice between Celia and Freya. There were too many strings attached to my relationship with Celia: the business, the Davenhirst family, Celia's controlling tendencies, to have me securely stabled and in harness. With Freya freedom beckoned. Freya would let me be whoever I wanted and would love and accept me however I was.

But it was not only a question of the choice between the two women in my life. I sensed I was now a man who knew too much. Like Adam and Eve I had bitten into the fruit of the Tree of Knowledge. I had a suspicion of the true nature of the Commission. The fate of my good friend Simon Spiegelhalter demonstrated what might happen to someone who knew too much. Simply my association with Simon could have been enough. Having registered myself as his friend in lieu of next of kin would only have increased the danger.

Even had I been initially spared, I might have felt compelled to resist the Commission's will if I had remained in Economica.

There was a choice between living in Ecologia and Economica that was more fundamental than my love preferences and personal safety.

The division of the planet between Economica and Ecologia has established two separate environments for people to live in. The Commission kept the people in these environments apart. It is clear that the destiny of these peoples is to diverge into distinct species of humans. My choice between the two realms is not merely of which home I prefer to reside, but a choice of the species of human I identify myself as.

Most people would have chosen the life in Economica without hesitation, but then those were people who would never have ventured into Ecologia. My life there would have been prosperous, comfortable, safe and secure. My life in Ecologia is tough, rough, dangerous and lacking the modern conveniences that make life easy in Economica.

Yet, Ecologia is where I want to be. Life is challenging. It has an edge. It is not so much being close to nature as being an integral part of it. For me, it has a reality Economica lacks.

At a more fundamental level, I now feel certain Economica is an evolutionary dead end for humanity and Ecologia is where humanity has its future, where humans can develop into the animals they were supposed to be before Adam and Eve bit into the forbidden fruit and launched humanity onto a path of planetary domination and destruction.

The Commission has a treaty obligation to preserve human cultural heritage, which I believe is its reason for maintaining Economica. If the Commission's only objective was to restore and preserve the Earth's ecology, they could have taken the opportunity to wipe out the economically developed world after the Nuclear War.

To fulfil the Commission's objective of cultural preservation there is no need to maintain the economically developed areas on the scale that they have been in the past. Some part of each nation or region would need to be maintained to sustain its unique culture, but in the long term that only needs to be a small fragment of what currently exists.

We have seen the Commission resisting development plans, transferring territory from Economica to Ecologia and imposing a system of Child Permits to limit the birth rate, all of which is consistent with my suspicion that

Economica is being scaled down.

The wording of the treaty requires the Commission to preserve human culture but makes no provision for its future development. For this purpose the Commission would not wish for or permit development of humanity within Economica. The characteristics of the human population there would need to be frozen as they were when the Commission took over, maintained in their current cultural state in a permanent zoo.

Before the Nuclear War nature reserves existed only as token pockets of territory surrounded by swathes of human occupied territory. I foresee the Commission transitioning over time to a complete reversal of this situation, where small reserves of economically developed enclaves are maintained within swathes of the wild landscape of Ecologia.

Humans were never suited nor designed by evolution to govern the Earth. No sooner had they developed a certain technological capability they despoiled the planet, fouling their own nest. Saving the planet from destruction had fallen on humanity's successor, the global artificial intelligence that manifests itself as the Commission.

Those same economically developed humans, the current inhabitants of Economica, have now lost their supposed advantage of scientific and technological knowledge, withheld by the Commission lest it be misused, a loss most of them have not noticed.

The culturally advanced people of Economica imagine themselves infinitely superior to the Stone Age folk of Ecologia. Yet they perceive the Commission variously as a ruling class of technocrats, or a conspiracy of other nations.

For all the simplicity, the people of Ecologia more accurately understand the Commission as the deity Commissum, something that in Economica would be derided as superstition. If the Commission is an integrated planet-wide artificial intelligence, as my friend Simon suggested and I now believe to be true, it is a deity, all-powerful and immortal.

The people of Ecologia live as humans were evolved to live, not as super-beings apart from nature. The future of humanity is in Ecologia because, like all the other flora and fauna we share our planet with, humans can develop and evolve here as Mother Nature intends.

Dear Reader,

Thank you very much for choosing my book to read.

As I am publishing a novel for the first time it has been a struggle to get noticed, so, if you enjoy this book it would be wonderful if you helped spread the word on social media or amongst friends. In particular a review on a web site such as the following would be fantastic:

https://www.goodreads.com/book/show/90340382-destiny-of-a-free-spirit

Thanks for your help
Stephen Ford (the Author)

About the Author

Stephen, son of a geologist, had a varied and nomadic childhood in Africa and the Middle East, among people struggled for existence in the midst of nature that was literally red in tooth and claw.

From childhood, Stephen has been inspired by wild places, mountains, rivers and forests, places where nature reigns, not people.

The computer systems that Stephen worked with during his career in information technology posed the questions, can machines be intelligent? If something is intelligent, does it need to be alive?

Now, inspired to write, Stephen explores these themes: What is nature? Is nature alive? What is life? What distinguishes a human from an animal? Do people have spirits? If people have spirits, then perhaps animals do too? Can spirits exist also in inanimate entities, rivers, trees, mountains, valleys? Can machines have intelligence? If so, do they also have a spirit?

Lightning Source UK Ltd.
Milton Keynes UK
UKHW012034101222
413708UK00004B/43

9 781788 649568